SHE KNEW HER KILLER

An unputdownable crime thriller with a breathtaking twist

REBECCA BRADLEY

DI Claudia Nunn Book 3

JOFFE BOOKS

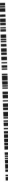

Joffe Books, London
www.joffebooks.com

First published in Great Britain in 2022

Cover art by Nick Castle

ISBN: 978-1-80405-314-0

CHAPTER 1

Harlow, now

Harlow was lying to her friends.

She stood in the shower thinking about this. The warmth of the water as it powered over her skin relieved the aches of her body and mind. And her mind needed it the most. It had been an exacting four days since she'd arrived in Sheffield on Wednesday afternoon. Harlow couldn't remember a time that had taxed her so much. Stress was not part of her dictionary, not since she'd walked away from her job in the city and opened up the owl sanctuary. It had been the best decision of her life. The corporate rat race had exhausted her and she'd wanted a change in tempo. But this, this had been beyond anything she had experienced. And she'd done it alone, without the others having any idea.

She'd organised the reunion — sending emails, checking dates, suggesting the venue. They hadn't seen each other since leaving school, nearly twenty years ago, but being with her friends felt like coming home. She'd needed them here, but when it came to it, she couldn't tell them why.

They were meeting downstairs for breakfast in forty-five minutes. Guilt niggled at Harlow that she hadn't shared the real reason she was in Sheffield with her old school friends, but not enough guilt to actually tell them the truth.

Shame was a great silencer.

As she was towelling herself dry, there was a knock at the door. Strong and even.

She wasn't expecting anyone.

She hadn't ordered any room service and as they were due to check out later that day — they'd all paid for a late check-out — she wasn't expecting a cleaner.

When the quick rap came again, Harlow realised she'd been staring at the door as if it would give her the answers she wanted. Whoever it was knocked again — they were impatient.

Harlow moved to the door and peered through the peephole. Her breath caught in her throat when she saw who was standing on the other side. It was the last person she'd have expected. Yet here they were. Outside her hotel room door and willing, by the look of it, to speak with her.

After all she'd been through these past four days.

She was naked from the shower. Her hair was wet and falling over her shoulders in damp tails. Quickly she wrapped the towel around herself, tucking an end into the front to secure it, then grabbed the courtesy robe from where she'd slung it on the back of the chair.

Tying the belt, she peered through the peephole once more. They'd already raised their hand to knock again, so Harlow, full of a lifetime's worth of nerves, yanked the door open before they could make contact with the wood.

She was face to face with her caller.

Nausea swept over her as she ushered her visitor into the room. Not a word was spoken. Their turning up was enough.

Harlow closed the door.

And as she did, a flash of leather whipped past her face, and tightened around her throat.

Her hands flew to her neck. The leather was already burning her skin. She grappled, but it was so tight there was no room to get any purchase.

2

It cut into her, deep and merciless. She couldn't make a sound. She gasped for air, but it wasn't coming. Her eyes were bulging. Her head thrummed with pressure, like it was about to explode.

Stars and darkness edged into Harlow's vision as her legs gave way and she tumbled down towards the carpet. She should have been getting answers to years of questions, but she was about to lose her life for asking them.

In the turmoil, Harlow's mind cycled over the shock of who was behind her.

How could they do this to her?

The darkness was creeping in. Her body twitched. The end was near. No one was going to save her. She'd brought this on herself. Thought was soon impossible as the world faded out. Harlow's head and shoulders were in the lap of her killer. Her death, while brutal and wretched, was soft and close to intimate.

Then everything went black.

And Harlow knew no more.

CHAPTER 2

Claudia

The room was comfortable. There were cushions to lean into or hold. An obligatory box of tissues on a small table to the side of the chair. In the corner was a shelf filled with teddies and dolls and other plastic bits for children of varying ages. What there was not was a clock. Time was carefully and discreetly tracked by the man in front of Claudia by the watch on his wrist.

He was relaxed, lounging in the comfortable armchair that matched the one DI Claudia Nunn was sitting in. Claudia, on the other hand, was perched on the edge of her seat. Comfort was never a word she assigned to these meetings.

A stereotypical tweed jacket was slung over the back of Robert's chair; there was a large diary closed on the desk. Robert was analogue in that way. Claudia herself kept a paper diary as well as a digital one so she wouldn't miss an appointment. This had become a habit after missing a meeting with DCI Maddison Sharpe and the Police and Crime Commissioner one afternoon and having a strip torn off her by her rather furious boss.

Robert was still watching her. His attention never wavered. He was waiting for her to answer his question. She'd hoped with a little time he would have moved on. But he was stubborn like that.

Claudia had been seeing Robert for five months now. Ever since she'd killed a man.

She'd been in a fight to the death and had been the one to walk away from it, for which she was eternally grateful. But she'd ended someone's life — now that the shock had passed, it had begun preying on her mind. Soaking up the edges of her days as she'd attempted to carry on as usual. Distracting her. And she didn't want to be distracted when she was working, so she was getting the help she needed.

At first she'd told herself all was fine. The IOPC and CPS had cleared her of any wrongdoing. Her actions had been in self-defence. She'd had no choice.

Seeing the light go out of his eyes though, that haunted her. That dead stare. Where once he was a living, breathing, human being, the next he was a corpse on the woodland floor.

Of course she'd seen death up close many times before; being a homicide detective, you do. But it was completely different when you were the cause.

Robert never pushed her. In fact, she often went off into her own head in these sessions. Maybe it was part of the therapy. To work through things silently for herself while he sat with her. Keeping her safe.

Safe. A strange word, but one Robert was adamant about using in here.

Claudia didn't feel threatened. She'd killed the man who had been the threat to her, after all.

But safe in here meant something else.

It was about her mind.

And here she was, wandering off into her own thoughts again. Getting sidetracked while Robert waited patiently.

'No,' she said eventually, answering his question.

Robert steepled his fingers. There was no notebook in his lap. He'd told her at the beginning of their sessions, when they first met, that he made notes as soon as the meeting was over. When it was all fresh in his mind. And that her notes were secure. No one would see them other than him. They were only created so he could see what therapeutic direction they were taking, where they had been, to assess how she was doing, and if there were specific areas he thought Claudia might consider working on. Because this was her therapy. She was the one in control, and she always had to remember that. No steps would be taken without her express permission.

He contemplated her now. She prickled under his gaze. He was so intense and sincere. Claudia, though here of her own free will, still found the whole process difficult. They were digging around inside her head and going to places that she hadn't necessarily expected to go. But she trusted him.

The silence between them dragged on until it was about to become uncomfortable. That was the thing with Robert: he did sometimes allow the silence to meander into discomfort, in order to make you speak. A tactic Claudia was used to, being in the police. But this time Robert broke the silence. He knew when and how to use the technique. 'You don't think it would be helpful to talk to your father about the incident you both experienced?'

'No,' she said again, giving nothing further away.

This time he went straight in. 'And why is that?'

Oh boy, they were looking at her daddy issues. Really?

She loved her father. She did. She didn't have issues with him. But he had walked away from the incident in a different way than Claudia, and this unsettled her. Of course they'd both been severely injured. They'd both come away with knife wounds. But DS Dominic Harrison, her father, hadn't been the one to kill him. And it was this point, Claudia mused, that gave him the edge in recovering from the event.

Even though she understood why he was in a better place than she was, it was hard to see him appearing unharmed and happy, getting on with his life as if nothing had happened. It wasn't like she was a walking, talking depressive. Claudia put a smile on her face for her team, but she was close to her father — she could sense how real his sentiments were. He wasn't pasting on a smile for the benefit of the group. Dominic had recovered from his knife wound and the incident itself. He might worry about Claudia, but other than that he was fine.

She wasn't sure why that annoyed her so much. Maybe she wanted an ally in this? Someone to soak up the traumatic mess she was swilling about in? Because she'd never been as lonely as she was right now and she didn't like it, and in turn, she didn't particularly like her dad.

Perhaps that was a little harsh. She loved her father. But she just wanted company. What was that saying? Misery loves company. Never a truer word spoken, or so it seemed in the depths of hell where Claudia appeared to have found herself.

She shouldn't have to sit here with a total stranger every week to rake over that day. She should be able to talk about it whenever the need took her with her father. You'd think he'd be there for her, having been there with her for the incident itself.

But no. Dominic was doing Dominic. And that meant he was getting on with the job when he was at work and pretending everything was fine when they weren't at work. And work, well that was a whole other can of worms. Claudia was the detective inspector on a new Complex Crimes Task Force, created by Detective Superintendent Connelly after the conclusion of a particularly difficult case. Connelly's only proviso was that Claudia should head the unit up with Dominic as her detective sergeant. Claudia had huge reservations about supervising her father. She was on the fast-track promotion scheme and Dominic had not progressed. He had failed an inspector interview board a few years ago, but had never done anything about taking it again. It was like he wanted the position but didn't have the drive required. It was difficult at times.

So, in response to Robert's question — how many minutes ago? — no, it wasn't that she didn't want to talk about things with her father, it was that he was impossible to talk to. 'He's in a different place than me,' she said.

'How does that make you feel?'

Always with the questions.

What she actually wanted from Robert was for him to tell her how to make this all better. Why couldn't he do that?

She already knew the answer. He'd explained it when she'd asked him at the beginning. He wasn't here to tell her what to do, but was here to help Claudia explore her feelings around the incident; in exploring the incident she would then be able to process it and her days would be smoother.

Smoother days. Oh, how she wished for those.

She rubbed her face. 'I'm tired, to be honest.'

Robert discreetly checked his watch. 'We're nearly at the end of the session. Do you want to call it a day? We can open next time with how you feel about you both being in different places.' His gentle smile encouraged her, told her it was both okay to close it down today and that she would be safe when they examined the subject next week.

'That would be great.' She rose from her chair, her body heavy and leaden. It was a sensation she was used to after these sessions. Not only did they exhaust her mind, but they took all the energy from her body as well. What he'd suggested didn't sound great at all, but she didn't have the words in her to engage with Robert about this. Next time was in the future, and she'd deal with it when it arrived. For now she could leave and it would all be over for the day. The inner reflecting. The emotional examinations.

Robert held out his hand, and she took it as she always did. 'Same time next week?' he asked.

'Same time,' she agreed wearily, before thanking him for his time and leaving the comfortable room. Leaving the cushions, the box of tissues she never used, and the shelf filled with all manner of toys a small or larger child might want to cling to while discussing a traumatic event.

Once outside in the weak January sun, Claudia turned her phone back on. This hour of the week was the only time she would ever have her phone off. Her team all knew where she was and why her phone was off. They'd deal with anything that came in while she was there. But Robert had been helpful and had scheduled the appointments early on Sunday mornings with the hope she wouldn't miss much, if anything. He'd accommodated her and she was grateful he'd made room in his weekend for her. His response was that he still had his full Sunday ahead of him once he had seen her, they met so early. She would have to buy him a thank-you gift once this was all over.

Her phone pinged immediately with a text message as it came to life. It was from DS Russ Kane. They had a body.

CHAPTER 3

Claudia strode into the hotel, looking for her team. All thoughts of her last appointment were gone from her head. She was in work mode now.

She was glad of the warmth of the hotel. The January day was decidedly chilly and only seemed to be getting colder.

Russ and Dominic were waiting for her in the foyer.

'Talk to me.' She had no time for preamble. What her morning session had done was make her feel like she was on the back foot. Previous meetings hadn't been a problem. But this morning her skin itched at her late arrival on the scene.

Russ jumped straight in. 'Harlow Cunningham, thirty-four years, here for a long-weekend reunion with old school friends. When she didn't turn up for their breakfast meet-up this morning, one of them, Chloe Martin, went to her room to see if everything was okay. When Chloe received no response to her knock, she called Harlow and heard the phone ringing inside the room so asked the hotel to open it up. That's when they found the victim and called the police.'

'And where's Chloe now?'

A few people were queuing at the reception desk, being addressed by uniformed officers. One man was getting irate, waving his hands in the air as if this would convey his meaning better. Claudia raised an eyebrow.

Dom smiled. 'We've informed the guests who are trying to check out that they're unable to leave until we've talked with them about the incident in the hotel.'

'Ah.' Claudia understood the man's frustration. People didn't like being prevented from going about their business and unfortunately it was something the police tended to do a lot. And no matter her level of understanding, she still wouldn't allow him to leave. Whoever had murdered Harlow Cunningham could still be in the hotel. Or a guest could have witnessed something that would go a long way in helping police identify who had killed her.

'And Chloe?' she prompted.

'Chloe is with the rest of her friends in the breakfast room, drinking tea and being comforted. She's pretty distraught — she was with the hotel manager when they found the body,' Russ explained.

'And the team?' Claudia was attempting to catch up as quickly as she could without causing a problem for her officers.

Dominic jumped in. 'They're talking to hotel staff, getting first accounts from Harlow's friends and talking to other guests that are around this morning.'

There were a lot of people about. 'Okay, Dom, do you want to come see . . . Harlow, is it?'

'Harlow Cunningham.'

Claudia was conscious lately of friction between Dominic and Russ, and was aware that it was because Dom thought she didn't use him as much as she used Russ. This was true, but it was because she and Russ had come from the same team prior to the creation of the Complex Crimes Task Force. It was natural for Claudia to automatically lean on Russ. It took effort to remember to use Dominic as much as she did her usual second-in-command. 'Great. And Russ, if you can make sure everything is in order down here.'

Claudia and Dominic wandered over to a CSI, collected a couple of Tyvek suits and climbed into the papery coveralls.

'Is Nadira here yet?' Claudia asked. Nadira Azim was the Home Office registered forensic pathologist.

'She arrived about fifteen minutes ago.' Dominic pulled the hood of the suit over his head and clipped a mask around his ears. His face was all but hidden, other than his eyes. Claudia was backfooted that she was so far behind the pathologist. Of course her appointments were important, but they couldn't be allowed to interfere with murder inquiries.

They made their way up to Harlow's floor. Dominic took the short amount of time they had alone to question her. 'How was it this morning?' He knew when her appointments were and liked to know how she was doing.

Claudia, on the other hand, always hated these conversations. The sessions were for her alone, and she didn't want her father intruding on that space. Especially considering his own demeanour about the incident. She didn't need his questions, even if they were coming from a place of love and concern.

'It was fine.'

'That's it? Fine?'

'The sessions are kind of private, Dad.'

The lights in the lift indicated they were about to arrive on Harlow's floor. They'd taken a lift at the opposite end of the building while CSIs examined the one closest to Harlow's room. What they would find was a mess to search through. It was a public space. There would be hundreds of fingerprints on the buttons. But they'd gather all the prints they could and if a suspect was arrested they could be matched up against all prints seized in the lift and placed close to Harlow's room.

'I know.' Dominic sighed. 'I want to make sure you're doing okay?'

'I'm doing okay.'

'Going to counselling kind of says the opposite, doesn't it?'

Claudia gritted her teeth. This was why she didn't like to talk to him about it.

'I killed a man, Dad. You walked away with an injury, as I did. But I had the added extra of having killed him. Don't you think it might have affected you slightly if you'd killed someone?' Her voice was low so as to not draw attention should the doors suddenly open, but it was curt. This wasn't the first time they'd gone through this.

Dominic shrugged. The lift doors opened with a quiet ping and Claudia shook her head and walked out, leaving Dominic to follow her.

A hulking uniformed officer was standing in their way, clipboard in his hands. His job here was to prevent anyone entering the scene who shouldn't. Claudia gave her credentials and Dominic his. The officer scribbled their details onto his sheet and checked his watch, detailing the time they entered the room. Claudia thanked him, then quietly moved past him and into the hotel room.

There were no signs of a disturbance. Nothing out of place in the room that Claudia could pick up on. There was a low hum in the room and Claudia frowned. 'What's that sound?'

Dominic indicated the bathroom door. 'I'd suggest with her damp hair, she'd just showered. It's the extraction fan.'

Harlow Cunningham lay on the floor, just in front of the door. Her white hotel robe had fallen open to reveal a loosening towel wrapped around her torso. One leg was bent out to the side and her hands were resting level with her neck where a thin leather belt was wound tightly. Hair splayed out around her head like a halo. Her eyes were open, and petechial spots were clearly visible.

Nadira looked up. 'Morning. Your team has fallen for this one then?'

Claudia smiled. 'Yes, it's not particularly complex but the Major Crime teams are all running jobs currently and the bosses feel that with both me and Dominic still recovering from injuries—'

Dominic huffed. He hated to be referred to in this way. In his eyes he was one hundred per cent fit.

She ignored his outburst and carried on. 'With both me and Dominic still recovering from knife wounds, they're happy for us to pick up more run-of-the-mill murders for a while. Unless something comes in that would require our specific attention.'

Nadira nodded. 'That sounds sensible.'

'What can you tell us?'

'Well, you know I don't like to do guess work at the scene, but . . .'

Claudia inclined her head in acceptance and gratitude that Nadira liked to work with facts and facts only, but that she was about to give them something.

'Going by the fact the victim was last seen late last night, her hair is still damp from the shower and rigor hasn't set in yet, I am willing to provide a preliminary verbal assessment that this young lady hasn't been dead long.'

Claudia turned to Dominic. 'You think her killer could still be in the hotel?'

He shrugged. 'It depends if he's a guest or not. If not, he's long gone. Out as quick as you can. If he's a guest, then he's hoping to mingle in with everyone else and not stand out.'

There were no signs of a disturbance. Nothing out of place in the room that Claudia could pick up on. The bed was unmade, but the room looked the way you expected it to first thing in the morning when someone had spent the night in it. The table lamps were still on their tables. The television was still in one piece and the kettle and little packs of tea and coffee were all apparently untouched, apart from a used cup on the bedside table.

'There's no sign of a struggle,' Claudia said. 'The door's closed. I'd suggest Harlow let her killer in. Whether she was expecting them or not is another question. Hotels are strange places. You answer a knock on the door the same way you'd answer your front door at home, even if you haven't ordered room service. Staff come by to fill up tea, coffee and biscuits randomly. Cleaners bring in fresh towels as well as cleaning the room. So, whoever gained access managed to surprise Harlow with the attack quickly. She didn't expect it from whoever entered. I'm not sure what that tells us, to be honest. Someone she trusted, or someone she expected to be benign?' Claudia looked again at the woman on the floor.

Dominic stepped to the side as a CSI with a camera edged past him for a different angle. 'I have to agree with you. This was rapid and over quickly. One of the friends downstairs?'

Claudia shrugged. 'Maybe. Or it could be absolutely anyone else. We need to find out who knew she was here this weekend. Her activity while she was in Sheffield. Who she engaged with. If she ruffled someone's feathers.'

She crouched down beside Nadira and pointed to the belt still wrapped tightly around Harlow's neck. 'Cause of death?'

Nadira's eyes crinkled, suggesting a smile. 'Were you listening to me earlier?'

There was definitely a smile behind that mask. 'Anything?'

'I can't say until the PM, but there are no other obvious injuries. That's not to say she didn't have a heart attack while he was attempting to strangle her, hence waiting.'

Claudia pointed again, this time at the victim's eyes. 'But the petechial haemorrhaging would indicate whoever put this belt around her throat managed to do what they came here to do?'

Again, Nadira's eyes crinkled above her mask. 'You're observant. Yes, it's a good indication.'

Claudia wrinkled her nose. 'What's that smell?'

'She's urinated. Either while she was being strangled or at time of death.'

It was such a degrading process, death. It was a good job really that you weren't here to witness the aftermath.

The clicking of a camera sounded behind Claudia as the CSI continued to record images of the body in situ and the pathologist conducting her examination.

Nadira clipped Harlow's fingernails and took swabs from underneath before bagging them up. Harlow's hands would be evidentially important in a strangulation case like this because she would have been struggling against her bond.

Finally, Nadira bagged Harlow's head, carefully covering the belted area. This was where the killer had spent his time. If they were going to recover anything, then the likelihood would be that it would come from this secured area.

Though it was necessary, Claudia hated this step in the process of securing evidence. It never looked good when you bagged a victim's head. It looked like you were hurting her all over again. But to do right by Harlow Cunningham after her death it was the best thing for her. Nadira was great at her job and Claudia was hopeful she'd recover something they could use. This was an up-close and personal kill.

She looked around the space again. 'It's impossible to say if he took anything so we'll have to check with her friends if she lived with anyone, or who her next of kin is. They'll know what she packed for the trip. Or her friends might think of something that might be missing.'

'There's no laptop,' said Dominic. 'There's an iPhone on the bedside table, there. We'll seize that, though iPhones are notoriously difficult to examine. It'll be all about working with her service provider.'

'Do people take laptops on weekend trips with them?' asked Nadira, as she pushed herself up from the floor.

Dominic shrugged. 'The youngsters are always connected nowadays. They don't seem to like to leave them behind if they have a slim version to carry around.'

Claudia double-checked the room. 'I suppose part of it depends on what she would want one for. We need to know what she did for a living. So much can be done on a smartphone now. We dig into her life and find out why anyone would want her dead and we find out who killed her.'

CHAPTER 4

Harlow

Sunday 6.15 a.m. — 45 minutes earlier

Harlow checked the time. Luckily her dad was an early riser. She felt the need to connect with him. He wouldn't mind. Of course he'd worry about her because she was calling so early, but she'd reassure him. She picked up her mobile from the bedside table, pressed through to her favourites and dialled her dad.

It only took three rings for him to pick up, which meant he was still in bed, but she could tell from his voice he was awake and alert so she knew he'd be sitting up with a cup of coffee and a book.

'What is it, Harlow? Is everything okay up there?' Worry edged his voice.

'I'm fine, Dad. I just wanted to talk to you. I missed you.' She felt it like something deep and true welling up inside her. Threatening to overwhelm her. If this weekend had taught her anything it was how much he meant to her.

'I miss you too, munchkin.' The name he'd used for her since she was small. It had made her giggle when she was a child so he'd never stopped using it. He liked to see her smile and laugh, and if her pet name made her happy then he would use it all the more. Gone was Harlow and in came munchkin.

'You think when you give me away you can call me Harlow in the father-of-the-bride speech?'

He laughed out loud. She pictured him — the duvet tucked around his legs, the bedside lamp glowing in the corner — and she grinned in response.

'Not a chance, munchkin. Munchkin all the way. You think you're ever going to give me a chance to test out my father-of-the-bride skills?'

Her love life hadn't been anything to write home about. Her biological clock was ticking and she did hope to settle down one day. But she'd had things she wanted to sort through first. Now it was done. It was over. 'I hope so, Dad. One day.' She could practically hear the smile down the phone.

'How are things with your friends, anyway?'

She jolted with the change in subject. The bed sank slightly as she lowered herself onto the edge. 'It's been good. So great to catch up with everyone. You wouldn't believe we haven't seen each other for so long. It's been like old times.'

'I'm glad you found them. Though you seemed pretty anxious before you went up there. You're glad you did it?'

'Yeah. I'm glad I did it.' She paused. She had to tell him but she knew it would come out weirdly. 'Dad?'

'Yes, munchkin.'

'You know you're a really great dad, don't you?'

There was a quietness on the other end of the line. Harlow could only imagine the thoughts running through his head. The sentimental retorts clogging up his throat.

'What's wrong, love?'

'Nothing, Dad. I just wanted to tell you. I don't think I tell you often enough. I want you to know how much I appreciate you. How I appreciated you and Mum. You mean the world to me. Being here with my friends, it's brought home how much I have and how much I have to be grateful for.'

'I love you too, munchkin.'

'I'll come and see you as soon as I'm home.' She had a desperate need to see him. To hug him. To hold him close and tell him how important he was to her. It was so difficult to do it over the phone with meaning.

'I look forward to it.'

'I have to go now, Dad. I'm meeting my friends for breakfast but I have to jump in the shower first.'

'Okay, love. Enjoy yourself and I'll see you when you're back.'

'Love you, Dad.'

'See you soon, munchkin.'

Harlow ended the call. A warmth wrapped itself around her. She was ready to go home now.

CHAPTER 5

Claudia

The hotel manager, a tall man with a head of bright red hair and piercing blue eyes, was wringing his hands by the time Claudia and Dominic returned to the lobby. They'd removed their Tyvek suits and securely placed them in evidence bags, signing the label and sealing it all up before heading downstairs. It was rare for the white paper coveralls to be examined at a later date in the investigation, but good practice demanded that everything that had been in the crime scene be bagged for evidential purposes.

'All this police activity is not desirable for the hotel's guests.' The manager peered out from behind his wide-angled glasses, looking for a target to vent his frustration on.

'I'm not sure the dead body of a young woman in your room upstairs is desirable for your guests either,' replied Claudia evenly.

The manager blinked several times. 'No, no, of course not. But guests were due to check out this morning and they're being told they have to stay. Is that correct?'

'It is, I'm afraid. At this point in time, we have no idea who might have witnessed what. So, with that in mind, we need to talk to everyone. If they haven't left their room for instance, it's going to be a quick conversation and we can obtain their details and they can be on their way.'

The manager nodded slightly. 'Is it possible the guests wanting to check out can be prioritised by your team so they can get on their way?' He sounded hopeful at his own suggestion.

Dominic huffed at her side and Claudia willed him to quieten down. 'I'm afraid my team's priority is to find the guests who have something to tell us. Those who might have seen something. We are, after all, here to solve a murder, Mr—' she glanced at his name badge — 'Mr Mackie.'

His shoulders slumped. 'Yes, yes, of course. I'll sort the guests out with some refreshments.'

He was about to move away when Claudia stopped him. 'I need to talk to you, Mr Mackie. Is there any possibility you can get one of your staff to sort out the refreshments?'

Confusion played out across his face. It was clear that the morning was stressing him out. As manager, he needed to be calm and in charge, but murder wasn't in the job description. Still, it was apparent he was adjusting to the situation.

Mackie clicked his fingers and a young man came scurrying to his side. 'Get all the guests who are being asked to refrain from checking out something to drink, please, and if they haven't had breakfast, then they can eat in the breakfast room while they wait for the police to—'

Claudia shook her head. 'We need them all in one place, I'm afraid. So we know who is who and what part they play in all of this. If you can settle them in the chairs in the lobby, for instance, that would be ideal. Maybe take some easily transferable food out to them?'

Mackie visibly shook himself free of the words he'd been about to say to his underling and tried again. 'Get them settled in the chairs, bring them any drinks they'd like and bring them pastries to go with their drinks, please.'

The young man trotted off.

Mackie turned back to Claudia and Dominic. 'How can I help you?'

'Does the hotel have CCTV?'

'Only in the lobby, not on the floors where the guests' rooms are. That would be too intrusive to our guests.'

'We need to seize that,' Claudia told him. At some point their killer might have walked through the lobby.

Mackie cleared his throat.

'Yes?'

'There are other ways out of the hotel. Back entrances for the staff. These aren't monitored either. We don't spy on our staff.'

Claudia stared at him.

'You're not spied on at work, are you, DI Nunn?'

She sighed. No, no, she wasn't. But it didn't help their investigation if the killer, whoever it was, knew about the back entrances.

'We'll take the lobby CCTV,' said Dominic. 'Thank you.'

Mackie wrung his hands.

'Is there anything you can tell us about Harlow Cunningham or her group?' Dominic asked.

'Such as?'

'Have you seen her with anyone other than the group of friends she booked in with? Arguing with anyone? Suspicious activity? Odd requests? Anything at all you can think of.'

Mackie was thoughtful for a moment. Claudia and Dominic waited him out. Then he shook his head. 'I'm sorry. I can't think of anything. The thing is, I don't interact with the guests much. I'm overseeing the staff more than the guests. You need to speak to the staff.'

'Don't worry, we'll be doing that. We'll also need a list of all staff on duty in the hotel from, say . . .' Nadira hadn't provided time of death, but going by the victim's damp hair, Claudia would take a flying leap and suggest it was this morning. 'Four a.m. this morning, please. That's everyone, no matter what they do. I also want to know which members of staff accessed the victim's room in the last twenty-four hours and what for. Then, tell us if you've seen any member of staff within the premises that shouldn't be on duty.'

Mackie wrung his hands even more, but nodded.

Claudia turned to Dominic. 'Can you go with Mr Mackie and seize the lobby CCTV and obtain those lists, please, and I'll head into the breakfast room and speak with Harlow's friends. Thanks.'

Dominic gave a curt nod and opened his arm wide to usher Mackie away, who took the hint and moved from Claudia towards the reception desk, muttering something under his breath to Dominic as they walked. She'd ask him later what it was he said. Everything was vitally important at the start of a murder investigation.

She was feeling more settled. The earlier stress of coming in late had dissipated now they were getting on with the tasks at hand. She could have done without the conversation with her father, though. He really didn't get it. That killing a man was so much more different than being stabbed. They both had knife wounds to heal from, but they both hadn't killed someone. Why couldn't he understand the difficulties in moving on from a trauma like that? It surprised her. He was usually a kind man. Always there for her. But this, it just seemed to be tripping him up, and she didn't get why.

Never mind, there was work to get on with. She spotted a sign for the breakfast room and moved towards it.

The room was bright and well lit. Claudia identified Harlow's friends immediately. A group of three, one woman and two men, were sharing hugs as they wept for their loss — DC Lisa James was sitting with them. At a table to the side was DC Krish Dhawan with another woman, who was sobbing into a fistful of tissues.

Krish had his notepad out. He would be obtaining a first account from the young woman and had separated her off from her friends to avoid the witnesses conferring.

Further in the breakfast room were DC Graham Dunne and DC Rhys Evans. They were talking to other guests, finding out who knew Harlow Cunningham and her friends, what they had seen of them this weekend, and what they had seen this morning. This didn't feel random. Someone had identified Harlow's hotel room and accessed it to kill her. Which meant that at some point this weekend or beyond, Harlow could have had contact with her killer and that person had been upset enough to locate her and place a narrow belt around her neck and squeeze the very life out of her.

Claudia approached Krish and the woman he was with.

Krish looked up. 'Boss, this is Chloe Martin, a friend of Harlow Cunningham's.'

Chloe's face was streaked with tears, her eyes filled with questions. From the nearby table, her friends were watching closely, although the hum of voices in the room would mask their conversation. Claudia kept her voice low as she held out her hand to Chloe Martin. 'DI Claudia Nunn. I'm leading the investigation into the murder of your friend.'

Chloe half stood to shake Claudia's hand. Her palm was warm and damp. She sat back down, dabbing the wad of tissues gently on her cheeks. 'I'm sorry. I'm just so shocked. I never expected . . .' More tears flowed.

Claudia grabbed a chair and dropped into it, bringing herself down to Chloe's level. 'Please don't apologise. It's a lot to take in. As Krish will have explained, we do have to ask you some questions, though.' She never asked if this was okay. Never give witnesses a choice. This was a murder investigation. Chloe was a witness and she had to answer questions.

Chloe nodded rapidly, the curls on her head bouncing around her face until she tucked some strands behind her ears out of the way.

'I'm sorry,' Claudia said. 'You've probably been through some of this with Krish, but I need you to go through it with me. I need a quick overview of what's happened.' Again, no confirmation whether Chloe was okay to do this. It was required. She'd take her time. Allow the woman to grieve. But Chloe was one of the first people on the scene and her account was valuable to the police.

Chloe wiped at her face again. Faint patches of pale skin appeared where she was wiping foundation away with the tissue and tears.

Krish leaned back in his chair, giving Claudia space to take over the questioning.

'Tell me what happened this morning.' Not a question as such. An open-ended request for Chloe to provide as much information as she could. And if she only gave scant details, Claudia would dig deeper as needed.

'We were supposed to meet for breakfast.' She hiccupped more tears.

'Take your time, it's okay.'

Chloe's mouth set in a tight line as she looked between Krish, who was poised with his pen and notepad, and Claudia. 'I'm sorry, it's just been too much for me. This had been such an amazing weekend. To reconnect after so long. It had been like no time had passed at all. And for it to end like this. Poor Harlow.' More tears flooded her face.

'You hadn't seen Harlow for a while before this weekend?' Claudia interrupted the flow of the original question, knowing it was the wrong thing to do, but needing the answer before they continued.

Chloe shook her head. 'This was a reunion. We haven't seen each other in about sixteen years, since we were eighteen.'

Russ had mentioned the word 'reunion', Claudia remembered. Sixteen years was a long time, and people changed. No matter what Chloe had just said about it being like no time at all.

'And this morning?' Claudia reminded the young woman of the question.

Though the generous thing to say to witnesses was to take their time, time really wasn't a commodity the police had. Harlow Cunningham's killer could still be in the hotel or at least nearby. The quicker they obtained details, the faster they could work and potentially identify who had been in Harlow's room with her today. Claudia began to itch, willing Chloe to move along at a more rapid pace.

'We all met down here as agreed.' Chloe dried her face again. 'But Harlow never appeared. Eventually we got fed up of waiting for her. She'd been like this all weekend and

Brodie was moaning about it. It was as though she was only half present most of the time. So I said I'd go and collect her.' Her voice cracked and crumbled.

'Go on,' Claudia encouraged her gently.

'I knocked on her door but there was no reply so I called her mobile in case she'd gone out. It wouldn't have surprised me. She disappeared a couple of times over the weekend. But I heard the phone ringing behind the door.' The tears started up again, but this time Chloe forged onwards. 'I came back down and spoke to someone behind the reception desk, told them I was worried about her, that she might be ill. They got a member of staff to come up with me and they opened up her room.' Chloe cried out, smothering the sound with her hand. 'I'm so sorry. It was just so awful.'

Claudia shook her head. 'It's okay. You've had a shock.' Chloe's cup was empty in front of her. 'We'll get you another warm drink.' She inclined her head at Krish, who smiled his acknowledgement and rose from his chair and went off to replace Chloe's tea.

'You said Harlow was only half present this weekend — what did you mean by that?'

Chloe rubbed at her eyes. Any make-up she may have been wearing was long gone. 'We weren't in each other's pockets this weekend. It wasn't like that. Harlow had time to do her own thing and she spent some time doing just that. Maybe taking in the city alone. I don't know. It's not like she answered to us.'

'When was the last time you saw her?'

'Last night. She was fine when she went to bed.'

'Can you think of anyone who would want to hurt Harlow?'

'No.' Chloe nearly shouted the word. 'She was so lovely. She ran an owl sanctuary. Who wants to hurt a woman who runs an owl sanctuary?'

'And nothing happened this weekend that we need to know about?'

'If an overindulgence in alcohol is what you need to know about, then yeah. But other than that, it was just a group of old school friends catching up after a really long time.'

Krish returned with a steaming mug of tea, and Chloe thanked him for it, grasping it between both hands as if her life depended on it.

The steam rising from the mug made Claudia realise she was gasping for a drink herself. It would be a while before she was able to have one.

Around the light and airy space of the breakfast room were the shocked and concerned faces of Chloe's friends and other hotel guests. A young woman had lost her life and someone in here likely knew the reason why.

CHAPTER 6

'Chloe said Harlow disappeared a couple of times over the weekend. Do you know where she went?' Claudia was sitting at a table with Jay Burton, another of Harlow's friends. A well-groomed man, if on the slightly slim side.

The tinkle of cups and saucers was the soundtrack of the breakfast room around them. People functioned better on a warm drink in the morning and there was no shortage of guests willing to take up the offer of free beverages.

Jay considered the question for a while before responding, sneaking a glance at the rest of the group. What did they know? What were they hiding?

'She appeared a little preoccupied, if I'm honest, but she joined in with our plans and I have no idea what she did in any downtime we had.'

Jay was more composed than Chloe had been. There were no tears. He was clearly upset by Harlow's death, his manner subdued, but without the need for the display of emotion.

'She never told you what she'd been doing?' Claudia pushed again.

'We didn't ask. What she did was her business. We were just thrilled to see her again. As I'm sure Chloe told you, it's been such a long time since we saw each other that there was so much else to talk about.'

Krish walked over and pushed a cup of tea in front of Claudia. Relief swept through her. She'd been desperate for a drink sitting in here but had been too busy to sort one out for herself. She smiled up at Krish and thanked him for the drink and the thought. He waved away her thanks and went back to his own interviews.

'We need to know of anyone who might have had reason to kill Harlow and that's where you and the others come in. You might be able to help.'

Jay rubbed his face, which was pale, with dark circles under his eyes. A bad night's sleep? 'I'm sorry,' he said, trying again. 'I wish I could help you. Harlow really did keep to herself.'

'Did she ever let anything slip?' Claudia took a sip of her drink, the wet warmth welcome after all the talking she'd done already this morning.

'We talked about a lot of things. There's a lot to catch up on when you haven't seen someone for the length of time we hadn't seen each other. But no, she never mentioned a person she was worried about. Or who . . .'

A look Claudia couldn't place crossed his face and Jay once again glanced across at his friends.

'Is there something else you want to say?' she asked.

'It's just . . .'

She waited him out. One hand wrapped around the hot teacup.

He looked again at his friends. The tears. The shock. A group who had been here for friendship and reunion but had finished with loss and death.

'It's just . . .' He tried again. 'I think she did argue with someone.'

Claudia held her breath. Silence was a good motivator for someone to speak. It was a void that people needed to fill.

'It's not that we . . . I . . . heard her, Harlow, arguing with anyone. But we had a meal together last night and

Harlow received a call in the middle of it. Most of the weekend if any of us received calls we sent them to voicemail. We were just enjoying each other's company so much. But this was different.'

Claudia took another sip of the tea to hide her interest. 'In what way?'

'Well, first of all, she took the call. That was odd in the first place. Then she left the table to take it.'

This disappointed Claudia. She'd hoped Jay would be able to tell her what the conversation was about. Maybe Harlow returned and informed them. 'Who was it?'

Jay shook his head, scratched the back of his neck. 'I've no idea. But when she came back she was definitely rattled. She looked like she'd been crying. She was subdued for ten minutes or more before she started to talk to us again. Whoever had called her had really upset her.'

'What time was this?'

Jay checked his watch as though it would tell him the time from last night. 'Oh, about nine.'

'And how long was she gone?' There was no point asking how long she was on the call for because being gone did not mean she was on the call the same length of time. They'd check Harlow's call log for that.

'It didn't take long. A little over five minutes I'd say.'

'Did she say anything when she returned? Anything at all?'

'I'm sorry, no. It's why I hadn't already told you. Harlow kept things close to her chest all weekend. Yeah, there was definitely something going on but none of us could tell you what that was.'

CHAPTER 7

Harlow

Saturday 9 p.m. — 10 hours earlier

Harlow laughed as Ashanti moved the phone camera in her direction. 'Will you stop pointing that thing at me! Put it down for a bit.'

Ashanti pouted. A put-on, beautiful, photogenic kind of pout rather than an ugly, you-can't-say-that-to-me kind of pout. Ashanti had grown into a beautiful woman, her long hair dark and glossy, her skin flawless. 'Photos are my business, darling.' She smirked.

'Yes, your business, not mine. Now put it away.' Harlow put her hand up in the way of the phone.

'My followers will not be pleased.' Another pout as Ashanti placed the phone on the table.

'Is that as far away as you can put it?' Brodie asked, lifting an eyebrow. 'You know you have a handbag on the floor beside your chair.'

Ashanti wrinkled her perfect nose at him.

Harlow watched Brodie and wondered again, not for the first time this weekend, how the skinny kid at school had grown into such a good-looking man. She couldn't help but imagine nestling her head into his neck while those toned muscular arms wrapped around her.

She shook herself free of her imaginings. Ashanti was still being given some light ribbing about her chosen career of influencer. The boys in particular couldn't understand what she did for a living, and the girls, Harlow included, were obsessed with the fact she could make such a great career from social media.

'My three followers,' Chloe stated in her excessively under-exaggerated way, 'wouldn't earn me a penny. I'd love to flounce about uploading photos all day and living the dream.'

Ashanti, who had heard this all weekend, looked to be tiring of the same old conversation. 'It's so much more than that. I have to be *on* all the time. Posting video content, telling them what I'm up to *all* the time. It's quite exhausting. You feel like you're never off. You have no peace. Honestly, I could do with a nine-to-five job. And Chloe—' Ashanti pulled a shocked face — 'you work with dead bodies.' She laughed. 'You did what you set out to do. You must be so pleased with the way your life worked out.'

Chloe smiled, and Harlow felt warm at the sight of her friend's happiness. The quiet, studious girl at school who had always wanted to work with the dead in some capacity had studied hard and achieved her dream by becoming a mortuary technician. Chloe had been taunted as a teenager for her unusual ambitions, but as an adult she was in a field where she was thriving and she looked well for living the life she loved.

Harlow understood that. She'd left the corporate game to open the owl sanctuary. It was hard work, but she loved it. No more high heels and suits, more wellies and jeans in the depths of winter when the owls needed that extra care.

Jay was quietly sipping on a lime soda when the waiter brought their starters out. He'd been a little subdued over the weekend but the girls had fallen in love with him all over again when they'd learned he was a hairdresser and he'd done a couple of blow-dries on request with much ooh- and ahh-ing happening around him. He was watching Ashanti vigorously defend herself now, and moved to the side to allow the waiter to place his mushrooms down in front of him. Harlow decided that she would try to talk to him before the trip was over and see what kept him at a distance from the rest of their friends.

They were tucking into their starters when Harlow's phone rang. Normally she'd have had it on vibrate only, especially in a situation like this, meeting a group of people she hadn't seen in so long. And what a great reunion it had been. But the weekend had been so much more than a reunion to Harlow, and she'd been hopeful of a call at some point. She nearly jumped out of her skin when her phone finally rang.

It was from a withheld number, but she knew who it would be. Or who she hoped it would be. Clutching the handset, she made her excuses to the table and scurried to the hallway just outside the dining room so no one would overhear her conversation. She hadn't told a soul why she was really in Sheffield this weekend, even though they'd spent many an hour talking and confiding in each other. This wasn't something she felt able to share.

'Hello.' Her breath caught in her chest.

'Harlow?'

'Yes. Yes, sorry. I was just with my friends. I had to find somewhere quiet to come and talk.'

'You're alone?' the caller asked.

'Yes. We're having dinner, but I excused myself.'

A couple, arms wrapped around each other, faces turned to the other, oblivious to Harlow, passed by. They were older. Harlow hoped to someday find love that lasted like that.

'Never mind that,' the voice snapped. 'Have you considered our previous conversation?'

Harlow paled. This wasn't what she'd expected. Because they'd called, she'd thought they had changed their stance. Not the other way around. Her hand shook. 'I . . . I thought . . .'

'Harlow, Harlow, Harlow. You have been doing too much thinking recently and look where it's got you.'

There was an ominous silence. What Harlow wanted was only natural. How could they think otherwise?

'I need to know,' the caller continued, 'if you're going ahead and continuing with your actions?'

A cold shiver ran down Harlow's spine. The voice was like broken glass. She couldn't speak.

'Because from what I've heard, you've completely ignored my very kind advice and continued to do as I asked you not to. This has displeased me. You have absolutely no idea what you have blundered into.'

Her whole body was shaking. She had nothing to say that would stop the heartless tirade that was raining down on her.

'My advice to you, Harlow, was to leave this well alone and to forget what you know and to walk away, but you ignored me. That comes at a cost. Don't say I didn't warn you.'

Silence descended. Her caller had hung up. They'd delivered their threat and delivered it well, and they'd gone. As if they were never there. It had taken only two minutes and fifteen seconds, but they'd said everything they needed to say. Harlow had to sit down. Her legs were shaking so much it felt like they were going to buckle beneath her.

She stumbled into the dining room. The starters had been cleared away. She couldn't have finished her plate, anyway. Not now. How was she to get through the rest of the meal? Her whole body was fighting against her. She grabbed the back of her chair and leaned heavily on it.

'Hey, are you okay?' It was Jay. Quiet, observant Jay.

The others turned to look at her, their laughter subsiding as they stared at her, clinging to the seat like a life raft.

Harlow tried to paste a smile to her face. 'I'm fine. I think those couple of glasses of wine on an empty stomach got to me a little.' She dropped into her seat and took a sip of water. 'I'll be much better when the main course comes.'

'Anything interesting?' Jay again.

Harlow furrowed her brows at him.

'The call.' He nodded to the phone, still clamped in her hand.

She pushed it back into her bag. 'No, nothing important. I shouldn't have taken it, to be honest. Not while we're eating.' She tried for another smile. 'It's staying in my bag for the rest of the night.'

'Unlike Ashanti's.' Brodie laughed and the whole table started up again, the focus gone from Harlow, for which she was glad.

She sipped her wine, trying to pay attention to the conversation around her, to steady the shaking that was threatening to overwhelm her. She'd just been threatened. But what the hell was she going to do about it?

What could she do about it?

Laughter floated up around her. She'd have to bring her attention back to her friends, or they'd start asking questions. Notice something was wrong. She'd done a pretty good job of hiding what she'd been doing all weekend. She couldn't fall apart now and let it all unravel.

But this was the first time that it had been clearly spelled out to her that her presence here was unwanted, and in such final terms.

CHAPTER 8

Claudia

Claudia gathered everyone together in the incident room at Snig Hill police HQ for a briefing later that afternoon. They'd been at the hotel for hours, talking to Harlow's friends as well as staff and other guests. CCTV had been seized, the list of staff on duty had been obtained, CSIs had worked the scene and Harlow Cunningham had eventually been transported to the mortuary.

Claudia advised everyone to grab a drink before they started and was conscious that they also needed to eat so she ordered pizzas to be delivered to the station once the briefing was completed. A mug of tea steamed on a desk beside her, where she stood at the front of the room.

'It's been a long day and it's not over yet. Thank you everyone for digging in. Let your loved ones know a job has come in and to not expect you home for tea.

'Harlow Jean Cunningham, aged thirty-four years, was murdered this morning at the West Park Grand Hotel. The post-mortem will be conducted first thing in the morning as time is ticking on today, but early indications are that she was strangled with a narrow belt. Only don't let Nadira hear

I said that. She'll have my hide for making an assumption prior to the PM.' There was snickering around the room as Claudia acknowledged the pathologist's distaste for guessing the MO prior to the official post-mortem.

Claudia continued. 'Harlow was on a long-weekend reunion with four friends: Ashanti Obeng, Chloe Martin, Brodie Keep and Jay Burton. Apparently none of them has seen each other since they were at school last. It's been a while. They're not from Sheffield, but they scattered from their old stomping ground of Devon when they left school and found Sheffield to be a good middle ground to meet up. Jay and Ashanti actually live quite close to each other, but said they hadn't realised and had never seen each other before the reunion. They're booked in at the hotel up to Tuesday, when they'll check out and head back to their respective homes. The hotel has waived all their bills for the duration of their stays, which is extremely generous of them. We'll need to obtain full statements from each of the friends before they leave.'

'I think the hotel feel it's the least they can do as one of their party has been murdered on their premises,' Dominic said.

'Quite.' Claudia tapped her fingers against her leg. 'Not an ideal advertisement for them. They won't want any further bad press.' Her team were listening intently, raring to go at the start of an investigation. 'Let's assess what we have so far, shall we, and then we'll move on from there. We have several lines of inquiry this investigation can take us down. Harlow, as I've said, was found in her hotel room. If a random, let's say, man, wants to kill, he'll look for opportunities. Women alone, walking at night, getting into a car, crossing a park, even walking up their own driveway. But once they're secure in their premises, an opportunist killer will look elsewhere. To walk into a hotel that has CCTV in the lobby, identify Harlow's room, gain access and get out undetected, that takes planning, guts and determination. So with that in mind, we could be looking for someone who specifically targeted Harlow and we find the answer with Harlow.'

There were murmurings of agreement around the room.

'But . . .' Claudia continued, 'there is the possibility of it being a staff member of the hotel though. But even if it was, we have to ask ourselves, did they choose the room randomly, or pick Harlow out for some reason? I would suggest, someone saw Harlow and took action. She'd allow them access to the room and no one would look twice at them walking around the hotel, before or after her murder. And it's not as though it was a bloody crime scene. The problem we have with hotel staff is any evidence found could be accounted for. Fingerprints in the room, stray hairs, that kind of thing. They could say they bumped up with Harlow at some point during her stay. We have to take this carefully and go where the evidence takes us.'

'One of the friends?' asked Krish.

'Possibly, but we'll know more when we get a time of death from the PM. The friends were waiting for Harlow downstairs in the dining room and have multiple eyewitnesses. Harlow was murdered this morning, going by her hair. It's really thick and was still damp. We need to narrow down a timeframe. But don't rule anything out yet.'

She picked up the tea to the side of her. 'So, what do we have?' She turned to Dominic. 'The hotel manager, Howie, or something, he muttered under his breath when he walked away with you. Anything important?'

Dominic laughed. 'Mr Mackie . . .'

'Ah.' Claudia waggled her finger in the air. 'Continue.'

'He didn't say much, just something about how this wasn't good for the hotel image. I mostly ignored him. Thought it was pretty poor taste, to be honest.'

Claudia couldn't agree with him more. 'Okay, what else?'

'Harlow was distracted this weekend,' said Lisa. 'The group didn't spend every waking hour together but some of them had the feeling that when they weren't together Harlow might have had other plans.'

'That fits with what Jay Burton told me. He also said she took a phone call last night and seemed upset when she returned. But she didn't discuss it with anyone.'

'Ditto Ashanti Obeng,' said Graham. 'It seems like her friends noticed but were pretty discreet and didn't question her.'

'Which is a shame for us. We could do with knowing who was on the other end of that call and what it was about. Krish, can you make the request for Harlow's call logs, please? The call was about nine p.m. And while you're at it, get the paperwork started to access her emails. We can see if there are any conversations of interest in there. The problem will be if she mostly used WhatsApp.'

'I'll get straight on it.' Krish looked at his watch. 'The phone logs'll no doubt be with us in the morning. It'll take a lot longer to obtain the emails.'

Claudia gave a quick nod and moved on. 'Lisa, if you can view the CCTV. I have no idea what or who we're looking for. It might be that Harlow comes in or out with someone other than one of the four friends we've spoken to. Go through the entire weekend, please. Also, use the CCTV to pin down each friend's arrival time for breakfast. They have to walk through the lobby from the lifts to get to the breakfast room.'

Lisa made a note. It would be a task that would keep her busy, but it was all part of the job.

'Russ will attend the PM with me first thing in the morning and I'll speak to Sharpe about increasing our numbers for this job. There are a lot of witnesses to get through, staff as well as guests.' Sharpe would push against it with budgetary constraints, but needs must.

'So, what are we looking at?' Claudia asked the room. It was always better to get the whole team to think through the case. No idea was too stupid, no question too inane.

'Whatever she was keeping a secret from her friends, it's come back to bite her,' said Krish.

'And our job is to find out what that secret was and if it got her killed. We also need to investigate her friends. Is it a coincidence that they meet up and Harlow ends up dead?'

'It's a little obvious though, if it is one of the friends. And anyway, none of them could have made that phone call, if they were all at the table when it came.' Lisa didn't seem impressed with the idea.

Claudia expected her team to speak their minds. In fact she encouraged it. Only by adopting a free exchange of ideas could an investigation flourish and push forward.

'We don't know anything at this stage. We don't know that the person who called is our killer. You spoke to the friends; what are your initial thoughts?' Claudia asked. 'Jay was subdued. Closed-off, even. What you'd expect for grief really. But there was something else I couldn't quite put my finger on, though it wasn't screaming murder at me.'

'The others were the same,' said Lisa. 'Grief-stricken, as you'd expect. But you're right about sensing an underlying reticence.'

'We need to just do a little research into them.' Claudia put the mug down and started to pace around the room.

'Ashanti told me she's an influencer.' Graham looked puzzled. 'She was deadly serious. Not a touch of irony in sight. It's a real job?'

'It is.' Lisa laughed at him. 'People can make a fortune just posting their lives online. Companies give them goods and money to post about their products while they're going about their day. It's really lucrative. And because their followers go and buy the goods the person has posted about, that person is then called an influencer.'

'And why do you know so much about it?'

'Because I'm so much younger than you and I don't live in the Dark Ages.'

Krish smirked.

Claudia shook her head. 'We'll have some photographs to trawl through on Ashanti's feed from this weekend if that's true. We can check, see if there's anyone skulking in the background. Graham, is it asking too much for you to do that?'

Graham frowned at his nails, already bitten to the quick. 'Yeah, I can search her social media and see what I can find.'

Lisa laughed again and Graham scowled. 'Give over will ya, mate.'

She chuckled. 'I'm sorry. I just know how much you hate social media.'

He shook his head. 'It's the spawn of the devil. Why people can't live their lives instead of documenting it all this way, I just don't get it. And now people are on it so much they can make careers out of it. It's a bit weird, if you ask me.'

With the tasks divided up, Claudia moved on. 'Harlow's next of kin needs informing, but she's from Devon. Dominic has requested Devon and Cornwall police speak to her father, who's her only living relative. She's not married or in a serious relationship. Apparently she threw herself into the owl sanctuary when she quit the London rat race a few years ago.'

'An owl sanctuary doesn't scream secrets and murder, does it?' Graham leaned back in his chair, a grin on his face.

'It doesn't. But something got her killed today. And, to me, this feels like a personal murder. With an up-close strangulation like that, they wanted to feel the life drain out of her.'

The grin slipped off Graham's face.

Claudia felt bad, Graham was a good cop and cops used humour to deal with difficult cases. 'We'll have a bite to eat, then we'll head back to the hotel and continue talking to witnesses. Of course there are a lot of people who don't know anything. But we won't weed out those who do without talking to those who don't. And tomorrow we find out who Harlow Cunningham was talking to when she left the dinner table last night.'

CHAPTER 9

Claudia was exhausted by the time she arrived home. It had been a rostered rest day, but those often went out the window in a busy city like Sheffield, especially when a murder occurred. And her session with Robert talking about the incident in the woods had taken a huge chunk of her energy before she'd even started on the new investigation.

There was a car she recognised parked outside the detached house as she pulled into her drive on Middlewood Drive East. It was a lazy quiet street to the north of the city, where she could enjoy the green spaces, and visitors were easily recognised. Her drive wasn't a driveway in the typical sense of the word, but a flat, paved and concrete area in front of the house, off the road. Claudia shook her head. This she could do without. What the hell was he doing here? Hadn't she made it clear she didn't want to see him? That she was doing okay and didn't need his support. Why did Matt never listen to her?

Claudia turned the engine off and waited a beat, gathering what limited strength she had left. If anyone could find their way under the shell she had erected around herself since she'd killed a man, it was Matt, and she didn't want that. Yes, it was Robert's job to get underneath, but he was doing it in such a way that it was less painful and more healing. Matt just took a shovel, dug down and found the painful spot, with little in the way to soothe it.

Matt was at the top of the drive, waiting.

'I heard you caught a job today, so knew you'd be late home. Thought you could do with someone to feed you.' He grinned and showed her a white bag with the local Chinese takeaway logo.

'I've had pizza.' She walked towards the house.

'If I know you, and I do, then you've only had a slice or two and left the rest for your team. While in the meantime you're wasting away.'

She hated how well he understood her. Unlocking the door, Claudia stepped over the threshold.

'Are you inviting me in?' He held up the bag again.

There was a whiff of sweet and sour. Prawn crackers. Her stomach rumbled.

'Why are you here, Matt?'

Matt smiled gently. 'Like I said, I thought you'd be hungry.'

'No. Really. Why are you here? Tonight. Right now.'

His face relaxed, the smile disappearing. 'You had your counselling session today. Then you fell for a job that kept you busy all day. I figured you'd be exhausted.'

He'd figured right, and again, she hated that about him. She turned and walked into the house, leaving the door ajar behind her.

Claudia grabbed plates from the cupboards and a half-drunk bottle of wine out of the fridge, pulling a couple of glasses from the top cupboard. Then she collected the cutlery from the drawer. Matt unboxed the food onto the plates. There was no need to talk. They'd done this a thousand times. It was supposed to be over, though. No more sharing meals together.

They sat at the table. Claudia delved into the sweet and sour chicken as though she hadn't eaten all day. Stress made her want to run, but it also made her hungry.

'Want to talk about it?' asked Matt as Claudia was finishing. They'd barely said a word as the food was devoured.

She rubbed a hand across her eyes. She was worn out and needed her bed. They had a long day ahead of them again tomorrow. 'What shift are you on tomorrow?'

'Afters.' Matt was a DS on the firearms car. He still worked shifts. 'I was on mornings today.' He didn't need to be up early.

'I'm tired, Matthew. Can we do this another time? I'm grateful for the food, but I really am exhausted.'

'The counselling?' His voice was soft. She remembered the old days.

'It didn't help.'

'Want to talk it through?'

'Not really. That's why I go to the sessions with Robert. To talk it through. I don't then need to talk those through with you.'

He smiled in acknowledgement. 'And Sharpe's still providing you space and time?'

Here he was, digging with his shovel.

'Yes. That's how we fell for this run-of-the-mill job this morning. She's not giving us anything too taxing.'

'She's a tough one at the best of times from what I've heard, but she seems to be fair.'

Claudia had had enough. 'I don't understand why you've been around so much since this happened.'

He flicked a crumb of food from the table into his palm and dropped it onto his now empty plate. 'You've been through something huge. I have a little understanding of what that's like working on the car. I wanted to be there for you. Is that so difficult to believe?'

'We're divorced, Matt. You don't get to be there anymore. We made that decision three years ago.' A headache was brewing, fatigue pulling her down. It really had been a long day.

She and Matt had married young after a brief relationship. Her dad had told her to be cautious, but she hadn't listened — too in love. As it turned out, her father had been right. It hadn't worked out.

Claudia rose from her chair and gathered the plates. Moved them over to the sink and ran the tap over them. She liked to rinse them before placing them in the dishwasher.

'It doesn't mean I stopped caring.'

'And what does your wife think of that?'

Silence fell over them like a weighted blanket.

Minutes passed. Claudia cleared away the dishes into the dishwasher, then stood with her back to the sink, her arms folded. She wanted her bed. Matt needed to leave.

He stood. 'She knows I'm here, Claudia. She can't possibly imagine what you're going through and, as long as I return home to her, she's secure enough in our relationship that I can support you through this.' His voice was quiet and gentle.

Claudia waved a hand around the room. Getting more and more agitated. Mostly at herself. Why had she allowed him in? Again. Maybe because he was right. He was the one person in her life who understood what taking a life in the line of duty felt like. But killing with a gun was at a distance. She'd been up-close and personal. She'd been in a physical struggle. She'd been holding the knife in her hand when it entered her attacker's flesh. He'd had no chance. But it had been him or her. She'd had little choice. 'You never came when Ruth died,' she spat out.

Matt had been moving towards the door, but he turned now. 'I made contact. I phoned you several times to check in. But . . .' He paused. Searched for the words. 'Your father.'

He never had liked Dominic. Had tried to get along with him when they were married, for her sake. But underneath, he'd struggled.

'What is it?' she asked.

Matt ran a hand through his hair. 'I don't know, Claudia. You don't want to go into that now, on top of everything else.'

'Tell me.' She had her own frustrations with Dominic and needed someone else's opinion on him.

'Something didn't sit right with me. It was like there were two versions of him and we were only seeing the one

45

he wanted us to see. I can't explain it.' He looked as tired as she was. 'I should go.' He checked his watch. As though this was his decision and not that Claudia had asked him to leave. 'I'm only ever at the end of a phone if you need me.'

Claudia closed the door behind him and rested her back against it, closing her eyes on the exhaustion that was threatening to overwhelm her. She didn't know how she felt about Matt's attempt to support her. There was a need for his comfort. But she had to remind herself that they were divorced and he was now remarried.

But that comment about her father. It was the most he'd ever said about Dominic. He'd kept his thoughts to himself when they were married. This was the only time he'd explained the frostiness between them. Matt was usually an excellent judge of character.

Her father was childish in his frustrations with Claudia being a rank higher than him and he was not being particularly supportive in her trauma at killing a man, but other than that, he was her dad. Nothing more, nothing less.

Claudia locked up, switched the dishwasher on, and went to bed. Dominic, laughing at her pain, invaded her dreams.

CHAPTER 10

The next morning Claudia and Russ attended the post-mortem of Harlow Cunningham.

The Medico-Legal Centre was a two-storey building on Watery Street. When they arrived, Nadira was already kitted up and ready to go, as was Smithy, the morgue technician.

Harlow's body had been X-rayed and now lay on one of the many examination tables in the room, waiting for the process to begin.

'Sorry we're a little late,' Claudia said, pulling her gloves on. 'The traffic was more difficult than usual this morning.'

Nadira's eyes wrinkled behind her mask, indicating a smile. 'Don't worry, you haven't missed anything. It's good to see you. Shall we get started?'

The X-rays showed nothing out of the ordinary and after viewing them Nadira picked up the clipboard holding the body map onto which she would draw all marks, scars and tattoos on Harlow's body, front and back. They had removed the bags from her hands and head.

There was a discreet tattoo on the back of her shoulder of a phoenix rising from the ashes. Though the tattoo was small, the colours on it were bright and beautiful.

The belt was still in situ but Nadira drew in the bruising she could see around Harlow's throat along with the scratches going vertically down through the bruising onto the body map.

'Where she attempted to claw the belt from around her throat?' murmured Claudia.

'She put up a fight.' Russ's eyes narrowed as he took in the dark ring around the woman's throat with the defensive marks breaking the line.

'We'll know more when we get the results from the nail clippings and swabs, but I suspect she did.' Nadira continued drawing in what she could see: the petechial spots in Harlow's eyes and the swollen tongue in her mouth.

There were no other markings of significance.

The room was brightly lit, and the glare was giving Claudia a headache. Then she remembered it had started last night. She closed her eyes for a few seconds, the darkness a peaceful release from the tension she was carrying.

'Shall we move on?' Nadira broke through Claudia's brief moment and she opened her eyes again, hoping Nadira hadn't noticed the time she'd taken for herself as they worked. It wasn't professional, and she wasn't sure why she'd done it. Robert would tell her it was her body's way of communicating with her. Telling her the real deep-down feelings she had about events occurring in her life. Past and in the present.

She didn't need Robert in her head right now. She needed to focus and do her job. Robert had an hour of her time once a week. That's all he was getting out of her.

As for her body, it was plain old fatigue. She was busy. Yesterday had been a long day. Of course it had affected her. It was supposed to have been a day off, a rest day, but that had been scuppered. 'Ready when you are.' She smiled from behind her mask.

Next came further swabs. From Harlow's neck, inside her mouth and a rape kit was completed. Russ and Smithy were quietly competent at keeping up with Nadira as she worked, taking the samples and creating exhibits to be forensically examined.

Claudia's stomach was tight as Nadira carried out the rape kit.

Nadira finished. 'There's no injury that would suggest she's been raped but we'll know more when we get the results back.'

Claudia let out a small breath. The woman had been through enough without adding rape to the equation. It didn't appear that this offence was sexually motivated, though. They had to look elsewhere.

The leather belt used to strangle Harlow was finally removed, and Russ carefully bagged it. This would be a priority at the lab as far as having exhibits forensically examined went.

Harlow's hair was combed and then washed through. Particulates collected and exhibited.

Nadira then commenced the internal examination, making her Y incision precisely and cleanly. Organs were weighed and measured and samples were taken.

Finally it was all over, and Nadira handed over the care of Harlow to Smithy, who would stitch her back up.

'Cause of death?' asked Claudia as they moved away from Harlow.

'Preliminary findings are that she was mechanically asphyxiated. Prior to that she was a fit and healthy woman with no issues that would have caused her death. We will, of course, have to wait for all the tests to return, but I'm pretty sure on my conclusions this morning.'

'And time of death?' This was a question that could potentially rule Harlow's friends in or out of the investigation, depending on the CCTV findings.

Nadira paused. Was there an issue?

'Whoever went to find the victim in her hotel room was very lucky they didn't walk in on her killer.' Nadira was serious.

'It was that close?'

'As you saw for yourself, her hair was damp at the roots. It provided a good indicator, without it being a forensic measurement. But along with body temperature, room temp, an empty stomach, and signs of livor mortis starting, it informed me the victim died an hour and a half, to two hours, before we arrived.'

'Shit. That was close.'

'Indeed.'

Claudia pulled off her gloves. They'd been treating the case as a murder, but now the forensic pathologist had labelled it as such they were on firmer ground. Though it had been pretty obvious. And Claudia, though she understood Nadira's need to follow protocol, sometimes became frustrated by how that protocol slowed things down. She thanked Nadira. She was, after all, an integral part of the investigative process.

Russ looked at Claudia as they returned to the car. 'There's a lot of work to do on this case. Have you spoken with Sharpe yet about extra staff?'

She hadn't. Things had gotten away from her yesterday. But Russ was right. There were so many witnesses to whittle down that they needed help. 'I'll get straight on it,' she promised.

'Are you managing okay?'

He wasn't asking about her mental health. About her feelings on killing a man. He was enquiring about the physical injuries she had sustained when she'd fought with him. 'I'm fine. All healed. You know that.'

'It's just . . .'

Claudia unlocked the car and Russ placed the exhibits in the boot before climbing in the front driver's seat.

'It's just you seemed a little distant in there, so I wondered . . .'

No one other than Russ would dare ask her. 'I'm fine. A little tired is all. Just give me a kick if you see me drifting off again, yeah?'

He laughed. 'With permission granted like that, you betcha.'

Claudia climbed in beside him and clicked the seatbelt in. It had been a traumatic year. First, they'd lost Ruth, her father's second wife, her step-mother and her closest friend, then the case with the Artist, which she was still trying to get her head around. And the difficult thing was, she'd lost her best friend so had no one to share her burden. Other than Matt, who had taken it upon himself to be her saviour. It was probably why she'd allowed him in rather than sending him away, as she should have done.

Russ manoeuvred the car into the traffic and headed back to headquarters. The drive gave Claudia time to think about Matt. Last night she'd been too tired to even consider her relationship with him. Her head had hit the pillow, and she'd been asleep within seconds.

She thought back to why they'd separated in the first place. Nowadays he was kind and considerate. Apparently he wanted to be there for her when she needed someone. But when they were married, he had been more distant. His job had taken up his attention, and he'd been studying for his sergeant's exams. They had spent little time on their marriage, and it had fizzled out for lack of care. They had drifted apart. It was as simple as that. It wasn't all Matt's fault. Claudia took her share of the blame. As a busy DI on a murder-investigation team, she worked all hours. It wasn't conducive to a solid relationship if the other person was struggling to put time in as well.

They hadn't fought. There'd been no bad feelings. That was one reason they were still able to see each other, and how it was so amicable. Matt had married a woman who was not in the job, and Claudia had promised herself she would do the same if she ever started dating again. She'd keep her love life away from police officers. It was just too difficult with opposing shifts and protracted hours. Of course, the initial attraction was easy and you always had a lot to talk about. But long term, as she'd found out to her detriment, it didn't work out.

The stronger relationships were the ones where cops were married outside of the job. As long as the spouse was understanding about the extra hours when they were needed.

Her ongoing relationship with Matt wasn't fair on his wife, though, no matter how understanding she was. He was obviously being open with her about it, but Claudia couldn't help but feel she was doing something wrong and she should push Matt away. But other than Robert, he was the one constant in her life she could go to when it all felt a little unstable.

CHAPTER 11

Before she went to the incident room for a briefing, Claudia headed up to DCI Maddison Sharpe's office.

'Start pulling the team together,' she said to Russ before they parted ways on the stairs. 'Morning briefing in ten minutes.' She hoped. If she could get a quick meeting with the DCI.

Sharpe's PA Maxine Clarke was on the phone when Claudia arrived. She held a finger up and finished the call, then welcomed Claudia warmly. 'She's actually free at the minute. Do you want to see her?'

'If I can. A bit of an update on the case and a request she's not going to like, I'm afraid.'

Maxine smiled. 'I'll leave that one with you.' And with that she phoned Sharpe, and soon Claudia was being sent through to her office.

DCI Maddison Sharpe was as sharp by nature as by name. Her whole appearance was polished and perfectly presented, and she didn't suffer fools gladly. This morning she had a look on her face that said today was not a particularly good day.

Claudia sighed inwardly. You never knew what you were going to get with the DCI. She'd been helpful to Claudia over recent months, but she was also driven and had in the past pushed her into jobs she had been uncomfortable with.

'Claudia, what can I do for you this morning?' Sharpe's tone was clipped. She wasn't in the mood for a drop-in.

'Ma'am, the Harlow Cunningham murder—'

'What of it?'

If she'd let her finish.

'An update?'

Sharpe leaned back in her chair. 'You couldn't do this via email?'

'I also have a request relevant to the update.' Claudia was still standing. Sharpe hadn't invited her to sit.

Sharpe pursed her lips. 'I'm not sure I like the sound of this. Get on with it.'

'I've just come back from the PM. Mechanical asphyxiation. As we suspected from the crime scene. The problem is the scene is in a hotel and the number of witnesses we need to speak with is high. Just to eliminate them, you understand. We have a lead in that Harlow took a phone call Saturday night that appeared to upset her. No one knows who the call was from or what it was about, but we've requested her call logs and will review them this morning. The issue is staffing . . .'

Sharpe steepled her fingers and leaned forward on her desk. 'You want more staff?'

'Temporarily, while we work the hotel.'

'You do realise the whole force is struggling for staff?'

'I'm aware of that.' There was no denying the trouble they were in, but murder was murder and it pretty much trumped most things. 'She's not from Sheffield, ma'am. She's from out of town and has come to our city and been murdered. I think it's an important public interest case where the media will watch our every move.'

Sharpe opened a drawer and pulled out a newspaper, dropping it on her desk with a flourish. 'Oh, we're already being watched, DI Nunn. We're this morning's headlines.'

Claudia paused. Sharpe was upset. She could understand why. Claudia's fatigue had meant she had dropped the ball by not updating her boss earlier. 'I informed the media department yesterday. They were aware of all the facts we were happy to disclose. But we had to wait until Devon and Cornwall spoke with the victim's family to disclose her name to the press.'

Sharpe ran a hand through her hair, something that was out of character for the detective chief inspector. She never outwardly showed signs of stress. And yet here she was, ruffled by the reporting of a murder in the city and Claudia's request for extra staff.

'Of course you can have the staff you need. Connelly has already been to see me this morning. He wants this case closing as quickly as possible. A murder in the city is never a good thing, but this is a visitor, a tourist. No one likes tourists getting killed in the city. It's not a good look.'

Detective Superintendent Connelly pretty much stayed out of the way, unless things were dire. He'd visited both Claudia and Dominic in hospital when they'd been stabbed. Claudia had wondered at the time if she was dying, because of his visit. But of course she had recovered quickly. It was amazing how well the human body could heal.

'Thank you.' Claudia was about to leave when Sharpe cleared her throat. She hadn't finished. Claudia held her ground, wondering where this could go. She'd taken the warning on board about clearing up the murder. What else was there to say?

'Samuel Tyler.'

Two words that turned Claudia's heart inside out. The man they had charged with murdering Ruth Harrison, her father's wife.

'What now?' she asked, with more venom than she'd have liked.

'His trial starts in a couple of months. I wondered how you were doing?'

Claudia shrugged. She had nothing to say. 'Let the courts sort it out. It's what they're there for.'

'You haven't heard from him since?'

'He's tried, but I'm not interested. To be honest, I've kind of had other things on my mind.'

Sharpe rose from her chair and walked around her desk to stand in front of Claudia. 'I understand that, which is why I want to know how you're doing. It's been one thing after another. You're still seeing your counsellor?'

Sharpe knew damn well she was. It was being paid for by the force. And Claudia told her this.

'Do tell me if I can do anything. And as the trial gets nearer, if you or Dominic need anything, just shout.'

And finally she released her.

Claudia was no longer interested in Tyler. The trial was something she and her father had to get through together. But for now, well, she had other things to occupy her mind.

Back in the incident room, Claudia gathered the team for the briefing. They had time and cause of death, and now it was time to see what Harlow's call logs had revealed.

With mugs in hands the team came together. The scent of coffee wafted strongly under Claudia's nose even though it was tea she was drinking herself. The majority of the unit were coffee drinkers.

She started by updating them on the post-mortem, as she had done with Sharpe. No one was particularly surprised. 'It gives us a timeframe for Harlow's murder, so Lisa, work backwards from our arrival, or rather, more specifically, Nadira's arrival, on the hotel lobby CCTV and check to see if the friends were downstairs then or had yet to arrive, please. I know you have a lot to go through with the CCTV. And because of the size of the task ahead generally, Sharpe has agreed to allocate extra staff to support us. It was a long day yesterday, speaking to everyone, prioritising those who may be of use and then those who wanted to leave the hotel, and there are more to go today. We have to stick with it. Early indications are that Harlow was up to something this weekend and not just here to meet up with long-lost friends. We need to push the friends before they disappear to their respective homes. They may know more than they're letting on, even if they don't realise it. Full statements are yet to be taken so they're expecting to be contacted.'

She still had an uneasy feeling that the friends were hiding something from the team. 'Graham, did you manage to go through Ashanti's social media channels?'

Graham pulled a face and scrubbed a hand over his tightly cropped hair. A style that was a leftover from his army days. 'Yeah, I've searched through all her social media posts, of which there's nothing of interest. There are photos of the reunion group, including Harlow, in various locations, but as far as I can see, there's no one in the background who pops up in multiple shots. And all the images suggest they're having a good time together. No one's out the way being side-lined.'

'Thanks for checking. It was important to view it all. Make sure you have a copy of all images and post text and upload it to HOLMES, please.'

Graham made himself a note.

Claudia let out a small sigh. 'The press is obviously interested in this story, so keep your wits about you, please, and no leaks. This has the potential to be high-profile because she was a visitor to the city and not a local.' She turned to Krish. 'Do we have Harlow's phone records?'

Krish lifted a stack of papers and waved them in the air. 'We do. They were emailed to me about half an hour ago. I printed them out as I find it easier to go through that much data on paper on my desk. I'm going through them now. It's going to take a while.'

'Who called her at around nine Saturday night?'

Krish frowned, and flicked through several pages until he found the one he needed. His finger slid down the page as he searched down the call timeline. 'It was a withheld number. The call lasted two minutes and forty-seven seconds.'

Claudia rolled her eyes. Withheld numbers were the bane of her existence — she hated the way they snagged investigations just as they were getting going. Whoever had phoned Harlow had upset her and whoever it was might well know why she was murdered.

She moved on. Letting her frustration slide for now. 'How is Harlow's father this morning?'

Graham tapped a pen on his desk. 'He called to say he arrived safely in Sheffield last night after being visited by Devon and Cornwall yesterday and is available anytime this morning to do the identification and to see his daughter. Want me to take him?'

Claudia shook her head. 'As SIO it's up to me to show my face and update him on how the investigation's going, so I may as well kill two birds with one stone and do the ID. Anything from the father on what Harlow was doing in Sheffield other than meeting school friends?'

It was Graham's turn to shake his head. 'According to the attending officers who visited him yesterday, Paul Cunningham said that as far as he was aware, his daughter was excited to reunite with her old school friends. She'd arranged it in Sheffield because it was pretty central for all of them, as they'd scattered around the country. They said he was pretty shaken up by her murder especially as he lost his wife last year and Harlow is an only child. They were both devastated by the loss. Harlow took it particularly hard. That was why he was pleased to see her travel for the reunion: she was interested in something again. He couldn't think of anyone who'd want to kill her. He was adamant about that.'

'That's parents for you. Always see the good in their children.' Claudia snuck a look at Dominic, who was taking notes in his pad, paying her little attention. 'Interesting that he says Harlow was the one to organise the meet-up in Sheffield. Can we confirm that with her friends today, please? It may be she had a reason to come up here other than meeting her friends. It's certainly looking that way. We need to find out what that reason was. Krish, trawl through her phone records. Identify anyone she called this weekend. We want to speak to them as well.'

CHAPTER 12

There was some free parking space outside the Medico-Legal Centre in the afternoon, her second visit of the day, and Claudia drove straight into a spot.

She had collected Paul Cunningham from his hotel. Not the hotel his daughter had been murdered in. Paul Cunningham, most sensibly, had stayed elsewhere. Though he had, on the way over to the centre, made noises about visiting the place where his daughter had died, or more specifically, been murdered.

Claudia wasn't sure why people felt the need to do this. Wasn't it better to remember them as they were rather than visit the place where harm had come to them? She always felt a twinge of . . . what? Anxiety, she supposed, when she entered her father's home, the place Ruth had been abducted from. They had found a great deal of blood in their garage so it was obvious she'd been injured there. Claudia struggled to understand how her father could stay there every night with that old crime scene below him. Didn't it haunt him? She had never dared ask.

And here she was again, wondering why Paul Cunningham wanted to visit the scene of his daughter's murder when he could remember the good times he'd had with her and not go to a terrible place that would haunt him with awful memories.

Harlow's father was a tall, very upright sixty-year-old. He unfolded himself from the car seat and into the street, standing straight and staring at the building before him. His eyes were damp before they'd even entered.

It was a building of loss and pain. Where they conducted post-mortems and carried out inquests. The human heart was ripped from the body in this building, both figuratively and literally.

'Are you ready?' Claudia was gentle.

'Is anyone ever ready, DI Nunn?' he asked quietly as they remained standing on the pavement.

The question surprised her, but no, no one was ever ready to identify their loved one after a brutal death.

Claudia inclined her head in acceptance and opened the door for him. No other words were necessary.

Paul stepped through into the building. Claudia took him down various corridors to where they needed to be. To where his daughter lay waiting to be officially identified. This was why Claudia was here, in an official capacity, but she was aware that for Paul his journey here had been to say goodbye to his only child.

'When you're ready,' she said, 'I will draw the curtain back, and you'll be able to see Harlow through the glass. Due to the nature of the investigation, we're unable to allow you to hold or touch her at this time. I'm so sorry.'

Paul bowed his head. 'She's not coming home with me, is she?'

'I'm afraid not. It's possible that when we arrest her killer, he could request a secondary post-mortem of his own and we have to accommodate that.'

He gave a sharp intake of breath.

It was always so difficult informing the family of this. That the person who had murdered their loved one could have them opened up again.

Paul's hands went up to his face and his shoulders shook.

'We'll do right by Harlow,' Claudia said, determined not to allow Paul's grief to break open her professional veneer. It would do neither of them any good if she became upset in front of him.

He raised his head. 'Harlow's mother . . .' His voice was like crushed ice. 'We lost her last year. A car accident. We were both devastated, but Harlow was broken for a good six months. I was so proud of her when she organised this meet-up with her friends. It was the first real thing she'd done, outside of going to work, since we lost Angela.'

The poor man. 'And Harlow was your only child?'

The tears were response enough. Claudia reached out and placed her hand on his arm. 'I'm so sorry for your loss.'

Paul gave a weak nod. 'I want to see my daughter now.'

Claudia pressed the button on the wall and the curtains slid silently away, exposing the trolley behind the glass on which Harlow lay. A clean white sheet across her body up to her chin. Her hair framed her face as it might have done in life. But there was no way she looked like she was sleeping. The blood had settled in the lower half of her body. Her complexion was pale, almost grey, her lips bloodless.

Paul took a step closer to the glass and placed a hand on it. He straightened his spine, and Claudia watched him blink several times. This was a man who was attempting to view his only child in her death and not fall apart in front of the police officer he was with. She'd witnessed many variations of reactions at this point, and none of them failed to touch her. Even though Paul was trying to hold himself together, the pain was clearly visible in the lines of his face and the tension in his shoulders. Claudia took a deep breath to steady herself.

'Is that your daughter, Harlow Cunningham?' she asked.

'That's Harlow. That's my baby.' He rested his forehead against the glass. 'Who would do this to her?'

'We don't yet know but we have an excellent team of officers working the case, with extra staff being drafted in to support us.'

'You'll catch whoever did this?'

She could never promise such a thing. There were times that it just wasn't possible. But they would work to the best of their ability. 'We will do everything we can to bring her killer to justice, Mr Cunningham.'

Paul straightened again. Stared ahead at the woman on the trolley. The woman who had once been his only child, full of life, with emotions and dreams, who cared for owls and her friends.

Claudia gave Paul the time he desired. To be close with her. To watch over her and talk to her through the glass as much as he needed to.

When he was done, she ushered him out of the viewing room and they walked slowly down the corridor. Paul had regained his composure.

'Can you think of anyone who would want to hurt Harlow?' Claudia asked.

'Someone targeted her?' Puzzlement crossed his broad face, the wide nose and ruddy cheeks.

Paul and his daughter didn't look much alike. Harlow's features were petite and classical. She must have taken after her mother. 'It's a possibility. She took a phone call the night before that we're told upset her. We don't have a number for the caller but I'm wondering if you have any idea who it could have been. Has she had any problems recently?'

Paul rubbed the back of his neck. 'She threw a lot of her time into the sanctuary. She was well-loved in the community. I never heard her speak of problems. Yeah, she might have struggled a little financially keeping the sanctuary going. Doesn't every charity? But that was all part of her day-to-day life. Not something she'd get upset with anyone about.'

'You don't think she would have borrowed money from anyone she shouldn't, to save the sanctuary?'

Paul stopped in his tracks. 'My daughter was not like that, DI Nunn. She worked hard. She loved what she did, and she liked to do the right thing. I said she *might have* struggled, not that she *was* struggling. Harlow didn't confide in me about her woes. To her, I'd done my time taking care of her, it was her time to care for me.' He gave a wistful, heart-breaking smile. 'Do I look like the kind of person who needs caring for?'

Claudia had to agree with him, yet again, that he did not. He was a strong-looking man who was bending a little under the grief of loss. A double heartbreak in the space of a year. What guy wouldn't?

'What about friends down in Devon? Anyone we should talk with, who might know more about her business?'

Paul set off walking again, and Claudia kept pace.

'There's the lad she runs the sanctuary with, Steve Pacey. A good individual. If she was having issues Harlow might've confided in Steve.'

Claudia ran Paul back to his hotel. Offered her condolences again, along with her contact details. Took Steve Pacey's particulars and wished Paul a safe journey home.

Back to a place that was forever changed.

This past year had given her an insight into the experience of the victim's family in a murder investigation. The hollowness of a home that was once a familiar space. The desire for impossible questions to be answered, and answered immediately. And a need for a kind word to help you through your day.

Paul Cunningham had lost his world and Claudia couldn't change that for him, but what she could do was listen if he needed her to and investigate to the best of her ability to provide the answers he was looking for.

Harlow Cunningham was dead. Killed by an intruder in her hotel room. Harlow had been hiding something that neither her friends nor her father had known about, and Claudia was going to find out what that something was.

CHAPTER 13

Harlow

Saturday 5.12 p.m. — 14 hours earlier

They'd been shopping as a group, and Harlow had slipped off to make a phone call as they reached the hotel. She'd tried a couple of times, but the call was never answered.

The January cold was chilling Harlow to her bones. This weekend would have been much more pleasant if they'd arranged it for spring, but Harlow had posited that you couldn't trust the UK weather, it could rain the entire time in April or May, so they may as well get together while they were all excited about it.

The truth was, Harlow just didn't want to wait. She hadn't wanted to delay doing this.

And now there was no response.

It deflated her.

She pushed the phone back in her coat pocket and rubbed her arms. It was time to head back in.

'Harlow? Harlow Cunningham?' The shout came out of nowhere. A woman's voice, loud and high-pitched. Like she was scared of what she was about to do. A nervous energy streamed from her.

Harlow frowned as the woman approached. She was younger than her by a few years. Late twenties, maybe. Her long hair flowed behind her as she rushed towards Harlow. Who was she and what did she want?

'Harlow?' She was panting now as she stood in front of Harlow.

Harlow was puzzled. 'Sorry, do I know you?'

'Sophie Sinclair.'

Harlow recognised the surname. Her heart leapt into her throat. She held out her hand for want of knowing what else to do.

The woman erupted, her arms flying into the air in a stop gesture. 'I haven't come to make friends with you,' she hissed. 'I want you to stay away from my mother.'

Harlow's mouth opened, but no words came out and tears pricked at her eyes. Her thoughts a moment ago clear, now jumbled.

'Do you hear me?' the young woman shouted in her face. 'Leave my mother alone.'

She'd already been cold, but a freezing sensation now hit her bones and her mind was in freefall. She had to get away from here. Get to her room.

She turned and moved to the hotel entrance.

Sophie Sinclair followed. 'You have no idea what you're doing to her. What you could do to her if you continue with this.'

The noise of the hotel lobby struck Harlow like a wall of thunder. Her senses suddenly overloaded. She was disorientated. Sophie was following her, shouting at her. People could hear what was happening. She couldn't lead Sophie up to her hotel room. Who knew what she was capable of? She was furious and her voice was so loud. Harlow wanted to cover her ears. Why had it gone like this? This wasn't what she had wanted, or expected, when she'd planned the trip to Sheffield.

She looked around her, needing an escape, but there was none. Nowhere to go where Sophie couldn't follow. So, with nothing else to do, Harlow stepped to the side in an attempt to quiet Sophie and talk about this peacefully. The way she had wanted from the start.

Sophie followed Harlow away from the centre of the lobby. Away from the reception desk. Away from listening ears. But still she was raving. Her arms twisting in the air. 'You have no idea of the damage you can do. What kind of person would want to destroy another woman like that?'

Harlow didn't have the words to respond. That wasn't why she was here. She didn't want to destroy anyone. She shook her head.

'You have to stop. Do you hear me? She can't take it. You're hurting her. Stop it and stop it now.' And with that Sophie turned on her heel and stormed away, leaving Harlow dumbstruck in the lobby.

Quivering and alone. With no one she could talk to about this. She'd decided when she came up here that she would do this without telling her friends. Not until she had something positive to tell them anyway, and it didn't look like that was going to happen.

Sophie Sinclair had been furious. There was no getting around that. Or was there? Harlow couldn't think straight at the moment. She had a few hours before they were all to meet for dinner tonight. But first she would have a rest, recover from this altercation, take a nap, a bath, and then spend time with her friends. Time to forget all that was happening in the background.

CHAPTER 14

Claudia

Back at Snig Hill and Claudia gathered the team for an afternoon briefing. Very quickly they updated her that they'd located a witness who had seen a woman arguing with Harlow on Saturday afternoon in the lobby.

'Who's the witness?' Claudia asked, pacing the incident room after listening to Krish relay his account.

'One of the hotel reception staff. Obviously we tried our best to prioritise yesterday, but some people haven't been interviewed until today. This receptionist wasn't on duty yesterday morning when we arrived.'

Claudia waved a hand, shooing away the excuse. 'Don't worry about that. Tell me what the receptionist said.'

Krish flipped open his notebook. 'The woman stormed into the hotel following Harlow, shouting at her. Harlow looked mortified and moved to the side out of the way of other guests, but the woman was so wound up she didn't pay attention to Harlow's attempt at discretion.'

'You said this was in the lobby?'

Lisa spoke up now, a wide smile on her face. 'It certainly is. We have CCTV footage. The witness gave me the rough time it happened. I searched for it while you were out and found it. Do you want to view it?'

Of course she did. She and Lisa headed to the viewing room. A bland box of a room with tables lining three walls, holding televisions and DVD players as well as a computer not connected to the rest of the force systems, for viewing thumb drives. There was even an old VHS player in there in case they ever needed it. Lisa lined up the clock to the relevant time. The screen came to life, and the hustle and bustle of a busy hotel lobby played out in front of them. From this, more witnesses would need to be identified. There was no sound on the video, it was just a visual account.

Claudia watched closely. After about thirty seconds the woman she'd seen dead on her hotel room floor sprang to life as she walked across the screen from the right, her steps hurried, distress on her face. Harlow was a beautiful woman. Full of life and energy. This always tugged at Claudia a little. Watching CCTV footage of the victims, alive, after she'd seen their murdered bodies in whatever state their killers had left them.

But Harlow wasn't hurried enough — a younger woman quickly caught her up, waving her arms in the air, her mouth rattling off words at rapid speed.

Harlow moved to the side of the lobby, hands held up in a defensive gesture. She was slightly out of sight of the camera, and they could only view her side on.

The woman continued to move forward, so much so that Claudia didn't think she would stop and would eventually collide with Harlow, but she pulled herself up short. The tirade, however, continued. She spoke with her hands, her face scrunched up with emotion.

Harlow was backing away, until she was pressed against the wall, her stance passive and defensive. Eventually the steam seemed to run out of the unknown woman and she turned on her heel and stormed back out of the hotel without a backward glance.

Harlow deflated, put her face in her hands for a moment. Then, apparently gathering herself, she headed to the lifts and pressed the button. The doors slid open and Harlow disappeared inside, swallowed into the confined space as the doors closed.

'What time was this?' asked Claudia.

'Just after five p.m.'

'And what did the receptionist hear?'

Lisa referred to the notebook in her hand. 'The woman came in shouting, "You can't do this, Harlow. You have to stop what you're doing." Then Harlow moved them away and she heard nothing else. She remembered it because it was such a public display and it was so recent. Plus Harlow looked so upset by it she'd considered calling one of the security staff in to help her, but by then the woman had stormed off.'

Claudia thought about what Lisa had said. 'The woman definitely called her by her name, Harlow?'

'That's what she said.'

'So she knew her. The next steps are that we need to identify further witnesses to this event and find out what else they argued about. And we need to identify the woman who accosted Harlow.'

CHAPTER 15

Claudia and Lisa finished up in the viewing room and returned to the incident room. If anyone would know what Harlow had been hiding this weekend, it would be her friends. It was more than likely that they were attempting to protect her. But what were they protecting her from? Something was definitely going on, and Claudia intended to find out what. 'I spoke to Steve Pacey this morning. He co-owned the owl sanctuary with Harlow. Said she didn't confide in him much. They talked a lot about the owls and about local life, but other than that, Harlow never told him anything he felt was personal.' She turned to the HOLMES inputter. 'Can you update the system, please?'

The inputter started tapping at her keyboard. 'Do you have his—?'

Claudia smiled. 'I've emailed you his details.'

There was a quick laugh that said, of course you have, along with further tapping of keys.

'Plus, he was in Devon at the time of the murder. His wife confirms this. That's all in the email as well. Devon and Cornwall paid her a visit to corroborate this.'

More tapping.

'Russ,' she asked her second-in-command, 'fancy a trip to the hotel to speak to the friends again?'

Russ rose and grabbed his coat from the back of his chair. 'Absolutely. You think there's more to come from them?'

'I think they might have more information than even they realise. I want to know what happened before the woman appeared in the lobby with Harlow and we can ask them if they recognise her. Also, what they'd been doing on Saturday.'

'There's a fair few of them,' Dominic said. 'Need a hand?'

Claudia thought on this. There was a lot of work to get through if they were to interview the friends about the entire weekend in detail. So far their interviews had only comprised what the friends knew about Harlow and the murder yesterday morning. But Claudia wanted to go deeper. More staff would be helpful. 'Yes, and take Lisa as well, seeing as she caught the witness and the CCTV evi—'

She was interrupted by a tap at the door, and two officers in ill-fitting suits stepped into the room.

'Can we help?' asked Russ as he shoved his arms into his coat sleeves.

'Yeah,' said the man. 'I hope so. I'm DC Jake Berry, from Doncaster CID. We've been seconded here to work on the Harlow Cunningham investigation.'

'DC Belinda Naylor, Rotherham CID,' said the woman. 'At your disposal.'

'Brilliant.' Claudia stepped forward. 'I'm DI Claudia Nunn. You answer to me. These two guys here —' she indicated Russ and Dominic — 'are DS Dominic Harrison and DS Russ Kane, so you also answer to them. I'm just on my way out, but . . .' She spotted Krish on his way past and waved him over. 'This is DC Krish Dhawan — he'll get you up to date with where we're at and sort you out with some actions. Come and find me in my office when I return and we'll have a chat then. In the meantime, jump straight in. There's plenty to be getting on with. I'm sorry you've caught me as I'm heading out. Something interesting came up and I want to follow through with Harlow's friends while it's still early enough.'

'That's fine, boss. We'll catch up with you later. We can easily dig in with work here.'

Claudia made a mental note to email Sharpe and thank her for pulling this out the bag so quickly. Securing extra staff was not a straightforward task, and yet she had done this within the day. She would also thank the officers themselves for dropping whatever it was they had been doing previously and jumping straight onto this job. It wasn't the most exciting of homicides but it was labour intensive and it was by working through all the lines of inquiry that a conclusion would eventually be reached and an offender be brought to justice.

* * *

'What do you want to do?' asked Russ as he manoeuvred the car through the Sheffield roads. 'Talk to them as a group or separate them out?'

Claudia stared out at the grey city buildings, bleak in the drizzle that was still blighting the streets. Sheffield wasn't an attractive city at the best of times, but winter made it seem especially dark and grim. People with their shoulders hunched up to their ears, hands shoved deep in their pockets, scurrying along, desperate to arrive at their next destination regardless of the others passed on their journey. 'Let's separate them, see if they contradict each other. They've had time to confer about any secrets they're hiding, but with a little investigative questioning we might wheedle our way in there. Trip them up and find out what exactly Harlow was up to this weekend.'

CHAPTER 16

Harlow

Saturday 11 a.m. — 20 hours earlier

Harlow was nursing a headache. The drinking game they'd played last night had left its mark. But she would struggle onwards. They were here to spend time together, to catch up after all these years, and she wouldn't be the one to cry off. Though last night had been a little more eye-opening than she had planned for it to be. A drunken game of truth or dare had not been in her plans for the weekend. She'd revealed a limited amount about herself but, she thought gratefully, not too much.

There was a rapid knock at her room door. Chloe's room was on the same floor and she had said she'd stop by to make sure Harlow was up. Little did Chloe know she'd not only had breakfast, but she'd been out this morning. Again, something she wouldn't be sharing.

Chloe stood in the open doorway, a wide grin on her face, looking for all the world as if she hadn't been drinking heavily the night before. Fresh as a daisy was the phrase you could tack onto Chloe. 'Ready?' she chirped.

Harlow smiled at her friend. 'I'm ready. Think the boys are suffering?'

Chloe laughed. 'They did rather overdo it.'

They walked to the lifts and waited for one to arrive.

'It got a little weird last night, don't you think?' Chloe asked, wrapping her arms around herself.

'Let's just move past it, shall we?' Harlow was all for forgetting the silly game of the previous evening. There was no need to dwell on the secrets that had been exposed. It was a ridiculous game by anyone's standards, anyway.

By the time they arrived in the lobby, Jay, Ashanti and Brodie were all waiting for them by the doors. Good mornings and hugs were exchanged.

'Did we decide what we're doing today, then?' Brodie asked.

Harlow looked outside at the grey, overcast day. 'We could go into Sheffield, have a mooch about and get a bite to eat and a drink.'

Ashanti groaned.

Jay laughed at her. 'Too much, too soon?'

'Do you lot have steel stomachs? Did you forget how much we drank last night?'

Brodie wrapped an arm around her shoulder. 'Maybe we're more used to it than you are. Don't worry, a hair of the dog and you'll be raring to go again.'

Ashanti dug an elbow in his side and he feigned injury, laughing at her fragility as he moved away.

They ambled out of the hotel and down the road, wandering about popping into various shops. H&M caught Chloe's eye and the boys waited outside impatiently while she oohed and aahed at the clothing and held dresses and tops up against her by their hangers. She couldn't resist and came out with a knitted jumper. Next stop was Superdrug for nail polish — all the girls in the group bought some.

Eventually they found themselves in an area filled with glass and shiny steel, where nothing was square: large steel balls were dotted about, over which water was pumped into little pools; one building's roof curved upwards and another downwards. The glass and metal reflected what little sunlight there was, brightening the gloomy day.

Ashanti peered at her phone. 'This is Millennium Square and apparently we can get both food and drink here.'

Harlow laughed and looked around. 'I think we could figure that out ourselves.'

Ashanti shrugged, unoffended, and snapped a couple of photographs of the area for her social media feed before she slid her phone back into the pocket of her slim-fit jeans.

'To the bar?' Brodie pumped his fist in the air energetically, like he was off to save the world.

'I could do with sitting down and grabbing a bite to eat when you're ready,' said Jay.

'Sounds good to me.'

Jay was pale, and not for the first time this weekend. He'd told Harlow he didn't have a hangover, but that was, she realised, because he hadn't drunk half as much as the rest of them last night.

'Food will help my hangover,' Ashanti said.

Chloe gave them a bright smile. 'Let's find a place to eat.' She linked her arms through Ashanti's and Harlow's. The boys trailed behind them.

'Last night,' Harlow whispered to Ashanti, 'while we played that stupid game, you said Jay was hiding a secret. Jay was pretty upset by that. Said you couldn't possibly know. What's going on, Ashanti?'

Ashanti glanced behind her, at the boys, then stared down at the floor. 'I can't tell you. It's his secret to keep, and he obviously doesn't want to tell anyone.'

So Harlow wasn't the only one carrying a secret this weekend.

'But how did you find it out?' whispered Chloe.

Ashanti shook her head. 'I'd be revealing my own secrets if I told you that.' And she gave a cold, brittle laugh that sounded like it would crack and break if pushed up against something hard.

'We're friends,' Harlow tried. Though not very hard. She understood the need to keep your own counsel on private matters. If Ashanti and Jay had issues they wanted to keep to themselves, then that was entirely up to them. It wasn't any of her business. 'It's not like we're going to judge you or Jay or tell anyone else.'

'Personally,' Ashanti said, 'I think Jay is an idiot for not confiding in you lot about what he has going on right now. But it's really not my place to tell you.'

Round the corner they found an Italian restaurant, Bella Italia. It looked inviting and they piled inside. There was a bar in the corner that was gorgeously lit with downlights, and square tables with blue wicker chairs were dotted around the room. But what stood out was the large flowering tree in the middle of the restaurant. It was beautiful.

The group settled down at a table against the wall. Most of them ordered soft drinks, but Brodie and Chloe went for something a little stronger.

'What?' Chloe was taken aback by the look Ashanti gave her. 'We're on holiday, are we not? That means alcohol with lunch in my world.' She grinned. 'Unless, of course, you can't take it.' The grin widened, and it cracked into laughter. 'I'm sorry, Ashanti. It can't be helped. You were so fragile earlier.'

Ashanti smiled. 'I'm not used to hardcore drinkers like you lot. My local friends are quite restrained drinkers. A couple of glasses of Prosecco and we're tipsy. You took it to a whole new level last night.'

Harlow browsed the menu in search of food. She was happy to be surrounded by her friends this afternoon. This morning had not gone well, but the love she felt when she was with this group was nearly enough to wipe those memories away. Just listening to their back and forth, their normal, everyday conversation, when her world seemed like it was crumbling beneath her, was calming.

'What about you, Harlow?' Ashanti asked.

Harlow turned to her, a question on her face.

'How's your stomach this afternoon?'

Harlow smiled. 'I'm fine. Also a practised drinker, I'm afraid.'

Ashanti groaned. 'I'm ready to eat.'

'I think we could have done with more food and less alcohol last night,' said Jay from across the table.

It *had* been a little over the top last night. Alcohol had played a big part in it.

The server returned with their drinks. Harlow grasped her lime and soda, the glass slippery from condensation. There was a lull in the conversation as the server handed the drinks out. Everyone thanked him and ordered food, then he moved away.

'Let's not rehash last night,' said Harlow. 'Once was enough. I for one don't want to go through it again.'

'But some of us are keeping secrets while others opened up,' said Ashanti, 'and that doesn't seem fair, does it?'

There was an audible sigh from Brodie. 'It was a game, Ashanti. Leave it be. It was a bit of fun. It's not serious. Just let go of it. Move on.' He glared at her.

Harlow's skin prickled. These people were her comfort blanket. She didn't want this to explode for no reason. 'I'm sure we all have things in our lives that are personal to us. It doesn't mean we aren't being honest with each other here. Can we just enjoy the weekend? I love you all so much. It's been amazing spending time with you.' She raised her glass. 'To friendship.' Her stomach twisted as she waited for the rest of her friends to reciprocate. Gradually they raised their glasses.

'To friendship,' they chorused, and the meal continued without further incident.

Harlow, however, noticed that Ashanti was a little distant with Jay, and she wanted to know why. It was one thing to have your own secrets, but another entirely when it affected the group.

CHAPTER 17

Claudia

The group of friends gathered in the dining room, faces all turned towards Claudia, Russ, Dominic and Lisa.

'Thanks for coming down to talk to us.' Claudia smiled at them. 'We need to talk to you again and as we said an officer will obtain statements from each of you. I'm hoping that will get started today as I recognise you're eager to be on your way tomorrow.'

'Actually,' said Chloe, looking around at her friends, 'we might be here a little longer. We're talking about it.'

Claudia was surprised. They'd been eager to leave, to go home. 'Once we've taken the statements, we can call you if we have any more questions.'

Chloe shook her head. 'It's not that. I was approached this morning . . .'

Claudia glanced at Russ who frowned. No idea where this was heading. Their heads were bowed. 'By?'

'I can't remember the specifics. They did tell me. Some women's group or other. Anyway, they read about Harlow's murder and that she was not from the city, she was a tourist, as they put it. They want to hold a candlelight memorial for her in front of the town hall on tomorrow evening. To commemorate Harlow and raise the issue of violence against women, to those in power. They wanted to ask if we'd like to be there.'

Claudia had seen these candlelight memorials in the media before, but had never had one attached to her case. 'You're thinking of going?'

Ashanti spoke up now. 'We think so, though we're a little split at the moment. There's still some desire to leave and go home. But also the wish to do this for Harlow. We'll probably stay. Go Wednesday once it's all done.'

'You wanted to talk to us?' Jay brought them back around to why they'd come here.

Claudia focused. 'Yes, you spent a lot of time with Harlow this weekend and as some of you have already stated, Harlow was clearly involved in something else, not just catching up with you four, and that's what we're interested in.'

'She never told us what she was doing,' said Ashanti, hands gripped tight around her phone.

'Not directly,' said Russ, 'but maybe she let something slip that could help. You might not realise what that is until we go through it with you.'

'Is this going to take long?' Jay ran a hand through his hair.

Claudia studied him. 'You want to support your friend's murder investigation, don't you?'

'Yes, yes, of course. But, it's just that the whole thing has taken it out of me.'

The rest of the group snapped around to look at him, concern etched on their faces.

'Jay?' Chloe spoke first. Claudia could see the toll finding Harlow had taken on her. She looked like she had shrunk a little. She was somehow smaller than before.

'I'm okay. I could do with a lie down when we've done, is all,' replied Jay.

Why was Jay so tired? Claudia wondered. Was it genuine exhaustion, bereavement, or an excuse to escape the police interview as quickly as possible? Dark circles underlined his eyes as though he needed sleep. Maybe he hadn't slept well after they'd found Harlow's body.

Or did he have something closer to home to hide?

'I'll talk to you first, if you'd like, Jay,' Claudia said.

A server brought them a tray loaded with cups and saucers, pots of tea and coffee, and sugar bowls and milk jugs. She placed it down, the contents of the tray tinkling against each other as they settled on the table, and excused herself.

'We'll grab ourselves a drink and then get started, shall we?' Dominic leaned forward and poured himself a coffee. The strong scent curled under Claudia's nose, making it twitch in response. She loved the smell of fresh coffee, but was a devout tea drinker, no matter the circumstances or the weather. Dominic had never understood that about her.

The group, friends and officers alike, poured themselves drinks as Claudia sorted them into pairs.

'Russ, if you can interview Brodie, please? Dominic, you talk to Chloe, and Lisa, Ashanti. We'll separate out and meet back here when we're all done and see what we have. It's a long investigation and, as I said, we'll probably need to speak with you again. We appreciate you staying in Sheffield to help with the case. Has anyone spoken with Harlow's father?'

'I met him before he identified Harlow,' said Chloe. 'Gave him a bit of information on what he should expect — I work in a mortuary. He remembered me from our school days, and was glad to meet someone Harlow had been excited to get together with, and he was grateful for the help prior to the ID procedure.'

Paul hadn't mentioned speaking with Chloe before identifying his daughter. Maybe he hadn't thought it important. But to Claudia, knowing how involved the friends were with each other was of utmost importance. Had Chloe ingratiated herself into the investigation by befriending Harlow's father? Or was it simpler than that? A friend who was familiar with the process offering a hand of friendship and support? That was what they needed to find out.

With cup and saucer in hand, she ushered Jay away from the large circular table to one in the corner of the room and sat back down, taking out a notebook and pen. 'I have to note what you say as we go through this, otherwise I'm likely to forget,' she said. Though the truth of the matter was, she needed a record of the conversation.

Jay smiled weakly. Harlow's death really did seem to have knocked him for six.

'How close were you to Harlow?'

Jay had chosen the banquette seat along the table. He leaned against it now. 'It's been so good to see her again after all this time. I'd wondered how much everyone was going to have changed. Chloe's changed the least. She always knew what she wanted to do, and she went out and did it. I'd say Harlow fell in the middle. There were mannerisms I remembered, and it was nice. But we all loved her. She organised this weekend, and we loved her for that.'

'You mention Chloe has changed the least out of your group. Who would you suggest has changed the most?' Claudia took a sip of her tea, but it was still too hot. She placed the cup back onto the table.

Jay seemed to think about this question, then laughed. 'I presume I can't say my own name.'

'If it's true.' Claudia watched his face.

'I'm sorry.' Jay straightened his features. 'It's not, no. That was a crass joke at a time like this.'

'It's fine.'

He went quiet again and looked around the room at his friends sitting separately with officers, giving their own statements. Claudia waited him out.

'I'd say Brodie has changed the most. He was the joker in school, but he seems to have settled down now he's matured. He has a good job, he's a vet now. Something happened in our last year he refused to talk about — perhaps that straightened him out.' Jay seemed to remember who he was talking to. 'That has nothing to do with Harlow though.'

'Old arguments and divides can easily spill over into adulthood, Jay. If, for instance, Brodie and Harlow had a problem at school, it might be that it was still brewing this weekend and they fought over it.'

Jay shook his head. 'No. No, I don't see that happening. Besides, Brodie's issue at school wasn't fighting — he got on with everyone. I just meant that he became withdrawn in the last year of A levels — nobody could get through to him. Harlow and Brodie were happy to see each other this weekend. Brodie was good with everyone.' His eyes glittered. 'You asked who had changed the most. An innocent question, not related to Harlow. We've loved spending time together.'

Claudia nodded. 'I'm sorry if I upset you. That's not why I'm here. But I want to find out what happened to Harlow and sometimes that means asking odd questions.' She glanced at her notebook. 'We've been informed that Harlow received a phone call on Saturday evening that upset her. Tell me about the rest of the day. What happened? Particularly with Harlow.'

Jay leaned back against the cushioned wall again, his face pale, his hair limp and his eyes dark. Claudia wondered if he was ill. A pang of guilt needled at her before she dismissed it — this was a murder inquiry, and as far as she knew Jay just needed to catch up on a little sleep.

'We didn't meet until late morning. We'd decided the night before that an early-morning start would be too much after all we'd drunk. So we met in the lobby at about eleven a.m. and went out for something to eat. It was at that place with the steel globes. What's it called?'

'Millennium Square?'

'That's the one.' Jay rubbed his face, looking exhausted. 'We walked around a little. Chloe and the girls did a little shopping, but they didn't go mad, not with me and Brodie there, bored. Then we went to a lovely little Italian to get a bite and a drink. There was a little tension.'

Claudia was interested now. 'What kind of tension?'

82

'Nothing much. Ashanti thought some of us were keeping secrets while others had been more open this weekend. She didn't think it fair.'

'What happened?'

'Harlow was the peacekeeper. She calmed everyone down. If it wasn't for Harlow the whole thing could have blown up because people had hangovers. But Harlow wanted us to be together. A group of friends. I loved her even more right then.' His eyes filled up.

'And yet Harlow was one of the people keeping secrets this weekend, from what I hear,' said Claudia. 'She'd been sneaking off when she wasn't spending time with you.'

'I wouldn't call it sneaking off, exactly.' Jay's face was grey now. 'And we did know about it. Chloe's on the same floor as Harlow, and she told me Harlow went out that morning, before we met in the lobby. Harlow didn't tell anyone she'd been out or say who she'd met with. I figured she'd tell us when she was ready, or she wouldn't. It was her business, whichever way she decided. I really wish I'd asked her about it now.' He scrubbed away a tear before it could fall.

'Jay, are you okay? You don't look great.' Claudia was worried about him.

'I was recently diagnosed with cancer. I've just started chemo.' He shook his head. 'I haven't told any of the group, though it seems Ashanti knows as she had a real dig at me on Saturday. I can't figure out how she found out, but anyway.' He closed his eyes a moment before continuing. 'It was Harlow who organised the weekend, but I was the one who chose which weekends we could and couldn't do because I'm at risk some weekends in the cycle and less so in others. Luckily they could all do this weekend, which is my first cycle.'

Claudia's heart ached for the man in front of her. 'You haven't told any of them?'

Jay shrugged. 'This weekend was about joy and happiness.' He paused a beat. 'It was supposed to be, anyway. Why would I break into that with my troubles? They didn't need to hear about it. I would have let them know at some other point. Afterwards, maybe. But now, I can't tell them now. It'll look like I'm vying for attention with a dead friend.' His chin sunk down to his chest.

'But you could do with the support and wouldn't they want to give you that, the support you need, if they were aware of your circumstances?'

'It doesn't feel right, what can I say.'

There was nothing else to say. This was his decision, and he'd made it. All Claudia could do was her job and bring all the friends some peace by finding Harlow's killer.

She had one last question for Jay. The printed photograph from the CCTV footage of the woman who had accosted Harlow after they returned from their trip out. Claudia pulled it from the back of the notepad where she'd shoved it to prevent it getting creased up. A corner was bent. She smoothed it down as Jay watched her with interest.

'Do you recognise this woman?' The shot had been taken as the woman was walking towards Harlow, who was scooting to the side, just under a camera. It was a clear photograph — Claudia was pleased with the quality.

Using his fingertips, Jay slid the image along the table and closer to him. He peered down, narrowing his eyes. He stared at it for some time. The outline of his friend and the woman approaching her, her face screwed up in anger and frustration. 'I've never seen her before. She's with Harlow. Harlow knew her?'

'We don't know what their relationship was. We're trying to figure that out. Any help you can provide would be useful.'

'I'm sorry. Harlow never mentioned meeting anyone at the hotel.' He glanced up from the image as though stung. 'And I can tell it's the hotel from what I can see.'

Claudia smiled. 'Don't worry. It's a good clear copy. My colleagues will ask your friends the same question. Maybe she spoke to one of them about this woman. She looked upset after the encounter.'

'You think she's responsible?' Jay peered down at the photograph again, surprise etched on his face. 'She's quite petite, isn't she? I thought you'd need some upper body strength to . . .' He couldn't finish.

'We're not ruling anything out but at the moment we just want to talk with her and find out more about that conversation and how she knew Harlow.'

Jay pushed the photograph back to Claudia. 'I'm sorry I can't help.'

Claudia picked it up. 'Don't worry. Someone will know her. She can't hide forever.'

CHAPTER 18

The team regrouped in the incident room, back at Snig Hill, police headquarters, to discuss the interviews with Harlow's friends.

'Jay said Ashanti feels some of the group were keeping secrets this weekend,' said Claudia. 'Ashanti wasn't wrong, Jay confided in me he's started treatment for cancer but hasn't told his friends. He wanted to enjoy his time with them — didn't want them worrying and monitoring him all the time. Though if you look at him, you can see how unwell he is. I'm surprised no one has figured it out.'

'Wow, that's a big secret.' Lisa was scribbling in her notebook.

'It is. But it's his to keep and we'll keep it for him as long as it doesn't interfere with the investigation. I also showed him the photograph of the woman who accosted Harlow, and he said he'd never seen her before. How did everyone else get on?'

Dominic leaned forward in his chair, elbows on his knees. 'Chloe talked about the friction between Ashanti and Jay. Said something was going on, but she didn't know what.'

'Yeah,' Claudia agreed, 'Jay said Ashanti appeared to know about the cancer from some things she said, but he couldn't figure out how she'd found out.'

'Chloe heard Harlow go out Saturday morning, as they're both on the same floor and on the same corridor. She had no idea where she went, though. And no, she didn't know who the woman in the photograph was either.'

Claudia was losing hope that any of the friends would identify this woman of interest. 'Russ?'

He opened his notepad, read through what he'd written, then closed it with a sigh. 'I'm sorry. I interviewed Brodie. He had absolutely nothing of interest to say. It's like he's not on the same weekend as everyone else. He's barely paying attention to what's going on around him. Has no idea that there's any friction within the group at all and didn't recognise the woman in the photo.'

Lisa was her last hope, but Claudia didn't think she would come through for her. 'Lisa?'

'Well, Ashanti said nothing about Jay. She was very discreet. You can tell her life is her phone though, as she wanted to take a photograph with me for her social media followers. I put her in her place and reminded her why we were here. It was as if she'd forgotten for a while, if I'm honest. As soon as I said it she started crying. I had to wait for her to pull herself together.'

'And the photograph?'

Lisa shook her head. 'I'm sorry. No recognition at all.'

'So nothing of note happened to Harlow prior to the woman appearing at the hotel, except that Harlow went out alone in the morning. That's what we're saying?'

'That's all they're giving us,' said Dominic.

'You don't believe them?'

He pursed his lips. 'I'm not sure. They're supposed to be friends, and close friends at that. After all that time apart, don't you think they'd have spent their weekend catching up on the important stuff? Not just who's doing what job and who's married or not. I just think someone is holding out on us.'

Claudia jumped up from her chair and paced around the room. 'You could be right. We're going to have to push them a little harder.'

'Aren't they going home tomorrow?'

'I don't think so. Ashanti said they've been approached by a women's group from the city who are holding a candle-light vigil tomorrow evening and they've asked the friends if they'd like to attend. From what she was saying, it looks like the majority of them want to but it's still up for discussion. I think the decision is going to be made on an all-in or all-out basis. Which reminds me, I need to contact the control room and make them aware. I've no idea how large these things can be.'

Graham spoke up. 'Harlow's father called while you were out. He wanted an update.'

Claudia was bemused. 'Called here? Is there a problem between him and the FLO?' A frown creased her forehead. The family liaison officer should have been keeping Paul in the loop. 'Do we need a replacement?'

'Erm.' Graham looked as if he was trying to work out which question to answer. 'Yes, he called the office. I picked up. He was very conciliatory and apologetic, saying he was desperate for news and couldn't help but make the call. He was sorry for being a nuisance and putting us off our work, but he was going insane sitting at home waiting for information.'

Claudia felt for the man. The families of murder victims always struggled with the length of time an investigation could take. Though they were only at the start of this one. Sometimes the police apprehended the offender quickly, if it was a domestic situation, for instance. But in scenarios like this where it was not known who the killer was, the investigation could drag on and family members were left in the lurch, unable to bury the body of those closest to them. All they had was an empty space and a burning desire to fill the void with something, anything. A snippet of news from the homicide team would feed them for a while until the darkness encroached into their minds again. So yes, she understood Paul's desire to reach out. Perhaps the family liaison officer was doing their best — perhaps Paul thought Claudia's team was keeping him in the dark.

'So what did you give him?'

'I had nothing I *could* give him, so I was put on the spot. We're working as hard as we can, but we're no closer to figuring out what Harlow was doing this weekend, are we? I told him we had a person we were interested in talking with and that we had to identify her first and reminded him if he thought of anything that could be remotely useful to inform his FLO who would in turn update us and we would work on it. He apologised again and ended the call.'

'And on that point, about identifying the woman who accosted Harlow, she's our priority now. It's likely she knows what Harlow has been doing this weekend and why she's been so upset. We have to ID her. I'll send the CCTV image to media liaison and ask them to release it with a request for members of the public who recognise the woman to contact us on a direct line into this office.' A sudden thought jumped into her head. 'It's a long shot, but we could ask Paul if he knows her. Send the photo of her to his FLO and see if Paul recognises her.'

Graham wheeled his chair closer to his desk and started to tap at his keyboard immediately. 'On it.'

Claudia spotted the two officers on secondment. 'I'm sorry, but I'm afraid I'm going to task one of you with manning the phone line. It's imperative we learn who this woman is, and the rest of the unit are already tied up.'

They both nodded.

Claudia clapped her hands together. 'Okay, I think we're up to date with everything. Finish what you're doing, get off home and get some rest. We start again early doors tomorrow.' Again, she spoke to the two new members of the team. 'Can you come with me through to my office and we'll have a chat before you go?'

In response, they stood, ready to follow.

'Thanks for all your hard work, guys,' she said over her shoulder as she headed towards her office, which was a glass, or more honestly, a plastic box, in the corner of the room, shielded by blinds for when she wanted privacy. Though she had an open-door policy most of the time.

She walked in and seated herself behind her desk. The two new temporary team members followed her in. Beyond them Claudia could see paperwork being filed away in drawers, computers being shut down and coats being pulled on. Her officers were eager to get home now she'd given them the all-clear.

'Thanks for staying a few minutes,' she said, waving at the chairs in front of her desk, indicating for the officers to have a seat.

They both perched on the edge of the chairs and waited for her to speak. Staff were always wary of new supervisors. She'd try to put them at their ease.

'Thanks for coming to help us out. As you can see, we're pretty busy and this has the potential to become high-profile for the city since the victim was a tourist.'

Naylor spoke up first. 'It'll be interesting, ma'am.'

'Boss is fine.' Claudia smiled. 'Have either of you been seconded to a homicide investigation before?'

Jake Berry appeared to be in his late thirties whereas Belinda Naylor's age was more difficult to pin down, late twenties, early thirties maybe? Her face was devoid of make-up and her hair was brushed back into an untidy knot at the base of her head. Age, however, did not denote experience in CID. You could spend as long as you wanted in uniform before moving into other departments and even then, you could move around specialisms trying to find what interested you most.

Claudia was sure that if she checked her emails, which she'd had no time to do today since getting in this morning, there would be one from either Sharpe or HR explaining who these two officers were, where they were from, how long she had them for and their experience. But for now, she could gather all she required from the people themselves.

There was a shout of 'See you tomorrow, boss,' through the open doorway and an arm shot in the air with a retreating back. Claudia lifted her hand in response before returning her attention to Berry and Naylor.

'I've done a couple of secondments,' said Belinda. 'I really enjoy them. I'm hoping to apply to one of the teams when a vacancy next arises.'

This was good. She would be easier to direct as they needed her on the inquiry. And each secondment was a feather in her cap when the time came for her to submit her application. Claudia turned to Berry.

'No, boss.' His shoulders drooped, as though he felt he wasn't good enough to be here helping out.

'Don't worry about that,' said Claudia. 'There has to be a first time for everyone. You'll get plenty of support from the team here. As long as you're ready to get stuck in, that's all we want. You're both fully trained detectives. You know what you're doing. All that happens here is we point you in one direction and set you going.'

'I'm sure I can do that.' Jake visibly perked up, his back straightening.

'Okay. I need to email media liaison. Thank you again for coming over at such short notice. I hope you enjoy working on the investigation. Don't be afraid to ask questions. We'd much rather you ask and then get it right than blunder in and get it all wrong to the detriment of the case.'

Berry and Naylor stood. 'Thank you, boss. We'll see you tomorrow.' They walked out.

Claudia woke her computer and scanned her emails. As expected, an email from Sharpe was waiting. It outlined the officers' details, their experience and the timeframe Claudia could expect to use them — according to Sharpe, this was likely to be as long as necessary. Their own supervisors had released them, so they were hers to use. She tapped out a response, a quick thank-you for the speed with which Sharpe had pulled this together.

Claudia shook her head, then completed the task she'd sat down to do. She sent the CCTV image to the media liaison department requesting that it be distributed to all news outlets along with a direct line number into the office for anyone who might know the woman in the photograph.

Now to wait and see if anyone recognised their person of interest.

CHAPTER 19

It was nights like this that Claudia really missed Ruth. She had been much younger than her dad and after initial caution over the relationship, because it had hurt her mother, Claudia had got to know Ruth and had, in turn, loved her. Ruth had been her closest friend and would often laugh at Dominic and side with Claudia if Claudia and Dominic had a falling out for any reason.

After Ruth's murder Claudia had spent her time supporting her father through his loss rather than focusing on her own. After all, Ruth had been his wife.

But she was only her friend.

And she felt the loss keenly.

Tonight, in the darkness of her bedroom, with a mug of tea in her hand and two slices of warm buttered toast on her bedside table, Claudia missed her more than ever. She was lonely, and she was struggling with her feelings over killing a man.

Ruth would have had something sensible to say about it. No matter that Dominic didn't even consider it a topic worth talking about. Ruth would have discussed the subject with Claudia as much as she needed her to. She'd listen as long as Claudia talked, and being a cop herself, she'd be able to talk it through with her in terms that both of them understood. In a way no one else could. Robert was a therapist and experienced in dealing with trauma, but Ruth was a friend and a cop and experienced in being supportive and experienced in the very real dangers you could find yourself in within the job. Particularly as she was an undercover officer. That made the whole thing more galling. If Ruth was going to be killed, Claudia had expected it to be in the line of duty. She'd worked some dangerous cases. Not be taken like this, inside her own home. It was all just so ridiculous.

Claudia saw that Dominic was frustrated with her. In his eyes the IOPC and CPS had cleared her of any wrongdoing, so why the hell was she still fixated on it? The man she'd killed had got what he deserved. He'd brought it all down on himself.

But she wasn't Dominic. She couldn't let go of it all that easily. If she could, then she wouldn't be seeing Robert every Sunday morning.

But for all Robert's soothing words, it was Ruth that Claudia wanted. Even now, seven months down the line, Claudia missed her friend with all her heart. Her father appeared to be coping with life, getting on with the job, and going to the pub with his mates. But here, in the quiet moments of the night, in the darkest corners of her mind, Claudia struggled with it all — the fight in the woods, and the loss of Ruth. And to top it all off, Sharpe thought she'd be interested in what was happening with Samuel Tyler, the man who had killed Ruth.

As far as Claudia was concerned, Tyler could rot in prison for the rest of his life, regardless of whether or not he pleaded guilty to Ruth's murder.

In her heart she knew what had happened.

Her best friend had suffered like no one should have to suffer. A deep-seated hatred burned in Claudia's soul for the man.

Claudia sipped on the hot tea, allowed it to soothe her frazzled brain. Long work days tired her out and when she was overtired she struggled more. It was a pattern she tried to avoid. But as SIO on the Complex Crimes Task Force, she could only do so much.

Robert had encouraged her to try meditation to quiet her overactive mind, but she hadn't connected with it. Running was her way of releasing tension, but tonight her fatigue was considerable. She just didn't have the energy to go for a run.

She placed the mug on the bedside table and picked up the toast, taking a huge bite. It was thick and properly buttered. Claudia closed her eyes to enjoy the taste.

If Ruth were here, she'd tell Claudia to take a break, get away from it all for a while, or even start dating. Shit, the woman was always on her back about her lack of a love life, telling Claudia she was too invested in her job and she should put some of that energy into her personal life. If she gave a fraction of the energy she used at work to her personal life, Ruth was always saying, then good things would happen.

Claudia finally smiled.

CHAPTER 20

Harlow

Saturday 8.55 a.m. — 22 hours earlier

Harlow stood before an ordinary-looking suburban front door. To her right a large bay window allowed her to see partially into the living room. It was plush, warm and inviting. The complete opposite of how her body was reacting right now. She was rigid with fear, having been standing there for what felt like a lifetime, but for what in reality was probably only a minute or less. If you stand silently watching a clock tick round for a minute, it really is quite a long time in its own space. But when a minute is put together with other minutes, they seem to fly by. And right now, Harlow wished the time would fly and this would already be over.

Or did she?

Shouldn't she hope to enjoy and appreciate every single moment? Not wish for it to be over before it began.

Eventually she stopped arguing the point in her head, raised her fist to the door and knocked.

Decision made.

She strained to listen for any sound beyond the black door, but all she'd heard in the indecisive minutes she'd been standing there was silence. It really didn't help that she was nursing a headache from hell.

Whoever was within the house was keeping their own counsel. No snippets of life to gain insight from within were apparent.

Her fear was palpable. Harlow's heart thundered in her chest, blood pulsating in her ears. Her legs wobbled beneath her and she wished the door would open so she could be invited in and ushered into a seat to take the strain off her treacherous limbs.

Was the house empty? She'd made a phone call before coming here. The woman was aware Harlow was on her way.

Had she changed her mind, left Harlow to stand here alone, hopeful, for nothing?

Her stomach twisted.

As she was losing hope, about to turn her back on the door, on the house, on the woman who might or might not be inside, a key turned in the lock. The sound was loud and ferocious. Harlow took an intake of breath as the shock of the sound reverberated around her body. Tried to still herself. She had to be steady for the meeting to come. She'd waited so long for this; she couldn't turn into half the person she really was because fear gripped her in its fist.

She breathed. Clenched and unclenched her hands. Tightening and releasing muscles. Trying to relax her body. She couldn't enter the house while in full flight mode.

The door opened.

'Harlow?' Her voice was soft, gentle and low.

The woman standing in front of her was nothing like she'd imagined and yet everything she'd imagined all at the same time. Her face was make-up free and Harlow examined it in detail. Staring.

She was slim, like Harlow, but with a slight padding around her middle.

The woman gave a little cough in discomfort.

'Yes, sorry.' Harlow held out her hand. Not knowing how she was supposed to react in these circumstances. Had anyone written a book on it? She could have done with some guidance.

The woman stared at her hand for a moment as though coming to a decision. Then she shook Harlow's hand. 'Dawn. Do you want to come in?'

'Thank you.' She did. She really did. She'd wanted this for so very long.

Harlow followed the woman into the house. Into her home.

Dawn led Harlow through to a comfortable living room, decorated in neutral colours and filled with soft furnishings, cushions, throws, rugs on the floor. Family photos filled one wall. The woman with her husband and their now grown daughters; photographs of her daughters as children, teenagers. There was a dog on the sofa. He barely shifted when they entered.

'You don't mind dogs, do you?' the woman asked, as though he was jumping all over them. The Lab was giving her the eye to say he would not move even if this visitor did mind dogs.

Harlow shook her head, her legs still shaking. The sofa, even next to the dog, looked more and more inviting. She wished Dawn would hurry up and invite her to sit. Her brain could barely function enough to hold a conversation. 'No, he looks lovely.'

'He is. He's a darling. So lazy, though. He's getting on, you see. His hips aren't so good. He'd rather lie there than go for a walk. We adore Freddie.' Dawn was rambling. She could barely look Harlow in the eye. Eventually she smoothed the back of her trousers down and sat beside Freddie who lifted his eyebrows in response. Dawn patted him on the head and the dog closed his eyes again. 'Do have a seat.' Dawn waved at the spare chairs in the room.

Harlow had never been more grateful for a seat in her life. She couldn't stop staring at Dawn. Taking in every detail. She was smartly dressed in black trousers and a short-sleeved knitted top, a necklace with a 'D' hanging from it around her throat. A gold wedding band, engagement ring and eternity ring on her ring finger.

Dawn caught Harlow's glance and covered her hand with the other. Harlow turned her attention quickly to the dog. Ashamed to have been found checking her out. She felt the flush as it crept up her cheeks, burning and hot.

Dawn cleared her throat. 'Would you like a drink? Tea, coffee, a soft drink?'

She would. Harlow wasn't sure if she could speak right now. Her whole body was letting her down. 'I'd love one,' she forced herself to say, 'if it's not too much trouble.'

'Not at all. I'm having a tea, if you'd like to join me?'

'Yes, please.'

Dawn patted the dog again before standing and walking out of the room. It gave Harlow time to study the photographs on the wall. The life of this woman stretched out before her in colour with the people she loved. A shard of something sharp pierced Harlow's chest as she moved from one photograph to the next. Dawn with her husband and children, the laughter, the locations, the children growing to the adults they were now. Shared experiences and time together. She took in a deep breath. She had to get herself under control before Dawn returned. She had to be capable of holding a conversation.

The door to the living room opened and Dawn entered, a small tray in her hands with two cups, a jug of milk and pot of sugar. She placed it on the coffee table. 'I didn't know if you took milk and sugar so I brought everything through.' There was a slight shake to her voice. An acknowledgement.

'Thank you.'

With the tea-making ritual completed the two women faced each other. A hot drink in each of their hands. Something to cling on to. They could put this off no longer.

Harlow swallowed. She should speak first. After all, she had been the one to request this meeting. 'Thank you for agreeing to see me this morning. I'm in Sheffield seeing friends which was why I called you and asked for this weekend specifically. Otherwise it's a long distance to travel.'

Dawn looked frightened now that they had come to the subject they were here to discuss. Her hands shook a little. The surface of her tea rippled. Her eyes were wide and bright. 'I have to tell you, Harlow, I'm only going to agree to this one meeting.'

Harlow sucked in a breath as though she had been punched. She couldn't hold the tea any longer and placed it down on the coffee table. How had she not seen this coming?

'I'm sorry if that upsets you. I don't want to hurt you, but you have to realise, I have a family. The damage you can do is immense.'

Harlow shook her head.

'You took me by surprise when you called. I was surprised that you'd found me. You must be extremely tenacious.' A brief smile. 'But I haven't told my family and I don't know what it would do to us. The details of what happened . . .' She trailed off. Lost in her own thoughts. Memories.

Memories Harlow knew nothing about.

'I can't risk losing them over this. You must understand that?'

How could she understand? Seriously, this woman expected her to understand that she wouldn't see her again, talk to her, explain anything, her side of things, spend any time with her? It was incomprehensible to Harlow. 'Why did you agree to see me this morning?' It was the only question she could get out.

Dawn was quiet a moment. Stared down into her tea. The ripples had stopped and Dawn was no longer shaking. 'To be honest, I wanted to see you. It was as simple as that. Why wouldn't I? As you wanted to see me. But I can't go any further than this.'

'Where are they now?'

Dawn raised an eyebrow, visibly taken aback by the question — the impertinence of it. 'I . . . they're . . . my husband . . .' She looked up at one of the photographs. Took in the lines of the man she had married. 'He had to go into the office this morning, my eldest daughter no longer lives at home and my youngest stayed at her boyfriend's last night. I don't expect her to come back until lunch time. I usually have a relaxing Saturday morning so this was good timing.'

'And there's no room for me?' It was out before Harlow could stop it. Being here, in such close proximity, it made her desperate for more.

Dawn set her cup down on the porcelain coaster with a small clink. 'Harlow, whatever I say here today, you will never understand my decision. That I had an overwhelming desire to see you, but at the same time this has to be the one and only time this can happen. I'm truly sorry if that hurts you or if it's selfish. Maybe one day you'll be in a position to understand the complexities of what occurred here this morning . . . of what occurred back then.' Dawn picked at her trousers, flicking invisible lint from the material. They were perfectly clean. 'You have no idea about what happened. It was a difficult situation and knowing about it will only serve to hurt you. I don't want to cause you any more pain than I already have.'

Harlow clenched and unclenched her jaw. 'I already know the truth.' Her voice was low, brittle. Someone else in this family already knew. But she wouldn't tell Dawn that. She wouldn't break a confidence.

Dawn appeared taken aback and looked up at her loved ones on the walls. 'I wish you the very best life, Harlow.' Tears filled her eyes.

The sharp shard in Harlow's chest twisted and dug in deeper, taking her breath away. There was nothing else to say. Dawn had made herself perfectly clear. All she wanted to do was get out of there now. She didn't care for Dawn's tears. Dawn clearly didn't care for hers as she hadn't all those years ago. The truth of her beginnings playing out all over again. Her heart was breaking. It had not gone the way she had hoped. This woman hadn't changed.

Harlow stumbled down the hallway to the door. Dawn chased after her. Trying for what, Harlow didn't know. She was so disorientated she dropped her bag. The contents fell out, all over the hardwood floor, scattering around the entry space.

The two women bent to retrieve the items and shoved them back into Harlow's bag. Tears were streaming down Dawn's face, but Harlow held onto hers. She'd save them for when she was alone. She wouldn't share them with this woman — she didn't deserve them.

Clutching her bag, she jumped up and opened the door. 'I'm sorry to have disturbed you.'

She exited the house. All the hope she'd been clinging on to was gone.

'Harlow?' Dawn called as she walked away.

Harlow didn't look back.

CHAPTER 21

Claudia

Little happened on Tuesday.

Some days were like that. Full of the hard graft of a murder investigation that the public didn't see. Hours of CCTV viewing. Long periods spent locating and interviewing potential witnesses, not just present at the crime, but who may have knowledge around the victim's life. The endless paperwork, staring at a computer screen and filling in forms and ticking boxes.

A lot of waiting. They were waiting for someone to call the tip line with information on the identity of the woman in the CCTV image. They were waiting for the results of a couple of leads, that almost certainly would be dead ends.

They were waiting for the forensics departments to send results that could whip the whole of the Complex Crimes Task Force into action.

But all that came was an email. It was from forensic submissions.

Anxiety clawed her stomach. This would either be results from the PM, or some query that would cause more delays.

Claudia prayed for results. A day as slow as this one had rattled her down to the bones.

She opened the email, the anxiety now fizzing through her body.

They had scraped a miniscule DNA sample from under Harlow's nails. Not enough to suggest she'd actively scratched her killer, but she'd definitely caught them as she grappled with the belt around her neck and the killer likely hadn't even noticed.

That tiny sample had been processed and they had run the profile through the system to see if it matched with anyone in their databases. But there was nothing.

Whoever had killed Harlow Cunningham did not have a criminal record, not even an arrest under their belt.

Claudia fought the urge to throw the computer at the wall. What was the use in having DNA if you didn't get it matched with anyone?

She tried to look at the positive side. At least they had a DNA profile of the killer. When they arrested him all they had to do was match his DNA to the sample they'd seized from Harlow's body.

It was the light she needed at the end of a long day that still wasn't over.

Ahead of her was an emotional evening.

Harlow's memorial.

* * *

Claudia and Russ shuffled their way towards where the crowd had already gathered in the Peace Gardens in front of the town hall. A low-slung platform had been laid on the central raised grass bed, with a couple of wooden steps leading up to it. Microphone and speakers at the ready. An enlarged photograph of Harlow was propped on a stand. Her face alight with joy, one arm out wide, the hand gloved, and an owl sitting atop the gloved hand. Harlow doing what she loved. Claudia smiled at the image. It was one she hadn't seen. The organisers must have obtained the photo from Harlow's friends, or even her father.

She turned to Russ. 'I think Paul would have liked this. To see how Harlow was honoured.'

Russ was staring at the photograph. 'Yeah. I get why he said he couldn't. It's a long way to come, to grieve so publicly. To bare your pain for everyone. I don't think I could do it if it were Maisy.'

Claudia watched him. His face intense. She wanted to reach out and touch his arm. Make a connection. There were jobs that sometimes just reached in and grabbed you by the heart and twisted it a little. It looked like tonight was that point for Russ.

Claudia turned on the spot and looked around her. The Goodwin Fountain behind her, their jets of water, sprouting from the concrete ground, made a gentle background sound to the growing crowds at the event. The huge Gothic structure of the council building behind them enhanced the setting for a such a significant occasion. It was a beautiful place indeed to hold a candlelight vigil for Harlow.

The vigil proper was set to start at seven p.m. This, Claudia had been informed, was to give workers the time to finish, eat and return to the city centre. She and Russ had grabbed a snack on their way between work and the vigil. It hadn't been much. Something and nothing, available in a coffee shop that had still been open and had food left.

She could see a uniform presence. A couple of officers floating about on the periphery of the gathering group. Here in case any trouble erupted. Not that she thought it possible. In fact, most people believed that just by having a uniform police presence at these events, problems were more likely to occur. Claudia wondered on the truth of that. It would be something she'd be able to assess for herself this evening. Glad that she and Russ were operating in plain clothes.

They were early. It was still twenty minutes until the official vigil was due to start but the crowd was building steadily.

This wasn't surprising. It had been well advertised on social media, inside Sheffield community groups and wider. The murder of a young woman visiting the city had struck a chord with many of the young people, many women and some men. It was a varied group here, candles in hand, ready.

Claudia nudged Russ, horror dawning on her that they'd come unprepared. 'Do you have matches for these candles?'

Russ grinned. 'You think we might be short of a light, at a candlelight vigil?'

She shoved him. 'Okay. You can have that one. My mind was elsewhere.'

Russ clamped his jaw together to prevent himself from laughing at her. Claudia just stared at him which made him laugh even harder — very quietly, of course.

There was a sudden hushed rumble around them and Claudia and Russ stopped what they were doing to check their surroundings. Chloe, Ashanti, Brodie and Jay were walking towards them. All dressed as darkly as they could, bearing in mind they had not travelled with the plan to grieve anyone. They had been in Sheffield to have fun. A bright pink scarf was wrapped around Ashanti's neck, but she'd shoved it deep into her coat, in an attempt to put it out of view, but also have it keep her warm.

'Oh,' Chloe said when she saw them. 'I didn't know you'd be here.'

'We wanted to pay our respects,' said Claudia.

The real reason, or rather, the other reason, was to see who turned up. It was highly possible Harlow's killer could attend this. But with the size of the crowd growing, Claudia could see, it had been a bad decision to only have her and Russ travel out to this.

'That's so kind,' said Ashanti. 'Thank you.'

A petite woman with a voluminous afro rushed over. 'I'm so glad you could make it.' She grabbed Brodie by his hands.

Brodie looked a little taken aback, eyes widening, Ashanti laughed, Brodie's shoulders dropped. The woman waved a hand behind her and music started to play from the speakers. Beautiful, instrumental music. The crowd hushed and oozed forward.

The woman, who Claudia didn't have a name for, leaned in to Brodie's ear, whispered to him. Brodie nodded. She patted his arm, then moved along the group of friends, making physical contact with each of them, whispering in each of their ears, before gliding off towards the wooden steps, the stage and the microphone.

Candles were being lit all around them now. Out of his pocket Russ produced a lighter and smiled at Claudia. She pointed her candle at him so he could light it. If this wasn't such a sombre occasion, she would have something to say to him.

'Let's split up and mingle,' Claudia said. 'That way, we'll cover more ground.'

Russ nodded and they started to move, just as the microphone cracked into life and the woman they had met on the ground started to talk, to welcome everyone and to explain why they were all there.

Claudia listened to the welcoming speech as she kept her gaze on the attendees while she walked. People tutting as she slipped past them, disturbing them.

There was a change in tone as another speaker took the microphone. Claudia never looked back, focusing on her task at hand. Come on. You have to be here. You wouldn't miss this opportunity to see what your handiwork created, surely? But she couldn't see a familiar face. She couldn't see a face she recognised from the investigation so far. But that was where it became difficult. They had little in the way of knowledge of what or who Harlow was doing or seeing when she wasn't with her friends celebrating their reunion.

Silence descended and Claudia found herself in the middle of a minute's silence. She stilled herself and thought of the woman she was here for. The woman they were trying to get justice for. They'd get there. It might take them a while, but in the end, whoever was behind this, would face a jury.

Another voice started to talk, but made the microphone squeal as Claudia stepped out at the rear of the crowd. A voice she recognised as Chloe. The quieter one of the girls. She was brave to step up there and talk about her friend. Claudia listened in. Heard Chloe talk of Harlow when they were at school. How much they used to laugh. How foolish they were. And how great it had been to reconnect again. She was feeling such loss and didn't know if she would ever get over this. How did you get over such a thing? She thanked the crowd for being there for her friend and then stuttering through tears, she thanked her friends for their unwavering support and kindness.

The vigil came to an end and Claudia and Russ found each other again.

'Anything?' she asked.

Russ shook his head. 'I'm not sure we'd know if we saw him, though.'

'It was worth a try.'

'It was nice to be here. I think it meant a lot to the friends.'

'It'll mean a lot more when we identify Harlow's killer and bring him in.'

CHAPTER 22

Claudia

Three days since Harlow's murder and no one had called the tip line with anything useful and Paul hadn't recognised the woman shouting at Harlow in the hotel lobby either.

Harlow's friends were on their way back to their respective homes later today.

Claudia's first call of the day was to the Devon and Cornwall allocated FLO, Darren, who answered on the first ring. Claudia had spoken to him previously and his role was to keep her updated. After a brief hello Darren jumped straight in.

'I've had a longer talk with Paul. It took a couple of days for him to be able to talk about Harlow. As I said before, I think the loss of his wife just made this all the harder to bear, though you never expect a child to go before you do and he feels incredibly alone now.'

This was true, about losing a child. It was something that came up time and again when it happened. 'What did he say about her visit to Sheffield?'

'He had no idea what else Harlow had come to Sheffield for other than to meet her friends. It had thrilled her to have found them all online after all these years. He said they'd been a real ragtag set when they were at school. A set of kids that wouldn't naturally blend with each other in normal circumstances — they didn't fit in with others at school, so they formed their own group.'

Claudia wondered at a group that could sustain a friendship long after school ended. She wasn't in touch with any of her old school friends.

Darren continued. 'Paul said that had worked. Bizarrely. Because they were such an odd bunch. But they were close and doted on each other — stood up for each other, even got into the occasional fight to defend one another. Not that Paul thought that a good thing, but the kind of friendship they had he admired. It was special. He'd been sad to see them slip away from each other when school was over and they made new friends.'

As Claudia had. But here they were, in Sheffield now. 'What happened to change that?'

'So many years had passed that by the time Harlow looked up they'd all gone their separate ways and she had no way of getting in touch with them. She didn't have their current mobile numbers and she wasn't on Facebook. She was too busy with the corporate job to bother with social media. But once she walked away from the job and when the sanctuary was set up and running well, she signed up to Facebook and had space and time to search them out again. That's when this was arranged, Paul said.'

Claudia pondered on Sheffield as a location. On Harlow's friends. Did bringing her friends here have something to do with that? And he'd mentioned Facebook. Yes, they could view all public profiles, but any conversations held on the platform, it would take them months to obtain.

'Do you have an update for Paul?'

Claudia closed her eyes and leaned back in her chair. She hated the snail's pace of the investigation. The lack of information she had to pass on. 'There are lines of inquiry we're following. We're working flat out and as soon as we have something concrete we'll get in touch. You know how these things go. I'm sorry it's nothing stronger.'

'I understand. I'll relay it to him.'

She thanked him. It was a tough role, that of FLO. She didn't envy him.

Next on her list was a visit to the kitchen to make herself a mug of tea. With drink made she picked up the local paper dated two days ago from her desk and settled down to read the article again. Ten pages in, and the CCTV still image confronted her yet again. The woman, facing the camera, emotion flashing across her features, hands up, speaking for her. A stance Claudia was so familiar with.

She read the text that ran alongside it requesting residents of Sheffield to call the tip line if they recognised the woman as police were interested in talking with her. Underneath the image, the tip line number was clearly printed.

Calls had come in but nothing of substance, nothing that had led them any further in the investigation. Though they'd had to check out the veracity of every call made. That was the problem with tip lines.

Russ walked through her open door. 'You're still brooding over it, I see.'

'Of course. All we can do is wait for the phone to ring.'

He dropped into a chair, facing her. 'You think this woman'll be able to tell us what this is all about?'

'I'm hoping so. She was upset about something. Harlow had been upset and secretive over the weekend about something. The two things should marry up.'

'So all we have to do is find her.'

'With her face out there, the odds of that happening are in our favour.'

Russ grinned. 'It's not been a straightforward case. There hasn't been a lot to go on, but we're getting there.'

Behind Russ the team trickled into the incident room, hanging coats up on the coat hooks in the corner of the room or wrapping them around the backs of chairs. Once stripped of outerwear staff exited the incident room and returned again bearing steaming mugs, ready for their working day. It was a morning ritual.

'Briefing in half an hour.' Claudia picked up her own tea. 'I just want to check through my emails, make sure there's nothing we need to know about.'

Russ jumped to his feet. 'I'll see how Jake's doing on the tip line.'

'Thanks, Russ.'

As Russ walked out, the early-morning chatter filtered through the open office door with talk of the previous evening's activities — a sneaky can of beer, or catching up on some television before bed. Mostly it was just bed. Murder investigations were hard work. But you needed to wind down and not just fixate on the case.

The memory of Ruth talking to her about needing more focus on her personal life made Claudia smile again. For the life of her she couldn't imagine how she would go about it, but it was worth considering, for Ruth. She couldn't wipe the grin off her face. How did a person date nowadays? Was it all online? Or was it still possible to meet a guy in the old-fashioned way? And how did you do that? Wow, she was going to need some guidance, and her primary guide was gone.

She was still smiling as she logged into her computer and her emails. There were a lot that didn't need immediate attention, and she was cc'd in on a lot of things simply because she was a DI. She scrolled through, not finding anything actionable.

Her desk phone rang. She picked it up. Her mind wandering between work and her impossible dating life.

It was Sharpe.

'Meet me in the smoking shed right now.'

She was gone.

Had Claudia heard that right? Sharpe never picked up the phone herself. If she wanted to meet Claudia, either in her office or in the smoking shed, because she wanted a smoke and you got a decent level of privacy in there, she'd get her PA, Maxine, to call down and make the request. It was beneath her to make the call herself. What on earth was going on?

The only way she'd find out was if she went to the smoking shed and talked to her supervisor.

But it was bloody freezing out there and Claudia wasn't a smoker. Why the hell couldn't Sharpe have this conversation in her office at this time of year? It didn't bother her so much when the weather was mild, but now, get your smokes in your own time. Not that she would say that to her boss's face.

Claudia grabbed her coat and walked out of her office. On the way she passed Dominic and told him where she was going. He gave her a puzzled look, and she shrugged.

'If I knew, I'd tell you. I'm as much in the dark as anyone.'

She stalked down the stairs and out into the wintry morning air, wrapping her coat tighter around herself. By the time she arrived at the smoking shed, Sharpe was already waiting for her. Face pinched. A cigarette between her fingers, smoke circling up into the air. She took a drag, inhaling deeply, as she watched Claudia approach.

Behind her, Claudia heard footsteps. They were heavy and flat-footed. Men's shoes.

'Morning,' Claudia greeted Sharpe. Whoever was behind Claudia went to move around her into the shed. Sharpe gave them a penetrating look and shook her head. The smoker turned around and stomped off.

Now Claudia really was intrigued.

'I saw your piece in the press.' Sharpe didn't bother with any morning welcome, getting straight to the point.

'You mean the photo and phone number?' Claudia shifted further inside the shed, hoping it would provide some cover from the cold.

'Yes, the photo and phone number.' There was almost a snarl on her face.

What was this about? Sharpe took another drag. Closing her eyes as she did. Claudia waited her out.

'I received a call this morning.'

Claudia's interest was piqued. This early? The day had barely started. Had someone phoned Sharpe directly instead of contacting the tip line? Did they now know who the woman in the image was? Could they progress the inquiry? 'Has she been identified?'

Sharpe had been staring off into space as she talked, but now her head snapped around, Claudia in her sights. 'No, Claudia, the woman has not been identified.'

She didn't understand.

'Orders have come from above that every DC on your team is to be seconded to Operation Reverberate, the investigation into the nightclub shooting. Apparently they need all hands on deck, staffing is ridiculously tight right now due to the cuts — you know the spiel.'

Claudia's jaw slackened. The cold that had been invading her bones now ebbed away. This couldn't be right. Their investigation was in its infancy. It couldn't be mothballed yet. 'I'm sorry, what?'

'Oh, come on, Claudia, you heard every word I uttered. You're an intelligent woman. Someone, somewhere wants you stopped and they've gone to the very top to get that done.'

'Who gave the order, ma'am?'

'It came to me via Connelly, but he's as angry about it as I am. Even I'm just the monkey in this scenario. Doing as I'm told and passing the information on.'

'But . . . but . . .' Claudia stuttered. 'You can't.'

Sharpe flicked the cigarette butt away, and ground it out with a pointed shoe. The movement slow and deliberate. '*I'm* not, Claudia. Are you listening to the words coming out of my mouth or am I talking to myself?'

There was a quiet fury in Sharpe's voice. She might be passing on the message, but she was not in the least bit happy about it. As for Claudia, she was stunned. She couldn't wrap her head around what Sharpe had told her.

'Every constable?'

'Did you hear me?' Sharpe dug into her pocket and produced another cigarette and lighter. Before Claudia could see her use one on the other, Sharpe was puffing on the lit cigarette.

'It's one way to slow your investigation down, while at the same time, providing the illusion of operational needs taking priority. You can, apparently, continue on with reduced capacity and the team that needs the staff can put them to use where they're needed.'

'But . . .'

Sharpe glared at her.

Claudia paced around the shed, her mind swirling with random thoughts. Harlow Cunningham was being denied justice. Her father . . . what would they say to her father? The team? The press? The press was aware of the case. They didn't just forget a visiting woman had been murdered in their city. A candlelight memorial had only occurred last night. Plus, an entire group of friends would shout for answers.

'Will you get out of here!' Sharpe barked behind her.

Claudia spun around, her heart racing in her chest at the sudden outburst, but she soon realised it wasn't aimed at her but at another poor soul who was only trying to have a fag break. She watched the uniform scurrying away, terrified at being scolded by the DCI in charge of homicide teams, shoes slapping on the concrete ground. 'You know this is high profile? The press is following it? There was a candlelight—'

'I know all about the memorial last night, Claudia.' Sharpe sighed. Smoke drifting out of her nose. 'I imagine that's one of the reasons they've not been able to close the investigation down completely. It's been a good highlighter for your case. The nightclub shooting makes this movement of staff look legitimate, and we still have officers on the Cunningham inquiry.' She inhaled on the cigarette again. Head back, eyes to the sky.

'Who would want to do this?' Claudia asked.

Sharpe shook her head. 'The order to reallocate staff came from the acting ACC of the Specialist Crime Services, Mike Davidson. I don't know what your young lady had herself wrapped up in, but someone doesn't want you to find out.'

CHAPTER 23

Sharpe had decided the smoking shed was too cold to stand in after she'd smoked three cigarettes in a row, yet she wasn't prepared to continue the conversation with Claudia in her own or Claudia's office so they'd decamped to Albie's, a glass-fronted coffee house just down the road, a short walk down Snig Hill.

They took stools in the window so they weren't close to any other tables and they could see anyone who entered.

Claudia was on edge. Her stomach was rolling and her whole body twitchy. The revelation that the Harlow Cunningham murder inquiry was to be mothballed, without actually closing it, had thrown her for six. Her mind was a swirling cauldron of fractured thoughts and stuttered conclusions.

Sharpe returned from the counter with their drinks. A tea for Claudia and a latte for herself.

Behind them, Claudia was hyper-aware of the other customers. At one table a couple of women were deep in conversation and at another a young man with a baby in a pushchair was quietly sipping on his drink while the baby slept, oblivious to the piped music and roar of the coffee machine alike.

Sharpe lifted herself onto the stool next to Claudia. 'Tell me about the case.'

'It has to be the woman in the video.' Claudia stared out the window at the six-storey, flat-fronted building across from them and at the passing cars. 'No, she's too young to be so influential. Someone who recognised her, who cares for her. A parent? A lover, even?'

Sharpe steepled her hands, leaned her face on her thumbs and was silent for a minute. 'Well, we know this person is someone extremely powerful with friends in interesting places. And by interesting places, I of course mean the acting ACC, if they managed to get staff reallocated. What else do you have on Harlow?'

Claudia shook her head. 'All we know is that she came to Sheffield to meet up with old school friends this last weekend. A school reunion. And during the weekend she was engaged in something else that none of them are aware of. A side project of sorts. It's that which we are interested in.'

'She's stuck her nose somewhere very dangerous, and the result was her murder.'

Claudia had never known anything like it. 'This isn't usual. You know that.'

Sharpe glared at her. 'Of course I know that.'

'What are we doing about it?'

'We find out who killed Harlow Cunningham.'

Claudia shook her head. 'You'd expect more from me. It's not just about Harlow now. It's about corruption. We're going to look at Davidson, yes?'

Sharpe sighed. Looked around her surroundings. 'I'll dig a little. As discreetly as I can.'

Claudia was at least a little calmed by that. But they still had problems. 'How do we run a murder investigation with only three serving detectives? Me, Russ and Dominic.' She paused, thought about her team. 'What about Naylor and Berry? They've only just been seconded to our unit.'

'They're included in the reallocation. You're right, there are three of you to work this.'

Blood rushed through Claudia's head, thrumming in her ears. 'It's a homicide investigation. We'll miss leads without the staff.'

Sharpe stared at her. 'We have our instructions. We work with what we have.'

'You're serious?'

'You want to stop?'

'A young woman came to our city and ended up dead. I want to know what happened to her and I don't like being backed into a corner.' She was about to push it, thought better of it, but she went ahead anyway. 'Do you?'

Sharpe tapped the side of her mug, steam rising from the hot fluid inside. 'I don't, no. But neither do I want to lose my job.'

Claudia was taken aback. 'They can do that?'

Sharpe sighed. 'I don't know, Claudia. They've shrunk the investigation team on an active homicide down to three. Admittedly, they made it look like an operational necessity. You think they, whoever they are, can't get you fired?'

They sat in silence for a while. The coffee shop music little more than muted background noise, barely perceptible over the thoughts rampaging through their heads.

'I can't let it slide,' Claudia said eventually. 'I want to find out what happened to Harlow. I want to know who this woman is. Regardless of the obstacles in our way, I'm continuing with this case.'

Sharpe picked up her latte. Polished nails glinting under the lights of the shop. 'You're sure about this?'

'They haven't shut it down, have they?'

'Not for lack of trying, I suspect.'

'Well, I get to do more legwork than usual.'

Sharpe eyed her over the rim of her mug. 'Watch out for further barriers, Claudia.'

'I will.' She sounded so sure of herself, but Claudia had never felt so unsure or nervous about anything in her life. She'd always been at home in the police. It was her secure place. But the bigger picture was that the place where she was most comfortable had been infiltrated by something insidious and poisonous.

Claudia jumped as the coffee shop door rattled open to admit another customer. She had seen the lone woman passing the large glass-fronted window but was nervous now that her trust had been broken. Someone, somewhere, was attempting to scupper their investigation. They had influence within the top corridors of the service. They couldn't allow this to happen.

It was as though Sharpe had been thinking the same thing. 'We better inform the team immediately that they're moving, and then you'll have to focus the investigation on the important lines of inquiry. There will be many actions waiting to be tasked on HOLMES, but with lack of staff, you can only do so much. Work smarter. Do you understand me? We bring in Harlow's killer. Show whoever wants this slowing down that you don't stop the police. And remember, it's not just your career you're putting at risk as you go after this offender.'

'I understand. Thank you.'

'Oh, don't thank me just yet. You've no idea what you're getting into, who's behind this or what they're capable of. I've never seen a homicide team sucked dry like this before. Regardless of how much another team needs support. Don't underestimate your opposition.'

Claudia had never seen Sharpe so anxious. She promised to be careful.

'You want to give your sergeants the heads-up before we inform the team?'

There was no hesitation on Claudia's part. She'd known from the beginning who would support her in this. Russ Kane wouldn't back down from a fight. 'Yes, I'll text both of them.'

Sharpe nodded. 'Get them down here and we'll update them. Then we'll have to return to the incident room and send everyone to Operation Reverberate.'

Those words sent a shiver down Claudia's spine. Envisaging a quiet incident room was beyond comprehension. Sending the two seconded officers, Berry and Naylor, on their way when they'd only just arrived was wrong on so many levels. The team would feel let down, and there was no way she could confide in them that it looked like someone was sabotaging their investigation.

Russ and Dom walked through the door within ten minutes, a confused look on both their faces.

'South Yorkshire Police branching out and in need of extra briefing rooms?' Russ said with a half-smile.

Claudia had two drinks waiting, knowing what they both preferred, from years of working with Russ and from being Dominic's daughter. She shoved the mugs towards them and told them both to sit. Her tone brooked no argument.

The men did as they were instructed, Russ taking hold of his mug and pulling it closer. Within five minutes they were up to date. There really wasn't a lot to tell. The investigation was being hobbled in a way that if anyone looked, could just about pass muster for official needs. If they were up to the task, Russ, Dom and Claudia were going to run it and get to the bottom of who killed Harlow Cunningham and if possible, find out who was attempting to close a police investigation. If they wanted in, that was.

Russ didn't need asking twice. 'You're kidding, right? You want me to hunt a killer and, in turn, a sleazy scumbag who thinks they can tell the police what they can and can't police? I'm all the way in.'

'You understand the dangers?' pushed Sharpe, her voice low. They were still in a public place.

'I understand the risk, and I'm more than willing to take it. People can't be allowed to come into our organisation and handicap us this way.'

'Only it seems they are, DS Kane. That's the whole point. Whoever is pulling these strings has enough power behind them to do just that. We have no idea what they're prepared to do next, or what they're capable of doing next and I, for one, do not want my career derailing. Do you understand?'

Russ, who had been full of bravado, sucked in a breath. 'Yeah, I get it. I'm sorry. I'm just so angry.'

'You and me both,' said Claudia.

'Seriously, Claudia?' Dominic had been quiet and now fire was brimming out his eyes. The lines in his face were pronounced. 'You're allowing this to happen?'

She rounded on him. 'I'm not sure what you think I can do to stop this?' She was sick of him. Always needling at her. Now, as everything was crashing down around her, she really needed him to toe the line. To not be the argumentative arrogant twat he was currently being. 'You heard the DCI. This is coming down, not from her, it's much higher. Yet you want me to stop it? How do you propose I do that, DS Harrison? Tell me, in all your wisdom, how do you recommend I go against an acting ACC without risking my job or my career, just so you feel happy with the outcome?'

There was silence as the four of them recognised they were not in the office, but in a coffee shop.

Shit. Claudia was furious he'd pushed her buttons like this again. It wasn't the first time they'd publicly come to verbal blows. They'd done so in front of the team while hunting the Artist. It hadn't been pretty then, and it was damn well uncomfortable now.

Dominic stared at her. His jaw set hard. She couldn't tell if he had something to say and was holding back because of where they were, or if she'd silenced him, but the tension played out across the table.

'We have no choice,' she said. 'We have to trust that they know what they're doing. That this is way above our pay grades.'

She'd said it in such a resigned way that the pressure around them snapped and released.

Sharpe was the first to speak. 'Don't get me wrong,' she said, 'I'm furious. But we have to recognise what we're up against. This isn't a game. I've never seen a new homicide case sucked dry of staff so early on in its investigation before. You agree to continue the investigation, you do it knowing you're up against a formidable foe who has some serious clout and is capable of knocking you out with one punch.'

CHAPTER 24

Claudia watched from the side of the incident room as DCI Maddison Sharpe spoke to the team. She had never seen her boss look so deflated or her staff so shell-shocked or confused.

'I don't understand. We need our staff as much as any other investigation needs detectives.' Graham's tone was bordering on disrespectful but, being ex-forces, he knew where to draw the line and wouldn't cross it. Though Claudia understood where his anger was coming from. It was burning a hole inside her as well.

'The decision has come from above me. Someone in the command team has assessed the situation with current incidents and staffing levels and allocated detectives where they feel they're best needed. Most of the details are above my pay grade, I'm afraid. But I do—'

'But they're closing the investigation?' Graham was bewildered.

'The investigation is not closing. Yes, it's losing the majority of its staff but it can still be worked. And to you, the detectives being temporarily reassigned, I was going to say that you are a wonderful team. I recognise you do a great job and that's why Claudia chose you to come together for the Complex Crimes Task Force.'

There was muttering around her. She was losing them. She'd lost them the minute she said they'd been removed from the Cunningham case. No one wanted to walk away when there was still work to do on a murder investigation. When there were still active lines of inquiry to follow.

'What about the tip line for the woman in the CCTV video?' asked Krish. 'The press has only just put the image out. It's not like we've even been given a chance yet.'

'This isn't about you not having done the job well, DC Dhawan. I don't know how many times I have to say this, but I'll repeat it again: this has come from above me. It's not a reflection on the task force or your work on the case. In fact, you could see it as a positive point that you've been selected for the team investigating the nightclub shooting.'

'I don't get it, ma'am,' said Graham.

A headache was drilling a hole at the base of Claudia's skull. She rubbed the spot with a couple of fingers. Kneading at it gently, willing the pain to go away.

Sharpe took a deep breath. Claudia could see how difficult this was for her. 'Your presence has been requested elsewhere and as an officer of South Yorkshire Police you follow orders. You have two hours to update your paperwork and arrive at the relevant incident room.'

'Two hours!'

Sharpe walked out of the door. To the casual observer, her stride would have looked as confident as usual, but Claudia could see her shoulders were hunched, her arms had less swing.

Dominic turned on Claudia immediately. 'This is bullshit.'

She stepped forward from her place at the side of the room where she'd been hiding out while Sharpe delivered the devastating news. The dull ache in her head flared, and she rubbed at it again. Fingers digging into the pain in an attempt to push it away. 'It is what it is. We have no choice but to follow directions. It's up to me, you and Russ now.'

'We can come and give you a hand when we've done our hours on the other case.' Rhys was sincere. Usually the joker of the team, he was deadly serious right now. Claudia's stomach flipped. They couldn't go down this route. Someone was going to a lot of trouble to nobble the investigation and she didn't want to get her team involved in that.

'I'm sorry, Rhys, please don't.'

He glared at her.

'We have our orders. You have your job to do. Me, Russ and Dominic will be fine. Let's see how we get on with it, shall we?' She had to keep her staff safe. It was a strange thought, the need to keep them safe, but it was the feeling that had come over her since hearing the news that so many of her team were being reallocated to another case. Yes, it had the air of authenticity to it. Operation Reverberate was a serious investigation, there was no doubt about it. A gun discharged in a nightclub, killing two, it needed everything throwing at it. But leaving her own inquiry so understaffed, well, that had a distinctly bad whiff to it.

Dominic jumped out of his chair, as if the energy inside him was too much to keep him still. He paced around the room, scrubbing a hand through his hair. 'It doesn't feel right, Claudia.'

Of course it didn't feel right. It was so far from right but she had to do as she'd been directed.

Berry and Naylor hadn't uttered a word, but they looked demoralised. 'I'm sorry, guys,' she said, leaving Dominic to burn off his frustration on his own for a minute. 'You haven't been here long, and you were looking forward to working this case with us, but you've also been reassigned to this other investigation. It's a meaty case, plenty for you to do.'

There was little they could say. She understood that. They weren't in a position to give their point of view on this matter. They didn't know anyone well enough to get properly involved.

'It's not usually like this. If we need extra staff in the future I can make a specific request for both of you, if you'd be interested?'

Two sets of 'yes ma'am' came back at her.

'It sucks,' muttered Lisa.

'You're not wrong.' Claudia couldn't tell her just how right she was. It was then she took her courage in her hands and looked at Russ at the other side of the room. They locked eyes, and Russ gave her a small smile. One that told her he was with her all the way. Regardless of how difficult this was, and it was bloody awful. He was standing beside her to the bitter end, wherever that was. Her nerves soothed somewhat.

'Okay.' She clapped her hands together. 'Tough as it is, get all your paperwork up to date so you can leave the three of us with something resembling order when you leave in two hours.'

The room moved at once. The team's movements slow and sluggish. They might not agree with what was happening, but they followed orders and they'd been given directions and a timeframe.

Claudia headed into her office, deflating with every step.

She slumped in her chair. Defeat smothered her, her every muscle, her every synapse. Russ walked in behind her and closed the door. The sound of the team bitching about the decision was instantly muffled. Claudia put her face in her hands. Overwhelmed by the whole bizarre situation.

'They'll understand in the end,' said Russ quietly, sitting in the chair in front of her. 'When we find the person who wanted this case to fail.'

'Will we ever be able to tell them?' Claudia spoke through her fingers.

'One day it'll all come out. It has to. Stuff like this has a habit of rising to the surface.'

Claudia raised her head. 'You're very optimistic considering what we're facing.' She waved an arm at the office beyond. 'Look at them. They'll be on Operation Reverberate soon.'

Russ smiled. 'We can do this, Claudia. As soon as the team has gone, we'll crack on. It's a long shot, but do you think it's worth having one last face-to-face conversation with Harlow's friends, if we can catch them before they leave? See if there's anything else we can get from them, anything they might have remembered in the days since we last spoke to them?'

Claudia thought on this. It wasn't necessary, but one last conversation wouldn't hurt, before they left. Last night hadn't been the place to question them any further. It was a time and place for grieving. 'Okay, but we need to get going because I don't know what time their trains are.' A look into the incident room dented her motivation. 'We needed the staff, though, Russ. It took a huge amount of time to check the hotel CCTV for people coming and going, to work out who each person was, to whittle them all down to see if we could get an image of the killer walking through the lobby. We've lost that.'

'Claudia,' Russ snapped.

She stared at him.

'There are plenty of other ways in and out of that hotel other than the lobby. That was a long shot, just one we had to follow up. Don't now start being defeatist. Can we at least give it a go?'

She tried a smile. 'We can. Fuck them, whoever is behind this. We'll not only find out who killed Harlow, but in doing so we'll expose whoever tried to silence a police investigation.' The smile slipped a little. 'It's going to wobble a whole house of cards though, for anyone who allowed this to happen. Because someone did allow this to happen. There's no way this is just a matter of resources.'

'Well then, let's topple those cards and discover what Harlow Cunningham has been involved in.'

CHAPTER 25

Harlow

Friday 9.55 p.m. — 35 hours earlier

They'd eaten their evening meal at the hotel and were now occupying a booth in the Gardeners Rest, Neepsend Lane, which had a jazz night on. The drinks were flowing, and the mood was lively. Harlow had drunk a few too many and was considering slowing down. She'd decided the belief that food soaked up the alcohol was a fiction people told themselves so they could drink more. Harlow had never found it helped her level of drunkenness if she was eating as well as drinking.

Mixing her drinks was never a good idea, though. She'd started the evening on white wine and was now on grapefruit gin. There was a warm glow emanating from her, and combined with the buzz from the room, the love she felt for her friends was amplified. She wrapped an arm around Chloe. Her friend leaned her head on her shoulder in response.

'I love you, you know that, don't you?' Harlow tried desperately not to slur her words.

Chloe laughed without lifting her head from Harlow's shoulder. 'I do, lovely. I love you, too.' Her voice was a soft burr in the mix with the music.

'What do we have to do to get in on this lovefest?' asked Brodie, grinning, very obviously on the alcohol train with Harlow.

Ashanti, at the opposite end of the booth to Chloe and Harlow, lifted her phone and snapped a photograph of the two wrapped in their embrace. 'Beautiful.' Her eyes shone in the flash from the camera.

Harlow opened her spare arm and wrapped it around Brodie. 'You feeling left out?'

He laughed. 'Not now.'

'Lucky guy,' said Ashanti. 'Just look at the friends you have.'

Chloe shot upright, and Harlow dropped both her arms.

Chloe smiled. 'We're great friends, but it's been such a long time since we were together, there must be so much we don't know about each other. Let's play truth or dare!' The song that had been playing ended just as Chloe shouted and the end of her sentence rung out loudly in the bar. A few faces turned and smiled at her, knowing where this was likely to end.

Harlow's stomach shrank. This wasn't such a good idea. Not with what she'd been doing this weekend.

'Oh my God, yes,' shrieked Ashanti, raising her glass in the air in a celebratory salute. The music stirred up again.

It wasn't too loud that people couldn't hold conversations. Yes, they had to shout, but they could still be heard.

Harlow supposed she could manage the game if the questions weren't too specific. It all depended on what she was asked. She wasn't the type of person to keep going for dares. She hated the kinds of dares they came up with in games like this. Kissing each other, drinking lots of alcohol when you'd already had too much. Questions were easier to navigate. She just had to be careful how she answered them.

The boys didn't look too keen, but Chloe and Ashanti were full on and preparing to go ahead, regardless of the fact the whole table hadn't erupted in joy at the prospect. Their own enthusiasm for the game was enough. They had a small empty tonic bottle they decided they could use, and they were set to go.

'We should fill up our drinks first,' said Chloe, cheeks now glowing.

Jay shuffled out of the booth and headed for the bar, returning shortly with a round of fresh drinks on a tray.

'Okay, we're ready.' Chloe was giddy with excitement.

Harlow was attempting to keep the dread at bay.

With the little tonic bottle in hand, Chloe placed it on its side, gave a maniacal grin to every single person sitting around the table, then gently spun the bottle.

Harlow's stomach clenched. This was really not a good idea, but she didn't want to be a drag.

They all watched as the small vessel spun around. Each widening their eyes as it passed them. Cheek muscles twitched as nerves and excitement mounted. Everyone was playing, but it was clear that no one particularly wanted it to land on them. The fun was in setting the dare or asking the question. Watching your friends squirm under interrogation or under the strain of some ghoulish dare.

Harlow clenched her fists under the table, fingernails digging into the palms of her hands, and prayed to some god she didn't believe in for the bottle to not point at her.

It slowed.

Chloe grabbed the edge of the table dramatically. Eyes like saucers as she watched its final rotations until it eventually stopped.

'No,' shouted Ashanti, her face paling.

Chloe clapped her hands in glee.

Harlow looked around at the other tables. No one was paying them the slightest attention, everyone was involved in their own worlds or watching the musicians play. A young couple had found a dark corner and were so involved in each other that Harlow wondered if they realised they were still in public. After this weekend she'd start socialising again and start dating again. She missed being a part of a couple. Having someone to tell your world to.

Much as she loved her friends, Harlow wished she was anywhere else right now.

She brought her attention back to their table. Chloe was rubbing her chin like a pantomime villain, considering what dare to set Ashanti.

Ashanti was shaking her head, and the boys were laughing hysterically. Harlow smiled. Not wanting to appear as though she wasn't a part of the group.

Dread was winding through her for future spins. It was possible though, that the bottle wouldn't land on her. Really it was. It didn't have to stop on everyone.

'I know,' shrieked Chloe.

'No,' shouted Ashanti again, before Chloe could even tell her what the dare was. Fear emanating from every pore.

'Don't worry, my lovely young friend,' purred Chloe, grinning.

'No, Chloe.'

Chloe gave her a stern look. 'You agreed to play the game. Come on now. You don't even know what it is I'm going to ask you to do.'

Ashanti was silent. The entire table fell silent. Waiting for Chloe to release her will.

Chloe stared right into Ashanti's eyes. 'You're beautiful, you know that, right?'

Ashanti kept quiet.

'For your dare, and because you're a social media queen, and I believe you are a beautiful woman inside and out, I want you to wash off all your make-up. Right now.' Chloe's face was earnest. She watched Ashanti for her reaction.

They all watched Ashanti. Ashanti removing her make-up? She'd taken so many selfies and posted them to social media while they were out this weekend, it was impossible to imagine her without her make-up on. And yet Chloe had led with the fact that she was beautiful.

'I . . . Chloe . . .' Ashanti stuttered. 'Chloe, I can't.'

Harlow grabbed her hand under the table. Ashanti could do this because she *was* a beautiful woman and make-up didn't create the woman, and Harlow hoped to convey all this with only a hand squeeze.

Ashanti let out a breath and let go of Harlow's hand, bringing her own hand up to look at the brightly coloured nail polish that adorned it. A glossy pink that shone. Everything about Ashanti was created to perfection in her eyes. 'Okay, I'll do it. I don't have any face wipes in my bag, so I'll have to go to the bathroom. I'll be back shortly. Don't play without me.' She rose and wriggled out of the booth, striding towards the bathroom with her shoulders back and a confidence Harlow wasn't sure she was feeling.

'Shit, Chloe.' Brodie whistled. 'That was a harsh start to the night.'

Chloe giggled. 'Oops. I've not made things easy for myself, have I? For when it comes around to me.'

Jay laughed. 'You most certainly haven't. You've set the bar high going for Ashanti's looks.'

'But she is beautiful. She doesn't need her make-up.' Chloe pouted.

'That's not the point,' said Harlow. 'How would you feel if you were asked to remove all of yours? Pretty naked in front of us all, I'm sure.'

Chloe scratched at her arm. She didn't look so confident in herself now and when she finished scratching, she raised her glass to her lips and took a deep swig.

Harlow followed suit. This could be a long game. Who knew where it would end?

They chatted about their plans for the next day as they waited for Ashanti. Agreeing that they shouldn't meet until the afternoon if they were to continue drinking the way they were doing at the moment.

It was then that the toilet door banged and Ashanti, nervous and shy, walked towards them. Her bag clutched in front of her like a barrier to what was coming.

Harlow smiled. 'You're exquisite.'

Ashanti glowed. A wide smile on her face. She'd done the impossible and survived. 'I need my drink.' She laughed and pushed her way back to her seat.

'Friends?' said Chloe.

Ashanti put her drink down. 'Friends. Now give me that bottle and let me enact my revenge.'

God, this was going to be brutal.

Ashanti spun the bottle hard. It spun and spun and spun. They watched with fascination, waiting for it to slow and eventually stop.

The bottle ceased spinning at Harlow. 'Shit.'

The table laughed. They were in high spirits now the game had started and the first dare had gone reasonably well.

Harlow ran a hand through her hair. 'I'm not choosing a dare. Not after what just happened. So you can ask me a question, Ashanti.' It terrified her. But whatever Ashanti asked, she could either tell them the truth or if it was about this weekend, she could work around it somehow. Maybe a dare would have been safer.

Ashanti was grinning. She'd taken her medicine, and now the power was hers.

'You've unleashed a monster, Chloe,' laughed Jay, seeing Ashanti's face.

Harlow took another deep drink to prepare for what was to come. They'd need another refill soon. The hangovers would be strong tomorrow.

Ashanti turned a serious face on Harlow. 'Tell us one secret you have told no one else. And I don't mean that you leave the lid off the toothpaste. I mean a proper secret, Harlow.'

She swallowed. Fear clogging up her throat. Could she do this? Could she share what she'd kept to herself for so many years? At least it wasn't a question about her actions this weekend. 'Okay, okay.' She grabbed her drink and downed the rest of the liquid, raising the empty glass to show she was out.

Jay raised a hand to the bar staff. They'd get table service this time. No one wanted to leave as Harlow was about to bare all.

'This goes no further.'

They all nodded. Solemn in their promise.

'My mum and dad, well, they're not my birth parents.'

Mouths dropped open. Someone gasped.

'What?' Chloe blurted out.

'I'm what is known as a foundling.'

Chloe leaned in closer. 'What's that?'

'A baby that is abandoned somewhere, like outside a hospital, or fire station, or somewhere less safe. But ultimately, has been left by their parents for someone else to find and care for.'

There was silence as no one wanted to ask what was on all their minds. They wanted the answer to whether Harlow's parents had left her somewhere safe or less so.

The drinks arrived and Harlow grabbed hers with relish. She'd slow down after this. After her trial by bottle-spin. But they hadn't finished with her just yet.

It was Chloe who braved the elephant in the room, whispering into the silence. 'Where were you left, Harlow?' She held Harlow's hand as tightly as she could.

Harlow welcomed the warmth of it. 'They abandoned me outside a hospital.'

There was a collective sigh of relief. Chloe and Ashanti leaned in and hugged her. It was over. She'd done it. She'd paid her dues. Now she could relax and enjoy the rest of the game. Her real secret was safe.

CHAPTER 26

Claudia

Claudia and Russ arrived at the West Park Grand Hotel after promising the team they'd keep them updated. A new face manned the hotel reception. Claudia and Russ presented their ID and asked to speak to the friends of Harlow Cunningham. One by one, Brodie, Chloe, Ashanti and Jay arrived in the lobby, Ashanti dragging a suitcase behind her. They looked tired now. It had been a long few days and last night had been emotional. Their friend had been murdered. Claudia expected they were desperate for their homes now. To return to loved ones who would hug them and care for them, instead of being holed up here, where it had happened. Even if they were together, it was still pretty morbid.

This interview was their last chance. They had to push them hard. And they'd try a new tactic. They would keep them together. See how they bounced off each other. See what slipped, and who picked up the mistake and ran with it.

She and Russ had agreed on this on the drive over. They were out there on their own now. No team behind them. Just her and Russ and Dominic back at the office.

'Let's go to the bar. It's empty in there at this time of day,' she suggested, and led the way. The hotel bar was all mirrors and glass and sumptuous velvet in a multitude of colours. An overly large chandelier hung in the centre of the room. All set against huge black-and-white wall prints of former punters, from the Edwardian era to the 1960s, looking glamorous and sensual. It was an unusual setting for a police interview, but it was quiet, which was what they needed.

Claudia requested a jug of water and some glasses from the bartender.

'How are you all doing?' she asked, and then regretted the question. She'd never seen them so deflated. Of course they were grief-stricken when Harlow had been murdered. But today they seemed seriously depressed. They must be so wrung out. Home would bring some peace. A place to recover.

'I have a taxi collecting me in forty minutes.' Ashanti looked worried. The first of the group to leave the hotel, to leave Sheffield.

'We won't keep you from your taxi,' said Russ. He leaned forward. 'We really need your help. We're glad we caught you before you left. What we plan to do is talk to you together today, see if it brings anything different up.'

Jay let out a breath. 'Oh my God. This place. I'm so ready to leave.' He put his head in his hands.

They'd stayed to honour their murdered friend, but Claudia could see the toll it had taken on them.

The bartender arrived and placed a jug of water on the table along with a tray of glasses. Claudia and Russ poured and shared the drinks around before they began with their questions. It gave everyone a little time to settle with the news they'd just given them.

Once everyone was holding a glass Claudia dove straight in. 'Several of you have informed us Harlow was up to something this past weekend. What was that?'

Brodie looked at Jay, who looked at Ashanti. Chloe looked at her lap.

'Someone must know something,' Russ pushed. 'Someone walked into this hotel and murdered your friend and you're telling us you don't know what she'd been doing when she wasn't with you? There must have been some tells. Slips she made when she was talking. Anything at all?'

'You should understand,' said Jay, 'most of the time we didn't know she'd been out. If it wasn't for Chloe being on the same floor as her and hearing her door opening and closing, we'd have known nothing about it.'

Chloe fiddled with her hands. 'I wasn't trying to be a snitch. We were all friends, you see. I was interested in what she was doing. Thought there might be something we could help her with if we could get her to talk to us.'

'And we nearly did,' said Brodie.

'What do you mean?' Claudia was straight on it.

'Friday evening. We played a game of truth or dare and Harlow asked for a truth when it fell on her. So Ashanti asked her for one secret she'd never told anyone. We thought maybe we'd find out what she'd been doing this weekend. Support her if she needed it.' Brodie hung his head.

'You never mentioned this when we talked to you before,' said Russ. 'The game of truth or dare.'

'Is it relevant?' Jay picked up his glass of water and, with a finger, traced a trickle of condensation down the side.

'It's up to us to decide what is and isn't relevant.' Claudia was rattled these grown adults had kept this conversation with Harlow from them for so long. But she didn't want to shut them down now by scolding them too hard, so she softened her voice. 'So, bearing that in mind, I'd appreciate it if you could go through the events of this weekend again with us. We'd like to let you get home to your families.'

Ashanti put an arm around Chloe, who was close to tears. Claudia picked a napkin off the table and handed it to her. She took it and dabbed at her eyes and her nose, before leaning in to the crook of Ashanti's shoulder.

'Do you want to tell us about the game?' Claudia prompted.

It was Brodie who spoke for the group. Running a hand through his hair, as though to prepare for the ordeal. 'Harlow was the second person to have the bottle land on them. Ashanti had been first, and had opted for a dare. Chloe asked her to remove her make-up.'

Claudia looked at the heavily made-up girl and considered the genuine trauma that could have created for her.

'Harlow went for a truth,' Brodie went on. 'As I said, Ashanti asked her for one secret she'd told no one. We were all aware she was hiding something and were hoping she'd reveal what that was. No one ever asked her outright. We were too considerate for that. We thought and hoped she'd tell us in her own time. We were her friends and wanted to be there for her.'

Claudia was holding her breath.

'She never did, and I wish we'd asked her directly. That way we'd know and could tell you. And it might be of help so you could catch whoever killed her. Maybe, just maybe, if she'd told us, if we'd asked, if it was that serious, we could have persuaded her to go to the police and she'd have been protected and she'd never have been murdered in the first place. I have so many regrets about this weekend and about Harlow.'

The pain in his voice was real. Claudia's heart went out to him. 'What was her response to Ashanti's question?'

'She told us she was a foundling.'

Claudia was puzzled. 'A foundling?'

'An abandoned child. She was left outside a hospital as a newborn. Paul Cunningham isn't her birth father.'

Claudia looked to Russ, who was staring right back at her. Harlow's friends had kept this from them for days. If only they'd known. Now they were crippled as far as investigative powers were concerned, but Claudia couldn't tell them that. 'It might have helped the investigation if we'd known this sooner.' She tried to keep the blame from her voice.

Brodie looked away. Took a moment to gather himself. 'It was the most personal thing Harlow ever said to us. Revealing it to strangers didn't feel right. We were sitting in a bar, playing a game, and it was just us, no one else was involved, so it didn't seem relevant. I'm sorry if it is.'

Claudia moved the conversation on. 'Did she say where she was abandoned?'

Chloe frowned. 'Outside a hospital.'

'No. No, I'm sorry . . .' Claudia corrected herself. 'I mean, where in the country? She lives in Devon, doesn't she? You all grew up there.'

Realisation dawned on Chloe's face. 'Oh. No. She just mentioned the foundling thing and moved the subject on pretty quickly. I think we all presumed it was in Devon as that was where we're all originally from.'

Claudia considered this. 'Harlow arranged the reunion in Sheffield, didn't she?' Aiming to confirm what Paul had said, with the people involved.

'We all helped sort it out,' said Jay.

'Who selected Sheffield as a location?'

'We tried to figure out somewhere pretty central for us all. I think it was . . .' Jay looked around the group, the lines on his forehead deep in concentration.

'Who selected Sheffield?' Russ pushed him.

'I think it was Harlow,' he whispered. 'But what does that mean? What does it matter?'

Sounds of laughter permeated the bar area from the lobby beyond. This was still a place people came to relax and enjoy themselves.

Claudia leaned forward. 'Harlow was busy with something else last weekend. If what you're saying is correct, then it was something she had planned in advance to do.'

Chloe tapped her fingers on the side of her glass. 'You think it has something to do with what she told us?'

'We can't be sure. But it's a line of inquiry we have to follow. It's the only thing we have right now.'

'But we all have secrets, DI Nunn,' Chloe said quietly. 'That was clear on Friday night and Saturday afternoon.'

'The difference is,' Claudia said, 'it looks like Harlow's secrets got her killed.'

Brodie rubbed his head again. 'Look, you may as well know. Harlow went out alone on Friday morning as well.' He released a deep sigh. 'One of us would have mentioned it before now, but again, we didn't think a Friday morning meeting was relevant to what happened on Sunday. I'm so sorry. We've kind of screwed all this up. You have to understand how confused and upset we've been. One minute we're partying and the next minute one of us is murdered and the rest of us are grieving and in the middle of a murder investigation.'

His friends gave him weak supportive smiles. Brodie continued quickly. 'None of us know where she went. Harlow told us she had to pop out before she could join us for the day. I . . . I . . .' Brodie licked his lower lip and tried again. 'I . . . I think we felt guilty for not going with her. You know. . . if this is connected to her murder.'

Claudia could understand the group's feeling of guilt. It's what humans did. She wouldn't allow him to brood on it. 'What time did she go?'

Brodie looked at Chloe, clearly again the source of this information. Chloe closed tired and weary eyes for a moment before speaking.

'It was busy in the corridor Friday morning. It felt like there were several people booking out that morning. People who were maybe here for work? But I texted Harlow and asked if she wanted to share an early-morning cuppa and she replied she'd had to pop out and would see me later.'

Claudia thought of the incident room. Of Harlow's phone log received from the phone provider. It was still in the middle of being analysed. Numbers Harlow had called and texted herself, as well as received, with all of these numbers cross-referenced, requests submitted to identify the registered owner. Dates and locations pinned. A map of her activity drawn up. Analysing a phone log was not a quick job and as of this morning, that had suddenly stopped. 'Any idea of what time she returned?'

Chloe shook her head. 'I'm sorry.'

Claudia sighed. This group had kept details from them. Information they could have used while they were a working team. Now they were just three detectives with little in the way of resources. Even if Harlow's friends gave them everything they had, what could they do with the data? The thought of it drained her.

'Thanks,' said Russ, glancing at Claudia, who hadn't said a word. He'd know what was running through her mind. 'You've all been very helpful.'

'My taxi'll be here in fifteen minutes.' Ashanti was anxious, biting her lower lip, gripping her water with both hands in a vice-like grip.

'We've finished now,' said Claudia. 'We have your contact details so we can get in touch should we have any more questions. Again, we're so sorry for your loss. Travel safely.' At least with them leaving, they wouldn't know how reduced the inquiry was. Claudia wondered what the FLO was going to tell Paul Cunningham about that.

'You'll tell us when you find out who did it, won't you?' Brodie looked earnest.

'We will.' But would she, Russ and Dominic ever get to the bottom of who killed Harlow Cunningham, on their own, with little to no resources whatsoever?

CHAPTER 27

'What the hell?' said Claudia, as they walked back to their car.

'The foundling thing?' Russ pushed his hands into his pockets.

'Yes, the foundling thing. How could they keep that from us all this time? How could they not think it remotely relevant to the investigation?'

'They're not cops, Claudia. For them, they don't see how what happened thirty-four years ago could have a bearing on what happened to Harlow today.'

Claudia was furious at him for his level head, but kept her own counsel. This was not the time to be falling out between themselves. Besides, she could see his point. Even if she begrudged it.

The hotel loomed over them, blocking out the grey skies with its brick-and-glass exterior. A towering building in a city redeveloping, growing and expanding. They climbed into their car, shutting out the gloom of the day.

'So, ideas?' Claudia prompted as Russ manoeuvred the car into traffic and headed back to the station.

'If Harlow chose to reveal that she was a foundling during the game of truth or dare, that suggests it was on her mind at the time. Perhaps she'd only found out recently?'

'Yes,' agreed Claudia. 'Or she wanted to address it, at least. She had a crisis of sorts in the past few years — left her life in the city, started her owl sanctuary. And then her mother died last year.'

'So perhaps she'd become interested in finding her birth parents. That's one major line of inquiry right there.'

'We have to find out where she was abandoned. It's a bit of a coincidence that she's in Sheffield at the same time as finally telling her friends she's a foundling. And she's taking secret trips out without her friends. We have to do this quietly.'

Russ was thoughtful as he drove the short distance to Snig Hill. 'Even if this is about her birth parents, who would want to kill her? Surely not her parents? Giving her up is one thing, killing her another.'

Claudia didn't have a response. 'It may be we're on the wrong track, but we'll follow it up, anyway.'

Back in the office, Dominic was on his feet straight away. 'How did you get on?'

'They were emotionally wrung out and are ready to leave.' Claudia stared around the empty incident room. Hollowed out. It wasn't right.

Dominic followed her gaze. 'It's been brutal sitting here alone.'

'Come on. At least my office is smaller.' She walked past the empty desks and into her office with Russ and Dominic trailing behind her. 'Harlow's friends gave us a new piece of information today,' she said.

'Oh?' Dominic slumped down into a chair, notebook in hand.

'One of the things Harlow discussed this weekend was that she's a foundling. A baby who was abandoned at birth. She was left at a hospital, but we have no idea where — whether it's here in Sheffield or back in Devon.'

Dominic straightened up. 'You think it's relevant?'

Claudia shrugged and sat in her own chair. 'We need to bear it in mind. The problem is, there won't be any records of the investigation conducted at the time into the search for the mother. Not after thirty-four years. For starters it will have all been completed on paper and secondly, once they closed the case and the baby was the responsibility of social care, or social services as it was then, they'll have only kept the paperwork for so long. It won't have survived three decades. There was no guidance on the management and retention of material back then.'

Dominic grunted.

Claudia switched on her computer. 'The same goes for social care. 2019 guidance says files should be kept until the child is twenty-five. So, even if we were following 2019 guidance, the file would be gone. But we're looking at the 1980s. Social services have evolved, merged, separated and generally reformed beyond recognition since 1987, so to find a file would be impossible.'

'So, what you're saying,' said Russ, 'is that there's no way we're going to find out who Harlow's birth parents or mother are?'

'Not unless Paul knows. Plus he'll be able to tell us where Harlow was born, so which force would have looked into it and what he knows about Harlow's mindset on the subject. We could be looking in the wrong place altogether. We just have to bear it in mind.'

Her screen loaded. The badge of South Yorkshire Police flickered across the monitor. 'Okay,' she said. 'We'll use a Word document to keep a running log of everything we do and the policy decisions we make. I'll give it an innocuous name so no one will think to look at it. Someone doesn't want this investigation to progress, so I'll put the barest of details on the policy log and the full details on the document, until we know what we're dealing with.' She scratched her head. 'This transfer of staff is an unusual move. Keeping our information between us feels safer, though I can't believe I'm saying this.'

'Unless, of course, they've asked someone else to monitor us,' said Dominic.

'Stop pissing on my bonfire.' She glared at him and started tapping out the day's events in a document. 'I'm creating it now.'

Claudia titled it 'Annual review'. It made her smile. Everyone hated doing their annual reviews and no one was going to read such a drab document. Once she'd shared the document with Dominic and Russ, she checked her inbox. She needed to file all correspondence about this investigation into a secure folder. With that organised, she checked any emails that were left and binned any that were useless. She sat up straighter when she spotted one from Steve at the front counter with the subject: 'Visitor'.

'What is it?' asked Russ.

'Someone has been in to see me.'

Russ leaned forward.

Claudia opened the email and read it. Then pumped her arm in triumph.

'What is it?' Dominic asked.

'Someone came in to the station after calling the tip line and not being able to get through. She recognised the woman in the photo!'

'And we have her contact details?'

'We absolutely do.'

Russ stood, the chair wheeling away from him. 'Then what are we waiting for? Let's find out who this woman is.'

* * *

Sonia Brooke was a school nurse. She told Claudia and Russ that she'd popped into the station in her lunch break to speak to the investigation team.

They were sitting in a small box room at the local primary school that by some magical effort had fitted in a desk, a chair, metal drawers and a tall medical bed, complete with a roll of paper stretched out along it. Sonia had dragged in a couple of other chairs from somewhere and they were practically on top of each other's knees.

'The receptionist couldn't get hold of anyone on the investigation team,' Sonia explained, 'so I asked her to email someone my details to pass on.'

Claudia apologised that no one had been available, feeling annoyed again at the lack of officers. Dom must have been out of the room when the call came through. Three of them couldn't staff an investigation room and question witnesses without important evidence falling through the cracks — and somebody influential was counting on that.

'You said you know the woman in the photograph printed in the paper?'

'Yes.' Sonia said. 'It surprised me to see her staring out at me, to be honest. It took me a couple of days' soul-searching to decide whether or not to contact you. I've never had dealings with the police before. Giving you details of someone I know, well . . . it feels a little . . .'

Claudia didn't need Sonia to finish that sentence. There were many, many people who lived their lives with no contact whatsoever with the police and it would frighten them if they were to be stopped in their car for something as simple as their rear light being out. Deliberately getting in touch with a homicide team was a completely different kettle of fish. And as Sonia had said, especially to provide details of someone they personally knew.

The phone on the desk rang out and Sonia stopped to answer it.

Frustration gnawed at Claudia, but she kept her mouth shut. This was Sonia's place of work. Of course she had to answer the phone. Claudia listened as Sonia offered some advice and said she would be with the caller in five minutes.

Claudia didn't need long. All she needed was the name of the woman who had accosted Harlow in the hotel lobby, and she'd be out of here.

Sonia hung up. 'Sorry about that. A student fell over in the playground. It doesn't sound serious but I'm going to have to have a look.'

'That's fine. I appreciate you seeing us while you work.'

'I know it's important, which was why I came in when I couldn't get through on the phone.'

'So the woman?' prompted Claudia.

'Oh yes. She attends the same Pilates class as me. Her name's Sophie Sinclair. I've written down the class details for you.' Sonia handed her a piece of paper. 'You'll be able to find her from those details?'

It was possible — they could ask the Pilates teacher if she kept a record, though Claudia had attended classes where all the organiser did was take your money and there was no register. But now they had a name they could check it against the voters' register and the police PNC system if she had a record.

Sonia had the door open now. They could hear the sound of children's voices down the corridor.

'Do you have anything else?' asked Claudia.

'I have her phone number,' said Sonia. 'Would that help?'

It would. It was probably the best way of tracing her. Sonia handed over Sophie's number and showed Claudia and Russ out of the building.

'How do we go about this?' asked Russ as they made their way back up Snig Hill to the station. 'Every time we do a check on a police system we're leaving a footprint.'

Claudia let out a long breath. 'We have one advantage: our enemy is trying to keep under the radar. We have to work quickly, get to the bottom of this before whoever's keeping tabs on us can put more obstacles in our way. But they're going to notice our next move. We're bringing Sophie Sinclair into the station.'

Russ stopped halfway up Snig Hill. 'How're we going to do that?'

'We'll ask her in for a voluntary interview. She won't be under arrest and there will only be a basic log of her on the system for safety reasons. Not full arrest details. To keep it as low-key as possible, I suggest only one of us brings her in and takes her home.'

'I'll do it,' said Russ, starting up the hill again. 'You prep the interview. I'll fetch her in and meet you at the custody block.'

* * *

Russ was already there when Claudia arrived. The custody block, a bland space of smooth curved edges, oozed with the stench of microwaved meals, body odour and stale feet, all tamped down with a disinfectant wash. It was a strange mix. The sound of men and women shouting and banging from their cells when they weren't getting attention quickly enough from their buzzers provided the soundtrack. In front of Russ stood a small queue of officers with detainees in handcuffs waiting to be booked in. Normal, everyday people. Not all crimes were committed by villains who looked like a cartoon criminal. The criminals Claudia knew were the average person on the street, people who had taken a wrong turn. Made a mistake.

Standing beside Russ looking absolutely terrified in these circumstances, eyes wide, arms wrapped around herself, was Sophie Sinclair, the woman from the CCTV footage who had been shouting at Harlow Cunningham hours before her murder.

CHAPTER 28

The interview room was a square box containing a wooden table and four chairs. A red bar ran around the middle of the wall that could be pushed to sound an alarm should officers need immediate assistance with a detainee. Claudia didn't foresee any issues with Sophie Sinclair.

The woman was twenty-eight, but sitting in this small space she looked younger, smaller.

Afraid.

She'd shrunk into herself.

That was what this room did to a person. This building. It reduced them down to the smallest part of themselves. Especially if they'd never experienced a police custody block or an interview room before. And Sophie Sinclair had never had a run-in with a police officer in her life. Not even a speeding ticket in her name. This woman was the epitome of law-abiding.

Sophie had elected to have a solicitor with her, which was her right, even during a voluntary interview. Whereas most solicitors who came through the doors were pleasant — they were all here to do a job, after all — this guy, Toby Johnson, hadn't received the memo. He sneered at every opportunity, and Claudia had seen him wipe his hand on his trouser leg after shaking hands with an officer. It wasn't a discreet move, either. He made it to unsettle the officer in question. Luckily, Claudia was familiar with the cop and he wouldn't be rattled so easily. He'd grinned. The game was on.

Toby spent a good half an hour talking to Sophie before they went into the interview. Claudia and Russ were aware of the advice he'd have provided. To respond to all questions with the answer, 'No comment.' No matter what the officers said, reply, 'No comment.'

Claudia had to hope that something she said stoked an emotion in Sophie, one that gave her an urge to speak. Otherwise, this was a complete waste of everyone's time.

She ran through the official legal jargon at the start of the recording. Introductions, the right to legal advice, even during the interview, and that she, Sophie, was not under arrest and was free to leave at any time.

'My client,' sneered Johnson down his nose, 'is here of her own free will and is shocked by the events you want to talk to her about. However, she will take the advice I have provided today.'

Yep, a 'no comment' interview.

'How do you know Harlow Cunningham?' asked Claudia.

Sophie's voice was low and quiet in response, as though she was afraid that what she was about to say was the wrong answer. 'No comment.'

Claudia didn't flinch. She was prepared for this. 'Did you know Harlow Cunningham?'

'No comment.'

'What was your relationship with Harlow?'

'No comment.'

Claudia leaned back in her chair. Relaxed. Showed Sophie this was not over and she should make herself comfortable too. 'How did you know Harlow?'

Sophie looked at Johnson, who gave a slight nod. 'No comment.' Her lip quivered.

'When was the last time you saw Harlow?'

Sophie rubbed her hands over her face. The pressure mounting. Johnson laid a hand on her shoulder. Sophie jumped. Johnson removed his hand. 'No comment,' she whispered.

Claudia checked in with Russ. With a 'no comment' interview, the trick was to keep things at a steady pace, not rush through the questions just because you weren't getting any responses. Because if Sophie decided to answer a question and you were simply flying through the questions like a robot, you could be onto the next one before she had the chance to open her mouth and the opportunity was gone. It was tedious, though, when an interviewee stuck to their guns and gave their pro forma response all the way through.

Russ nodded. It was going as well as it could.

'When you last saw Harlow, what did you talk about?'

'No comment.'

Johnson had a soft flip-top notebook on his lap and was making notes as they progressed.

'Was Harlow upset when you saw her?'

Sophie paused. Johnson stared at her. 'No comment.'

'Why would Harlow be upset?'

It was becoming obvious that Sophie had something to say. She was fidgeting. Her gaze flitting between Claudia and Johnson. He'd obviously laid it on thick during their meeting, because she appeared terrified of going off-script. 'No comment.'

Claudia lifted a laptop off the floor and placed it on the table between them. Sophie looked panicked. Johnson shook his head slightly. He'd known the image in the paper was a CCTV still. It had said so in the report. He'd been expecting this and must have warned Sophie about it as well. But even so, she wasn't ready. When it was lined up, Claudia pressed play.

'You can see Harlow walk into the West Park Grand Hotel.' She pointed to the screen where Harlow Cunningham walked into the lobby. 'And just here, see here . . .' She tapped the screen with her pen. 'You follow her in. Do you agree that woman on the recording I'm showing you, labelled CN1 is you, Sophie Sinclair?'

Sophie stared at the footage as it ran through her following Harlow, arms waving, mouth shouting unknown words before turning and stomping off. 'I . . . It's not what . . .'

'Sophie, I'd suggest you keep to the advice I offered.' Johnson's voice was quiet and friendly. He didn't want to scare his client.

Claudia stared at him, then turned her attention to Sophie. 'Mr Johnson has indeed provided you with advice. You can choose whether to follow that advice or speak to us. The choice is yours at every single question. It can change as often as you want it to. Mr Johnson's guidance is clear. I'm still going to ask you the questions, Sophie. Is that you on the recording I've shown you?'

Sophie was shaking now. Johnson was scowling. 'No comment.' It was barely audible. But it was there all the same. Claudia couldn't push her on it.

'What were you saying to Harlow?'

Sophie checked with Johnson. He shook his head. 'No comment.'

Now to the tougher questions. 'Did you meet Harlow again, after this incident in the West Park Grand Hotel lobby?'

Sophie looked like she wanted to bolt. And if she wanted to leave, there was nothing they could do to stop her. She braved it out. 'No comment.'

Claudia bristled, but she kept herself still, her face impassive. What was the point in agreeing to a voluntary interview if all you were going to do was offer no comment? She supposed Sophie didn't realise that would be the outcome until she'd spoken with Johnson. And having a solicitor present was her right.

'Did you have any further conversations with Harlow after this one on the video?' It was practically the same question but she could get away with it, just because the last question was about seeing Harlow and this one was about talking to her.

Johnson picked up on the difference, and the similarity, and scowled at her. Claudia gave a slight shrug.

'No comment.'

She was good.

'Why was Harlow running away from you?'

This one was like a shot through the air to Sophie. Her hands clenched around the arms of the chair. Her mouth opened as though to speak and then closed again. Claudia could practically hear her mind ticking over. The woman desperately wanted to respond. She wanted to tell Claudia that Harlow wasn't running away, and in turn, what was really happening. But she was fighting that urge with the expert advice she'd been given by Johnson, who was watching her intently, ready to jump in should she speak any words other than the two he'd advised her to say. Her knuckles whitened as her grip tightened more.

'Sophie?' Claudia prompted.

She let out a small sigh. 'No comment.'

They were not getting anywhere. Sophie Sinclair was sticking to the solicitor's advice like her life depended on it.

Claudia threw a couple of other questions at her, but they were in a losing battle. If Sophie didn't break when shown the CCTV footage, then she wouldn't break at all.

Eventually it was over.

Claudia thanked Sophie Sinclair for her time. Sophie was cautious. Johnson had already gone. Sophie was obviously afraid Claudia would throw a random question at her now she was alone, but it was against the rules. That was the problem with cop shows. The public's perception of what was and wasn't permitted was a little warped. Sophie looked baffled when Claudia allowed her to walk out without further verbal battle, but Claudia was resigned that that ship had sailed. She left Russ to run Sophie back home, and returned to Snig Hill.

* * *

The incident room was empty. It felt like a ghost town.

It was a ghost town that Claudia hoped to populate again. She would not give up. Whoever had done this to them hadn't heard the last of her.

Russ returned with what looked like a heavy load on his broad rugby-playing shoulders. 'That didn't go as well as we'd hoped.'

Claudia agreed with him.

He assessed the deserted incident room. 'Dom went home?'

'It's been a long day, I told him to get off. He'd called Paul Cunningham, but couldn't get through. I'll try again tomorrow.'

She checked the 'Annual review' document — Dom had updated it before he'd left. 'He's ordered a copy of Harlow's adoption certificate and as far as birth certificates are concerned, he says that foundling babies don't have typical birth certificates.'

Russ dropped onto a chair near her. 'Wow, I'd never considered that. What do they have?'

Claudia read the screen again. 'They're recorded in the Abandoned Children's Register which is held with the General Register Office. He's requested a copy, but all it contains are details of Harlow's date of finding and location. Bear in mind, we're not even sure at this stage if it has any relevance to the case yet.'

Russ shrugged. 'What now?'

'Let's look into Sophie Sinclair's background, see if there's any shared history with Harlow or her friends.'

'But that's a task for tomorrow?' Russ rubbed his eyes.

Claudia smiled at him. 'It is. Get yourself home and grab some sleep. I'll see you in the morning. No need to come in early.'

'You can manage that?'

She laughed. 'If I can't, then I need stripping of these pips.' Claudia didn't wear a uniform, but if she did, the rank insignia on her shoulder would be two pips.

'If anyone deserves those pips, it's you.' He made for the door. 'I'll see you tomorrow and we'll make a dent in this case. With or without the support of South Yorkshire Police behind us.'

'That's big talk, DC Kane.'

It was his turn to laugh. 'I'm a big man, DI Nunn.'

She joined in his laughter. 'Rather you say that, than me!' And she headed out the door with him, turning off the lights as they walked out for the night. Little knowing what was in store.

CHAPTER 29

Russ

Russ parked the car on his drive at Sundew Gardens, High Green. A nice suburban detached property with a garage attached. A garage they didn't use as it was filled with all the junk they didn't know where else to store. He climbed out the car into the cold but bright and clear night, deciding after the drama of the day he'd go for a walk to clear his head. He zippered his coat up to his chin to keep the chill at bay and shoved his hands into his pockets.

His wife, Maura, and daughter, Maisy, would be fast asleep and wouldn't notice if he was another twenty minutes. In fact, Maisy slept the sleep of the dead and wouldn't notice an earthquake if it hit through the night and he adored that about her. If only he could sleep as well as she did. Maura had told him she never settled properly until he was beside her but he wasn't sure how true that was. She always seemed to be snoring gently when he slipped in beside her after a late night at the office.

But tonight he needed to stretch his legs, so whether Maura was unsettled or not, he had to just walk the streets a few minutes. Allow his mind to wander and then settle.

He'd never known anything like what had happened today, in all his career — an investigation reduced to nothing while still in its infancy. It was unheard of. The power of the people behind it must be immense. He could barely get his head around it. Who could control the police this way? Make the acting ACC of the Specialist Crime Services redirect staff. There was the police and crime commissioner who had the final say in what the police directed their budgets to and could even hire and fire the chief, but not the ACC. Were there people with money of the kind Russ could never imagine who could direct operations this way? Like Russian oligarchs? He didn't think so. It was like clutching at straws trying to figure this out. Someone had applied pressure to Mike Davidson. The chief constable herself? The prime minister? Those working for the prime minister? That all seemed a little too far-fetched though, for a young woman who ran an owl sanctuary in Devon.

The list, though fanciful, was longer than Russ liked and it depressed him. He'd hoped the days of police corruption were in the past. Whoever it was hadn't gone as far as closing the investigation. That would have drawn too much attention, especially while they still had leads to follow. It would be different if the investigation had been further along, if they'd reached a dead end. The job would have been mothballed if that had happened, to be reopened if new information came to light. But this was a new case and someone had done their best to tie their hands behind their backs.

Russ dipped his chin into his jacket to protect his face from the wind and hunched his shoulders up to his ears. The street was deathly quiet. Most homes were in darkness with only a few lights on. It was a street of workers or mums with kids who had to rise early, so bedtime was not a late affair. Not on a school day.

Russ passed his neighbour and friend Billy's house. The location of many a barbeque in the spring and summer. A smile flitted over his face. How he hoped for those days to come soon. Winter was not a fun season. Though Maisy, at only six years of age, had been waiting all winter for the snow to arrive so her dad could take her out on the red plastic sled that hung on their garage wall. Snow had been sparse in recent years, but if it was going to settle in Yorkshire, it would settle in the high areas of Sheffield.

The cold air snapped at his face and after ten minutes of trudging through the streets Russ decided he was suitably cold and settled enough to go home to his family, climb into bed next to the warmth of his wife, and sleep.

Tomorrow was a new day.

Soon home was in sight. Maura and Maisy were in there, sleeping, snoring, snuffling, snuggling. Russ let out a sigh, the frigid air nipping at his skin. Russ imagined the tip of his nose was red like Rudolph's, as Maisy would tell him if she saw him. He smiled at the thought of her. He'd pop his head into her room when he got home. He'd see the tumble of curls peeping out from under the quilt and he'd know he was home and everything was as it should be. No matter what was happening elsewhere in the world.

As Russ crossed the road a low rumble came from behind him. A car, possibly. It was late but there were people like him who had lives that didn't follow traditional lines.

He trudged onwards with home in view. The house was in darkness, the bedroom curtains drawn. Russ held the key in his pocket. A little piece of warmth in his palm. A promise of sleep to come. He was ready to lay down his head. Forget the day and allow darkness to take him.

As he crossed the street, the rumble behind him exploded to life like a dragon waking from slumber and roaring. Headlights bore down on him, dazzling him. There was no time to move. No time to react and no time to get out of the way.

The monster was upon him. Its breath hot, its sound loud and violent, screaming in his face, its eyes bright and glaring.

Then came the pain as it attacked. Sudden and savage as it powered over him. The world tumbled, the black sky tilted, streetlights shifted to the side, everything flickered as bones splintered, cracking and snapping, searing in his head.

Darkness descended. There was no way to know which way was up or down. Blackness covered him like a shroud.

He should probably get some help. Yes, that was what he should do.

The inky night closed some more.

He had a phone on him somewhere. He also had limbs but he couldn't find them. The darkness, the quiet, it was all too much for him.

Then it was all gone.

CHAPTER 30

Claudia

An ear-splitting sound roused Claudia from sleep. It took a moment or two for her to recognise her phone ringing.

Wearily, she picked it up. Sharpe's voice was loud and overbearing. 'Russ has been hit by a car. He's at the hospital, Claudia.'

She bolted upright. Like a lightning strike had found its way to earth through her. Russ. No, not Russ. 'What happened?'

Sharpe was all business. 'From what I can gather, he was crossing the road outside his house when a vehicle struck him, before driving away.'

It drove off. A jumble of thoughts ran through Claudia's mind at a million miles a second until it finally stopped at one conclusion. 'A hit-and-run. You think this was deliberate?'

'Accident investigation are there, doing their thing, measuring skid marks, of which I'm told there are few.'

This meant the vehicle hadn't braked or even tried to brake. Shit.

Sharpe continued. 'But early indications from an eye-witness looking out her window provide reason to believe it's highly possible. This is having all the cops thrown at it, Claudia, but we need to talk.'

They did indeed. 'At the hospital.'

'I'll meet you there.'

Twenty minutes later Claudia was at Northern General Hospital stomping around searching for both Russ and Sharpe. First and foremost, she wanted an update on Russ and to see how Maura was coping. She imagined she wasn't doing too well. Russ was her rock. She dreaded to think how Maura would manage if the prognosis was bad. She couldn't bear the thought of it herself and she was only a colleague and friend.

Eventually she found Maura sitting alone in a waiting room, a bag clutched to her chest as if for protection against the words that might come from passing staff. Claudia ran to her. Maura leaned in and allowed herself to be hugged. Claudia could feel the silent tears as they dampened the sweater she'd thrown on in her hurry to get to this family. 'Tell me,' she whispered.

Maura pulled back from Claudia's warm embrace and wiped her face roughly with her hand. 'There was a knock at my door.' The tears wouldn't stop, no matter how much she wiped at them. 'I was asleep. Maisy was sleeping. We were fast asleep, oblivious to his suffering. Dreaming of pleasant things while he lay on the road in agony.' She was angry at herself for something beyond her control. Claudia squeezed her hand.

'Don't do that to yourself. He wouldn't want you to. Maura, tell me what happened.'

Maura shook her head, freeing the haze of fear that clung on in there. 'It was my neighbour. She'd been looking out of her window. Saw the car parked and Russ crossing the road.' She bit at her lip. 'It waited until Russ was crossing before it started up and drove straight for him. Who would do this?'

Pain sliced through Claudia's chest as an inkling of an idea about what had occurred on Russ's street played in her mind. But here, with Maura, his wife, wasn't the place to go over it. Claudia's breaths were shallow, the pain present with each inhale. Like a barb was lodged in her heart. 'What's his condition, Maura?' The possible responses terrified her.

'He's in surgery.' Maura choked.

Claudia squeezed the limp hand that lay in hers again.

'Russ's mum and dad are on their way in. But they have so far to travel. I just hope they take it steady. His dad has a heavy right foot as it is. I hate to think what his driving is going to be like tonight.'

'Don't worry about that, now. They'll get here safely.' She waited for Maura to answer her question in her own time, dreading what was to come.

Maura's eyes eventually met Claudia's. They were rimmed red, her eyelids puffy and swollen, her face ghostly pale. 'They said he's critical.' Her words were quiet as she tried to draw from memory what the doctors had said to her. 'He has internal bleeding and some serious fractures.' She paused. Stuttered out more words. 'His leg.' Swiped at the tears again. 'They're worried. I can't . . .'

Claudia gripped Maura's hand. 'You're not in this alone. You'll have all the help and support you need. Anything. Just ask. We're here for you. Russ is family. You are family.' Hot tears pricked at the back of her eyes, threatening to overpower her and stream down her face. But that wasn't what Maura needed. Claudia took a deep breath and tried to hold herself together. She could cry when she was at home. Not with Russ's wife.

Hold on Russ. You can do this.

Shoes squeaked on the laminated floor and Claudia turned. It was Sharpe. Dressed as she'd never seen her, in jeans, a jumper and trainers. Claudia gave Maura's hand another squeeze, then rose to meet her boss.

'Ma'am.'

'How is he?' Sharpe asked quietly, pulling her gently out of earshot of Maura.

'Critical. He's in surgery — internal bleeding, fractures.'

Sharpe let out a deep sigh.

'That's all Maura's been able to tell me.'

Sharpe nodded, then moved past Claudia towards Maura. She sat beside her and took the hand that Claudia had just released. Claudia watched as Sharpe spoke, unable to hear the words, but presuming she was offering the support Claudia had offered. It wasn't much at a time like this, but it was all they could do. Sharpe would also tell Maura they would find whoever had done this to her husband and bring them to justice. Not that it would be on Maura's mind right now. Russ getting through his surgery would be all she could think of, Claudia imagined.

Sharpe stood, leaned down, and wrapped her arms around Maura in a hug. Tears striped Maura's face, as she nodded at the words Sharpe whispered. Claudia had never seen the woman so soft and gentle.

Then she was upright and back with Claudia. 'We need to talk.' Her tone abrupt. Serious. 'Let's walk.'

Claudia followed Sharpe down the corridor. Would anyone else join Maura? Russ's mother and father were on their way, but they were hours away. Claudia would ask if she could call a friend.

'I only have the incident report,' said Sharpe, once they were far enough away to prevent Maura overhearing. 'And it's pretty vague on details. What has Maura said?'

Claudia didn't want to say it out loud, but she had no choice. 'She knows no more than us — her neighbour, the woman who saw it happen, said a car was waiting for him and hit him deliberately.'

They reached an exit and stepped outside into the cold night. Sharpe looked around. There were No Smoking signs in place, but on the ground in the darkness were cigarette butts. She pulled out her own pack and lit one, leaning against the wall, her face in shadow. 'You know what this is, don't you, Claudia?'

'You think this is because we brought Sophie Sinclair in?'

'This is because we brought Sophie Sinclair in. It was a warning shot.'

'Some warning,' said Claudia. 'What if Russ doesn't make it?'

'Then they have the murder of a police officer on their hands. I had Connelly ranting down the phone for a good fifteen minutes after I called you tonight. He wanted to know what the hell was happening. If I was aware you and Russ had brought Sinclair in and—'

'He was more concerned about us bringing Sophie in than Russ being in critical condition because one of his cronies wants an investigation sweeping under the carpet?' Claudia's voice was rising, and her temper with it. Her closest friend inside the department was fighting for his life and she had never felt so impotent.

'If you let me finish,' Sharpe snapped. Her cigarette tip glowed as she sucked in another drag. 'I was about to say, he asked if I was aware you and Russ had brought Sinclair in and what the hell were we going to do about identifying whoever had hit Russ because they needed arresting ASAP.'

The two women glared at each other in the dark corner. The whites of their eyes flashing as they contemplated the position they were in.

Claudia sighed. 'I never, for one moment, envisaged it would come to this if we continued with the case. I didn't think that we were putting our lives at risk. Yes, they were hobbling us, but surely they expected those of us who were left to continue with the investigation. Russ has a family, for fuck's sake.'

'They won't get away with it, Claudia. It's one thing to pull strings and reallocate the majority of the team; it's completely different to attempt to kill an officer.' Sharpe spun the cigarette in her fingers, smoke twisting into the night. 'Connelly has already woken up a DCI and in turn a full team to investigate Russ's hit-and-run, attempted murder, whatever you want to call it.' She waved a hand in the air dismissively over the phrasing, though they both understood she most certainly was not dismissing what had occurred tonight. This was some next-level shit that had gone down. 'They'll want to speak to you and you'll have to be completely honest about what happened. It'll uncover some pretty shady stuff, with someone higher up allowing an investigation to be drastically reduced at its inception, but they crossed a line there's no coming back from.'

Claudia was exhausted. She ran a hand through her hair, imagining she looked like crap. 'We can investigate the hit-and-run. Especially as we're already up to date with the entire case.'

Sharpe stubbed out the cigarette on the wall and placed the end back into her pack. Claudia had never seen her be so tidy. Maybe it was the location she was being respectful of. Then she pulled out a fresh one and lit that. 'Connelly was adamant you were not to take on Russ's investigation. He said you'd try and I wasn't to permit it. He wants you and Dom, if you're still able, to follow the Harlow Cunningham case. We can't spook whoever is behind this any further. You are not to put yourself at risk were his exact words. But neither would he allow what had occurred tonight to happen again on his watch.'

Claudia had never been so relieved to hear anything in her life. She had the support of those above her. 'There's no way I'm backing off. They don't get to do this to Russ and walk away. Whatever they're hiding, we're going to drag it into the daylight for them.'

Sharpe inhaled on her cigarette, blew out the smoke and smiled. 'That's my girl. Let's go get these bastards.'

CHAPTER 31

Claudia pulled up to her house and was surprised to see Dom's car already on her drive. It was early. What the hell was he doing here? And why did people keep thinking they could stake out her house? After her experience with the Artist, she'd have thought they'd have known better.

She parked, took a deep breath and climbed out.

He was on her immediately. 'Claudia. Are you okay? How's Russ? I received a phone call and came straight over.'

Dom's hair was twisted up at the back. A sure sign that he'd been asleep before he'd arrived at the house.

'How long have you been here?' She pushed past him, having little patience for his mollycoddling at this time in the morning, after what had just happened. Though to be fair to him, Russ was a colleague. He was bound to be concerned. She should relax and talk to him.

He had the good grace to look sheepish. 'I came as soon as I heard Russ had been hit. I presumed you'd be at the hospital and I didn't want to overcrowd the staff there, but I needed to check on you, so I made a presumption you'd need to come back for some clean clothes. I'm glad you did. I could have sat here for hours.'

Claudia opened the door and strode inside, shaking her head. 'You could have phoned me.'

Dominic followed her into the house. 'There's too much I want to say and the phone isn't the ideal way to say it.'

Claudia walked into the kitchen and flicked the kettle on before stripping off the jumper she was wearing, a slim T-shirt left clinging to her frame.

'Russ is in critical condition. He was still in surgery when I left. They'll update us as soon as they know more.'

Dominic ran a hand through his hair, which did nothing for the look of it. Frustration coming off him in waves. 'Claudia,' he barked at her as she pulled a mug out of the cupboard.

What the hell was wrong with him?

Dominic lifted his hands, palms up. 'What the hell is wrong with you?'

'What?' she snapped. 'You turned up uninvited on my doorstep. What exactly is it you want?'

He put his face in his hands. Claudia frowned but left him to it. She made her tea. 'Do you want one?' she asked.

'No, I don't bloody want a drink. You do know it could have been you, don't you? How many people do I have to lose for it to be okay with you?'

That stung. Claudia put the mug back down on the side. She had to talk to him. 'We had no idea how serious this was or that the people behind this were dangerous. Do you think I'd have put Russ at risk that way if I'd have known? Or you?'

'I've never seen a case mothballed like this before, Claudia. Not this early, only a few days in and I've been doing the job a lot longer than you.' Dominic slumped onto one of her dining chairs.

'I'm sorry, Dad.' She hung her head, the effects of the night weighing heavy on her.

He shrugged. 'You know there's no way we're stopping now, don't you.' It wasn't a question.

'I was going to talk to you this morning,' Claudia said.

Dominic raised an eyebrow.

Claudia laughed at his expression. Though it didn't feel like the time for laughter, her father's disbelief in her amused her. 'Seriously. Connelly has given us the go-ahead to continue, even after this.'

'Well, I'm not letting you out of my sight after tonight's events and we assess everything you and Russ did yesterday that would make him a target. We'll work this methodically like anything else.'

Claudia filled him in on the interview of Sophie Sinclair. The only part of the day he wasn't up to date on. She then shared her conversation with Sharpe, that the hit-and-run on Russ might have been because they brought Sophie Sinclair in. She winced at the thought of Russ laying in the road. Damaged and broken.

Dominic rose from his chair. 'I'll let you get showered and changed and I'll meet you at the office shortly. Then we'll assess what we have and go from there. But you're not in this alone, Claudia. Shall I stay with you while this is ongoing?'

She paused. There was no easy way to say this. 'You staying over didn't stop my abduction last time.' Okay, she'd just come right out with it. 'I just think if they want to get to me, they will. But I appreciate the sentiment, truly. Thank you. I'll take care. I promise.'

Dominic huffed. Tried for dispassionate but failed miserably and shrugged instead. 'I offered.'

'I know. I'll catch up with you later.'

Once he was out the door and it was locked and secure behind him, Claudia sank onto the sofa and burst into tears. She'd held herself together while she'd been with Maura and then discussing the case with Sharpe. Then again with her father. She couldn't show vulnerability in front of Dominic. It was bad enough that he was aware of her struggles over the stabbing without him knowing she had crumbled over Russ. He'd think she wasn't up to the job and it would give him even more reason to believe he should have been promoted when he applied for the inspector's position. But he'd failed the interview board and had done nothing about it since. He wasn't desperate for promotion; what he hated, what he harboured, was a quiet bitterness that Claudia outranked him. It wasn't obvious, but they were both aware it seethed under silent waters. And Claudia wouldn't give him that reason to beat his own chest. She was competent and capable and would run with this case and bring whoever was behind this down.

She showered and changed. Had a bite to eat. As she closed the front door behind her, her phone rang. It was Sharpe.

'Things are changing rapidly, Claudia.'

This didn't sound good.

'I don't want to go into it all here. I don't trust phones now. Neither should you.'

Again, not good. The power behind this must be immense.

'I'm not even sure how safe the nick is. I suggest we meet somewhere off site. Any suggestions?'

'Does Connelly know about this?' Claudia's head was reeling.

Sharpe's response was whip quick. 'Not on the phone.'

Claudia felt as though she'd been punched it was so fast and abrupt. She tried to think. Outside of the building. 'There's the smoking shed?'

'I don't want to be on the grounds, if I'm honest.'

'We could use Albie's again?'

'Okay. That'll do. I'll meet you there in half an hour.'

'I'll let Dominic know.' Claudia pulled out of her street without noticing the car parked on the next road, waiting for her to leave, ready to follow where she went.

CHAPTER 32

Albie's coffee shop had a few early-morning customers grabbing their first coffees of the day. Sharpe was already there, waiting for Claudia at a table. A mug sat before her, steam rising, and a small plate with a croissant, half eaten.

The smell of baked goods and coffee was welcoming after the night they'd all had. Claudia ordered a tea and a croissant, then sat down opposite Sharpe.

'How are you?' asked Sharpe.

Claudia shook her head. 'I can't quite believe what's happened.'

'We will find who did this, Claudia. You mark my words. We'll not rest until they're behind bars. You might be able to cut resources on an investigation, but you certainly don't attempt to kill an officer.' Her tone was steel.

Her determination buoyed Claudia. 'Is there an update on Russ this morning?'

'He's out of surgery. They're saying it went well. But his condition is still critical, and he's in ICU recovering. Maura has gone home to get a couple of hours' sleep and then she's going back.'

'I presume we're doing a whip-round for Maura and Maisy?'

'I think it's already in hand. You know how generous everyone is at a time like this. I've sent an email warning them all off getting in touch with Maura. I don't want her overwhelmed. I told them she'd have a point of contact who would relay everyone's messages of support, but she can't be spending all her days answering texts and calls.'

The chime above the door tinkled and Dominic entered, scarf wrapped tightly around his neck. 'I've been fielding calls all morning from the team, wanting to know the latest on Russ and asking what they could do to help. I told them in no uncertain terms they were to stay away.'

Claudia thanked him and Dominic stalked to the counter to make his order. There was a subdued silence at the table as Claudia and Sharpe waited for him. It wasn't long before Dominic towered over them, mug of coffee in one hand, bacon sandwich in the other.

Claudia's stomach rumbled as the scent assaulted her. Bacon always smelled like the food of the gods. She hadn't taken a bite of her croissant yet, so pulled a piece off and shoved it into her mouth. It tasted good. Buttery and sweet. Just what she needed.

Dominic pulled out a chair and sat beside them. 'Is the hit-and-run in hand?' he asked.

'Another team has taken the incident on, Dom.' Sharpe's tone was cool.

Dominic, however, was not afraid to butt up against her. 'Are they as determined to get to the bottom of the matter as we'd be?'

He was here for a fight. Claudia picked at her croissant again, feeding the dread in her stomach.

'Dom,' Sharpe said, making sure she had his attention. 'Connelly has put one of his best DCIs on the task who has been given the go-ahead to create the team they need to get to the bottom of what happened last night. Russ is one of us and no copper in the country would allow that incident to go unanswered for. So trust that yes, it's in hand.'

Dominic took a chunk out of his sandwich, chewing on it as he mulled over what Sharpe had said. 'How's Russ?'

'Recovering in ICU. Condition critical,' said Sharpe, keeping it brief.

Dominic gave a quick nod of understanding, the frown lines on his forehead deep crevasses.

The door chimed again as another customer sauntered in out of the cold. Claudia watched their trek to the counter, making sure they were here for food and not to check out what the three police officers were doing. When she was happy they were simply ordering food, she returned her attention to their table. 'What's our plan of attack for today?'

Sharpe sipped at her coffee before speaking. 'You're the one who's been involved in the investigation from the start. What're your thoughts?'

Claudia considered the options. 'Four things,' she said. 'One—' she held up a finger — 'we continue looking into the evidence we already have on the Cunningham murder. It has to be done.'

Sharpe gave her a sceptical look. Claudia understood why. It meant using police databases. Trackable databases. But as she'd said, if they were to continue this, it had to be done.

Claudia continued. 'Two.' She held up another finger. 'We need to dig into Sophie Sinclair. Find out who she is and about her life. The receptionist heard her telling Harlow Cunningham to "stop" — we need to know what she wanted Harlow to stop, and why and find out if Harlow and Sophie overlap in their lives at all.'

Dominic nodded.

'Three.' She held up a third finger. 'We follow the line of inquiry we picked up on yesterday, that Harlow told her friends she was a foundling. It feels important and may be the reason she kept disappearing over the weekend. It may even be a link back to Sinclair.'

Sharpe and Dominic were listening intently.

'Four.' Claudia held up a fourth finger. 'The hit-and-run.'

Sharpe rolled her eyes.

'No,' said Claudia. 'It's relevant. It's relevant to our investigation because our case is the reason Russ was targeted — we all feel sure of that. So we need to keep abreast of all, and I mean all, findings on that inquiry. It could really help us.'

'I'll see what I can do,' said Sharpe.

Dom wiped his mouth where the last of his bacon sandwich had just disappeared. 'The question is, how do we conduct these inquiries discreetly without alerting the wrong people to what we're doing?'

Sharpe tapped her fingers on the table top. Polished nails glistening under the coffee shop's strip lighting. 'That's going to be more difficult than we'd hoped as we've no idea where this originated because I've no idea if this stops with Mike Davidson or someone over him. I've done a little digging and I can't find a link between him and Harlow. In fact he appears to be as straight as they come.'

'So, nothing.' Dominic's tone was hard.

'If you let me finish, Dominic.' His Sunday name. She was rattled. This investigation was getting to all of them.

'I'm sorry, go on.'

Sharpe gave him a look, then continued. 'I spoke to Maxine, my PA, the assistants tend to talk to each other and know the unofficial stuff, the rumours etc.'

Claudia raised her eyebrows. Wondered what they knew about Sharpe. One day she'd have to take Maxine out for a drink.

'Maxine said he's happily married, perfect suburban life, but he has a wandering eye.'

'Affairs?' Dominic asked.

'Not as far as anyone knows. But . . .'

'Maybe thirty-five years ago,' finished Claudia.

'You think he's Harlow's father?' Dominic sounded incredulous.

'He's in the right age range, certainly. But thirty-five years ago he was at college in the Midlands, and he has no connection to Devon. We'd need DNA to confirm or rule out the possibility and the acting ACC is not going to just hand over his biological material.'

Claudia and Dominic exchanged a glance. They were getting nowhere.

'If we could find Harlow's mother, that could get us somewhere. But for now, he's a dead end.' Sharpe cradled her mug. 'I want you both to be aware of your surroundings at all times. To me, it looks like whoever is behind this is now attempting to take out the remaining staff on the investigation. Those they couldn't legitimately remove. So keep your eyes peeled.' She sipped on her coffee. 'Which brings me to the question of how you're going to continue with this investigation with a light footprint. The answer to that is very carefully.'

Silence dropped around the group like a cloak as they all took in what Sharpe had said. The parameters of the board they were now playing on.

'I feel sick,' said Claudia. 'I seriously can't believe this is happening. I've never known anything like it. Someone attempting to kill an officer for simply doing his job? It's beyond horrific.'

'And because of that, I want you out of view. For everyone's safety,' said Sharpe. 'I'll set you up in a smaller space that is less easy for people to walk in and out of. That incident room is like Piccadilly Circus some days. I don't know how you ever get any work done.'

Claudia pursed her lips. 'I don't like the idea of hiding away like frightened rabbits.'

'You'd rather be out in the open playing target practice?' asked Sharpe.

Dominic watched her.

Claudia shook her head. 'Okay, we'll hide out in a cupboard, but consider this my official dissatisfaction with the matter. Anything else we need to consider?'

'I want updates on the hour every hour,' said Sharpe. Nails now tapping on the side of her mug. 'I don't care what time it is. If you're still working, I want keeping up to date.'

'And you'll keep us up to date with Russ?' said Claudia. 'I don't want to bother Maura.'

'Of course.'

'The team?' Dominic asked. 'What are we telling the team about Russ? Yesterday was a bit strange with the rapid reassignment and now this. They're worried.'

Sharpe frowned. 'I told them it was a hit-and-run and is being investigated as such. There should be no issues there.'

They were an intelligent bunch and Claudia worried someone might start sticking their nose in if the situation didn't feel right to them. All they could do was hold their ground for now.

Claudia fished in her bag, rummaging through the mess that accumulated in there and pulled out two twenty-pound notes, thrusting them at Sharpe. 'For Russ's collection.'

Sharpe took the money.

Dominic pushed his hand into his pocket and pulled out four ten-pound notes, sliding them to Sharpe. She took them, putting it all in her bag.

'I can't physically protect you, but I want you to be safe,' Sharpe said. 'Please be careful. For my part, I'll attempt to keep whoever is behind this off your scent. And if we need to talk . . .' She took stock of her surroundings. At people sitting alone, reading papers, books, just eating or drinking, people in pairs and groups, the morning rush before the working day really started. 'This looks as good a place as any to hold any kind of meeting. We can come here. Unless, of course, it's closed and then we'll reassess.' She rose. 'Stay safe. Whoever is behind this is serious. I don't want to lose another officer.'

CHAPTER 33

Claudia and Dominic found themselves a small office that looked like it was slowly being turned into a storage cupboard. Junk that officers couldn't find space for had been piled up in corners. There was a mound of large heavy-duty kit bags that were too big to push in a locker, so were stacked up in this room. In another corner box files created a mountain. Someone somewhere in the building had shoved paperwork in here instead of filing it properly and securely. Heads would roll one day when these documents were needed and they couldn't be located.

Dominic stomped around the small space as much as the office allowed stomping, while Claudia kept her mood under wraps. It would serve no one to get into a tizzy, as Dominic was doing.

'Hey,' she shouted at him eventually as the box files tumbled to the floor as he stormed past them once again, trying to get an extra wheely chair in.

Dominic spun around, the sound of boxes falling loud in the small office. 'What?'

'Tone it down. It's doing no good being in a mood. We can't work in the incident room. Sharpe found us this empty office.'

'Not that you can call it an office,' grumbled Dominic.

'Whatever,' she said. 'But it's ours. So we get used to it. Simmer down.'

You really couldn't call it an office. But it had a couple of computers so they could have one each. Dominic manoeuvred the second chair in, which was taking up far too much room.

Claudia logged on to the HOLMES2 case file on the Cunningham murder. She scratched her head.

'What is it?' Dom lifted the last box file from the floor and placed it back atop the tower, giving it a push into the corner in an attempt to stabilise it.

'HOLMES. I have no idea who is watching.' She scrubbed at her face. Fatigue wearing her down.

'We're police officers, Claudia. You're a police officer. We will not be intimidated to silence or inaction. We have a case to investigate until we're lawfully, and that's the word, lawfully, told to stop. Let's do this.'

Claudia leaned back in her chair, as much as the room allowed her to do, and thought about what her father had said. He was right, she knew that. But now they'd sat down and stopped for a minute in a quiet place, the whole thing had caught up with her.

'You think Russ will be okay?' Her voice was quiet, like a small girl asking her father if monsters existed under the bed.

'Russ is a fighter. Do I always agree with him? Do I hell.' He grinned. 'Which is why I know how much he'll fight. To get back to his family and to get back here to sort this bloody mess out and find who did this to him and to us.'

Her father's words reassured Claudia, for once. 'Thanks, Dad.'

'That's what I'm here for. As well as keeping you safe and wading through all this shit that is a murder investigation.'

It was Claudia's turn to sigh. 'Yeah, we really do have our work cut out for us.'

'Where do you want to start?'

He was playing by her book for once. Things had obviously shaken him.

'Harlow told her friends she was a foundling. I'm not sure what we do with that, but it feels significant.'

Dominic had his notebook out. 'I didn't find anything yesterday but there's still plenty to do.'

'If anyone knows about her start in life and where she came from, it's going to be her father. He's so far away it's going to have to be a phone call though.'

Dominic made a note.

Claudia opened HOLMES2 as she spoke and read the last few entries that had been recorded. Harlow's phone log being one of them. Other than that the call on Saturday night had been a withheld number, she knew little else about Harlow's calls. Krish had been examining it. She remembered Chloe talking about the text messages she'd exchanged with Harlow on Friday morning.

'Where's the nearest printer?' She searched around her. There was absolutely no space in this room for one.

Dominic walked to the door and looked out. 'There's one down the corridor.'

'Okay, I'm printing out Harlow's phone records. We'll go through those and see who she spoke to while she was here over the weekend and just before she came to Sheffield.' She tapped at the keyboard, locating the printer on the screen and printing out the document so they had a hard copy to work from in case anyone locked them out of the system. 'We also need to research Sophie Sinclair. There's enough to keep us busy for a few hours. We'll see what we can do and then discuss what we have later and go from there.' Claudia wasn't used to doing these kinds of tasks, at least not since she'd been promoted, but needs must. With only her and Dominic working the investigation, she had to get into the case properly and not just on a supervisory level.

'It's coming to life,' Dominic said as he strode out of the small office to fetch the paperwork. When he returned minutes later, he was holding a sheaf of papers and was flicking through the contents, focusing on a couple of pages.

'We need to pull out the numbers she called, and those who called her, and submit a request to the phone provider for user details. This may have already been done but we're going to have to do it again ourselves.' The image on the screen Claudia was looking through matched the hard copy Dominic had in his hands. 'It looks like she preferred to make calls rather than text messages,' she said. 'At least to what we're hoping are the important numbers. Looking at the text messages, we can see most of them belong to Brodie, Ashanti, Chloe and Jay. We have their numbers listed so we can cross those off the list we want to identify.'

Dominic sat in his chair. 'She made a call early Saturday morning and didn't Chloe say she went out Saturday morning? Maybe this was her making the arrangements?'

'Okay, we prioritise that one.' She checked down the list, mentally crossing off any calls to her friends, though there weren't many. Harlow had communicated via text message with them while she'd been in Sheffield. 'There's one Thursday night as well. We'll also identify that one. Didn't they arrive here at some point on Thursday?'

Dominic used a highlighter pen to mark up the numbers they wanted as Claudia talked through the call log. 'Yeah, they all met up on Thursday. Harlow's dad says she left home late Wednesday afternoon and her stay at the hotel started that day, but that was because she had such a long drive and wanted to be bright and ready for her friends on Thursday. The hotel corroborates this.'

'Okay then. So we've identified two numbers. Can you submit them, please? Hopefully it won't be too long before we get some results back.'

'Can do.' He started tapping away at his keyboard.

'We have two other steps we can take today. Investigate Sophie Sinclair, and phone Paul Cunningham to ask about Harlow's birth, where she was abandoned, which part of the country, and her thoughts surrounding it. How important it was to her. If it played on her mind. Was it something she used in the game because it was an interesting snippet of information, or was it something that lay deeper in her psyche? Is it the key to unlocking this case?'

CHAPTER 34

'I'll make the phone call to Paul Cunningham. You see if you can dig into Sophie Sinclair,' said Claudia as she searched out Paul's number in her notes. 'Then we'll come back together and look at what we have.'

She dialled and listened as the phone rang all the miles away in Devon.

'Hello?' The voice on the end of the line was tentative.

Caller ID wouldn't help for a police call. Paul would only see 'withheld number'.

'Paul, it's Claudia Nunn from South Yorkshire Police. I spoke to you a couple of days ago.' *When your world shattered into a thousand pieces.*

There was a brief pause. A moment where he considered what news she could break to him now. 'Yes, hello, DI Nunn.'

Across from her Dominic was tapping away at his keyboard, notepad open beside him. A serious, focused expression on his face as he read from the monitor.

'I need to ask you a few questions if you have a minute?' She wished she had some news to give Paul before asking her questions.

'I have a minute.' There was rustling in the background. She couldn't figure out what he was doing.

'I'm afraid we don't have a clear suspect yet,' she hedged. 'But we have several lines of inquiry we are running down.' It sounded so hopeless. But murder investigations could run on for months. She'd given updates like this before. It was the guilt of what was occurring behind the scenes that was eating her up.

Paul didn't respond. What was there to say, after all?

'It's one of these lines of inquiry I'm calling about, actually,' Claudia pushed on.

'You think you'll get him?' Paul finally spoke.

'I'm sorry?'

'The person who did this to my daughter, you think you'll get him in the end? It's all I'm living for, you see.' The soft Devonshire accent lilted up at the end of the sentence.

Claudia's heart broke a little. Paul's words hit home as he told her this. It was all the more desperate as she knew that someone, somewhere, was doing their level best to stop that happening.

'I certainly hope so,' she said with every ounce of honesty she had within her. If it was anything to do with her, or Dominic, or Sharpe, or Russ who had paid dearly for wanting this, then Harlow Cunningham's killer would be found. Regardless of who was protecting them. 'It's what we're working towards,' she added.

She felt his sorrow and bowed her head.

'What is it you want to ask me?'

Claudia tapped on the desk, trying to think of a good way to broach the delicate subject of Harlow's biological parents with Paul when he was grieving for his child.

'What is it?' He nudged.

'Harlow discussed something with her friends on Friday night and I need to ask you about it.'

'Okay.'

'It's a little sensitive and I don't want to cause you any further distress, Paul.'

Silence descended again. He was obviously finding this conversation hard going. 'Okay. We may as well get into it. Tell me.'

'Harlow told her friends on Friday that she was, in her words, "a foundling".'

A sharp intake of breath.

'She explained that you and your wife were not her birth parents.'

The quietest 'no' came down the line. 'No, we weren't. But it didn't mean we weren't her parents.'

'I don't doubt that, Paul.'

'Why would she . . .' He didn't appear able to finish the sentence.

She couldn't tell him it had been a game. The word game implied flippancy and Claudia doubted Harlow had been flippant about this. 'They were talking about subjects they might not have known about each other,' she went for instead. 'Because she brought it up the weekend she was murdered, we're wondering if it was relevant.'

The silence stretched out longer this time. Paul didn't seem inclined to break it so Claudia spoke again. 'Had Harlow mentioned anything about her birth parents before coming to Sheffield last weekend?'

The door to their office was open and a couple of uniformed officers strode past, their voices loud and raucous, laughing at a joke one of them had told. Claudia wished she'd closed the door before she made the call, but the room was so small, closing the door would have made it appear even smaller and she hadn't wanted to feel closed in. Now she regretted that decision. She listened in for Paul's response.

'Harlow hadn't mentioned them for a long time. It wasn't something we thought she was brooding on.'

Okay, so it was something that was on her mind, but not enough to talk to her father about before she came to Sheffield. Maybe they were going down the wrong alley.

'Can I ask about Harlow's birth?' Claudia asked. A difficult topic, but one that had to be broached.

'Is it relevant?'

Claudia had to strain to hear. 'It's something Harlow mentioned during the weekend, so we need to look at it and assess its importance.'

'As she said, she was a foundling.' Paul's voice was stronger now. 'That meant she was not only given up by her parents, but she was physically abandoned. She was left outside to be found by strangers, hence the name foundling. It's an archaic turn of phrase, but one that appealed to Harlow.'

'And what happened?'

'Someone left her outside a hospital — the Accident and Emergency department.'

Claudia couldn't imagine what would drive a person to do that. To leave a defenceless infant outside in the hope someone would find her. 'Can you tell me more about what happened?'

'Is it really relevant to your inquiry?'

'I can't say until I know all the details.' It was an emotionally difficult case and each day it appeared to bring even more pain for someone.

There was a deep sigh down the line. This was wearing on the father. He was grieving and yet here he was being pushed to remember the very difficult beginning of his child's life. Though Claudia had a feeling he had probably run through these memories at some point since Harlow's death. 'There was a note tucked into her blanket. It was a reasonably warm day, considering the time of year. It was October . . . her birthday was in October.' His voice cracked and he stumbled over the last few words as the thought that she wouldn't have any more birthdays hit home.

'I'm sorry.' The weight of the investigation was bearing down on her. She put her head in her hands.

Dominic looked up from his screen and narrowed his eyes in a question. She shook her head at him that no, nothing was wrong. Though of course everything was wrong. But there was nothing out of the ordinary with the call she was on. A father was hurting and this was all in the parameters of 'normal'. Dominic lifted his chin in understanding and returned his attention to what he'd been doing.

This time Claudia figured out the very soft rustling was Paul wiping away the tears from his face, attempting to steady himself for the rest of the conversation. Talking to her was, they both hoped, going to push the case forward, so it had to be done. He'd be brave now and break after the call. When he was alone and she wasn't listening at the end of the line. She'd seen her fair share of broken people. Lives shattered when loved ones were lost. It was the most difficult part of the job and it never got easier.

And neither should it.

'The note,' Paul said. 'It was from her mother. We kept it for her so she could read it when she was old enough. I'm not sure what she did with it once we gave it to her, but if what you're saying is correct, then my guess is she still has it. Is it important to you? Do you need it?'

Claudia thought on the question. What would having the paper achieve after all these years? Harlow was thirty-four. They could still recover fingerprints, but how many other people had been in contact with the letter? When she was first found, potentially the person who found her, nurses, doctors, social workers, any placements she was in before she was with the Cunninghams and then the Cunninghams themselves. The list was endless. She'd need to track all those people down to obtain elimination prints before they'd be able to identify the set of prints that belonged to either of the parents. And to what end? Claudia didn't even know how important this line of inquiry was yet. 'I'm not sure. Let's leave that question on the back burner for now, shall we? But can you tell me what the note said? Can you remember?'

'As clear as the day I first read it,' he said. '"Please take good care of me. I was born today and my mother loves me dearly, but circumstances prevent her from giving me the care I so very much deserve. She knows I will have a better life in a good home because you will make it so. She will never forget me."'

'It sounds like it was written by an educated woman,' Claudia said. 'Which I find unusual. But I have to admit, I know little about foundlings, or women who do this.'

'The police back then thought so too, going by the wording and the neat handwriting.' Paul cleared his throat. 'There was an investigation at the time to locate the mother — she would have needed medical attention. But no one ever came forward and Harlow became our daughter.'

'There were no clues to her biological parentage?' Claudia asked.

'The police, social care, or me or her mother, never heard a word after that. It was as if the woman had dropped off the face of the planet once she'd handed Harlow over, or more precisely, left her behind.'

'And what about Harlow?' Claudia made notes of what Paul had said so far. 'When was she informed, what was her reaction to the information?'

'She was shocked, as you'd expect. No one wants to think their mother could simply abandon them that way. And Harlow is an . . .' There was another pause as Paul gathered himself after the slip. 'Harlow was an emotional girl. It's one of the things I really loved about her. She was so sensitive. But this knocked her for six. She could barely speak to me or her mother for weeks after we told her. Not that she was angry at us. But her identity had been challenged, and she didn't know which way to turn. We understood that and gave her the space she needed while also being there for her should she need us.'

'How old was Harlow when you told her about her birth?'

'We never hid it from her, DI Nunn. It wasn't something we were ashamed of, taking her in and giving her a safe home. All we needed to do was wait until we thought she was old enough to understand what we were telling her. Let me think . . .' There was a slight pause as Paul Cunningham drifted into his past. 'It was in the later years of juniors.'

'And what happened then?'

'Nothing. Nothing happened. Gradually, she slipped back into life as it was before. There were questions, obviously. She wanted to know where she came from and we had little information we could give her. It bothered her, but not so much that she kept on about it. You should know,' he said a little more quietly, 'that Harlow was abandoned in Sheffield.'

'Here?' Paul had voluntarily provided Claudia with the information they needed.

'Yes. We moved when we adopted her. Took her away from the area where she was left like an empty bag of chips on the ground. Moved back to the coast, to Devon. Brought her up in the fresh air.'

'Back to Devon?' Claudia listened to the older man's Devonshire burr and realised that yes, an accent like that didn't come from a few years of life in the county. It was more.

'This is where me and her mum were from originally. We moved to Sheffield for work. Back then Sheffield was thriving. It was a huge industrial city. Plenty of work. Plus, we felt too young to be cooped up in a seaside location. We wanted a city life. But Harlow changed all that.' Another pause. A snuffle.

Claudia waited.

'Do you have children, DI Nunn?'

Claudia thought of Matt and their short-lived marriage. 'No. No, I don't have children.'

'Ah. Well, when you do, you'll know that having a baby changes all your priorities and your outlook on life. Everything me and her mum thought we knew was flipped on its head. All we wanted was to escape that city and bring that sweet child up in a beautiful place and we couldn't think of anywhere more beautiful than here.'

Claudia could understand that, regardless of being childless. But he'd failed to inform them of Harlow's connection to Sheffield. He'd slowed them right down and this rattled her. 'Why didn't you mention Harlow was born here when I saw you? Or you could have told your family liaison officer.' Claudia was aware her tone was abrupt. She brought her temper down a notch.

'I'm sorry.'

She could barely hear him now.

'It didn't cross my mind she'd chosen Sheffield as a location because of her birth. I genuinely thought she'd moved past all of it.'

'You don't think she wanted to know who her birth parents were?'

'Of course she did. It plagued her for a while. Particularly through the difficult teenage years. But in the end she realised there was nothing she could do, so she let it lie and got on with her life.'

'A delicate question . . .' Claudia said, returning to a more level place.

'Go on.'

'Would you have supported Harlow in her search for her birth parents or would she have hidden it from you?' Was this what had happened?

'We backed her in everything she did. Harlow knew there was nothing she could do that would upset or disappoint us. We loved her unconditionally and had done since the day we first saw her. That included when she was first inquisitive about her biological parents. We were comfortable in our relationship and understood who, if she found them, her birth parents would be to her. It wasn't a battle for a place in her heart. There was no need to be upset with her. That's why I didn't think anything of this visit to Sheffield.'

'So,' Claudia brought the questions to a close, 'as far as you're concerned, Harlow never found her birth mother or father? And she had stopped looking for them?'

'Correct to both, DI Nunn. She may have mentioned the circumstances of her birth to her friends, but I don't imagine it has anything to do with why she was murdered.' His voice dipped on the last word. So much that Claudia barely heard it and her mind filled in the blank. 'I mean,' Paul continued, 'how would finding her birth parents lead to that? None of it makes sense.'

Paul was right. If Harlow had found either of her biological parents and they hadn't wanted to acknowledge her, all they had to do was send her on her way, abandon her again. It would have been painful for Harlow but wouldn't have ended in her death. Something else had happened here.

'Thank you for your time, Paul. I understand this is extremely difficult and I'm sorry I've had to dredge up such personal memories, but it's been helpful.'

They said their goodbyes and Claudia promised to update him again when she had further information.

She was drained. With little in the way of sleep last night and the pressure of the investigation bearing down on her, Claudia wanted nothing more than to walk out of this broom cupboard and to never come back.

CHAPTER 35

Harlow

Friday 3 p.m. — 42 hours earlier

The place was huge from what she could see while standing at the gate at the end of a long winding driveway.

Harlow waited patiently for someone to answer the intercom. Her nerves somewhat dulled by the ostentatiousness. She'd never been in such a nice home and couldn't imagine the price if it ever went on the market.

The man inside was worth a pretty penny. Touted as the future prime minister of the country and the current leader of the opposition party. He was a shining star, someone who was going places.

A voice crackled through the box on the gate. 'Hello?'

'Harlow Cunningham. I'm expected.' MPs were some of the easiest people in society to get in touch with, even the leader of the opposition had to work for his constituents. It was all in the job description. Asking for this meeting had been the easy bit. That he'd agreed had been startling. But she was a little unnerved he'd wanted to meet here, at his home. It was probably because it was out of the way, where no one else could view them together.

'Come through,' the voice crackled again. The large wrought-iron gate swung open.

Harlow's stomach flipped over. Just once. This was it. She was finally going to meet him. Yesterday hadn't gone well, but today was another day. Who cared what Justin had said? Nigel Winters had agreed to see her, and it was about to happen.

She strode up the driveway with as much confidence as she could muster — which in this case wasn't a lot. Her legs were like jelly, but she held her back stiff and straight to give the impression of assurance. Even if she wasn't feeling it.

The door was a huge wooden affair and was answered by the man himself. He was just like his photographs and as she'd seen him on the television and from searching his online profile. Though he was much better looking in person. He was greying early. After all, he wasn't quite fifty yet. But it was a dignified grey at his temples. He had a good head of hair, which was a dark chestnut and his deep eyes were brooding. Intelligent and thoughtful. 'Harlow?'

She nodded, temporarily at a loss for words.

'Won't you come in?' He stepped aside and allowed her access.

The entry hallway was larger than her own living room. The flooring was all dark hardwood with the doors and skirting in a lighter wood. A chandelier hung from the centre of the ceiling and a stunning staircase swung up the side of the space. The cream walls seemed to have a depth and texture of their own. This space screamed money. On a table was an enormous vase of flowers, of beautiful colours and long green stems.

'Shall we make ourselves more comfortable?' Nigel said, ushering her towards a half-open doorway.

Harlow was unsure if she had been staring. Was her mouth hanging open? She closed it tight, teeth jarring. 'Yes. Of course.' She followed where he walked, unable to believe what she was seeing. This home was unlike anything she'd seen before. It was utterly beautiful. Like something out of a design magazine.

How the other half lived. That was the phrase, wasn't it? And it certainly fitted here. He led her through to what Harlow could only describe as a sun room. It was at the side of the house and consisted of the two outer walls, with floor-to-ceiling sliding glass doors. Opposite the glass doors, was the largest mirror Harlow had ever seen. It nearly filled the entire wall, making the room appear double its size. An illusionary feat as the windows made the outside appear part of the inside, giving the space even more depth. The January day was overcast but everything was light and airy in here.

'Can I get you anything?' Nigel asked as she sank into one of the chairs. There were only single chairs scattered around, rather than a sofa. Nigel was smooth and in control, his expression inscrutable.

'A glass of water would be lovely, thank you.' If she didn't have a drink she wouldn't be able to speak. Fear of what was ahead was drying her tongue so that it was sticking to the roof of her mouth.

A few minutes later he handed her a heavy tumbler filled with water and crushed ice. No doubt he had one of those fridges that contained a fitted ice-machine. She thanked him and sipped at the drink, the cool liquid a welcome respite to her nerves.

'You're very lucky to have caught me today,' he said. 'In my constituency, rather than London. As it's a Friday, Commons isn't sitting, so I came home to do some constituency work. I try to balance my time between the two. It's difficult, but I made a promise and it's one I intend to keep.' He smiled. It was bright. A whitened smile. Made especially for the cameras.

'I'm glad I did,' she said. 'Though I could have seen you in London if that had been the only option. This was convenient as I was meeting friends this weekend.'

Nigel had been standing, towering over her, but now he sat in one of the spare chairs. 'I'm sure you have some questions for me, but first, I have to ask you how you

found me?' Again, that smile. 'And I don't mean by looking online and emailing the address provided.' He held up
a hand. 'If you're honest with me, I promise, I'll be honest
with you.'

Did he mean it? Could Harlow be honest with this man?
Politicians often bent the truth to fit their narrative. But this
politician was different. He was known as the truth-sayer.
Unafraid to speak the unfiltered truth no matter the consequences, even when that truth had come with repercussions
that had played out against him. It was why he was so popu-
lar. It was a novelty having an MP be so openly truthful this
way. People liked it.

'I can do that,' she said, hoping for the best. She'd say
what she could without, hopefully, getting anyone into trouble. Because this was sensitive. The simple fact of her being
here was enough to throw Winters' career to the wolves.
They had to tread carefully.

He was openly staring at her now. Harlow felt like a
specimen on a slide being meticulously examined.

'You're a beautiful young woman, you know that, don't
you?'

She hadn't expected this and sipped at her water to give
herself time to formulate a response. 'Thank you,' was all she
could muster.

'You gave up a promising career to start an owl sanctuary. You have a strong, caring streak. That's something to be
proud of.'

He'd researched her before she'd arrived. She should
have expected this. All she could do was nod.

'Now back to the question, Harlow. How did you find
me?' He was leaning forward. His hands on his knees. He
wanted to hear what came next.

Harlow swallowed. 'I'd given up on you, both of you.
Thinking I'd never find you. Not after what happened.'

He frowned. 'Yes. It was an incredibly difficult time.'

So he hadn't been a part of it? Yet he still hadn't come
forward in all these years, not when she'd needed him most.

'But then I was contacted by a woman on one of those family history websites. The ones where you can upload DNA tests.'

He raised an eyebrow.

'I'd done one years before and Serena, the woman, she had just done hers, and we matched . . . as siblings.'

Nigel nodded his understanding.

'Instead of confronting her mother she went to her mother's best friend. A woman she had called aunt all her life. It was this woman who gave her the full story. Serena was shocked by what she heard. It took her weeks to process the news. That I was out there in the world and she hadn't known about me. She was angry at her mother and at you. In fact, she was furious with her mother.'

'Did the aunt give her the whole story? Why her mother did what she did?' His voice was gentle, his eyes soft.

'Serena didn't tell me anything other than who you were and that if I wanted the truth, I should talk to both of you. One of you should spill, she said.' This to the man who could one day lead the country, a powerful man. She silently pleaded with him to give her what she so desperately needed. Some closure at last. She would ignore what Justin had said yesterday. She was in the room with the man himself. He made the decisions. Her hands were shaking so much she placed the tumbler of water on the floor.

'Harlow.' His gaze was intense, as though he was soaking in every cell of her. 'I never thought I'd meet you and this meeting, seeing you like this, it's brought emotions to the fore that have been dormant for a very long time. But . . .'

Something inside Harlow shrivelled up and died as the word 'but' left his mouth.

'You know who I am. What you don't know is the truth from back then. It's not pretty and it could destroy me. It could destroy everything I've worked for, everything I've worked towards. All the people I'll be able to help in my future. The good I could do. All the public will see is the nasty story from thirty-odd years ago.'

He couldn't even remember exactly how long ago it was.

'Thirty-four,' she whispered.

'What's that?'

'It was thirty-four years ago,' she said.

'Yes, yes. Thirty-four years ago. The public is very fickle. A scandal like this will rage on in the press for weeks. It won't let up and you'll be there, Harlow. It won't just be me. They'll drag you into it. They'll dig into your life. Turn it upside down. And not just your life now, but everything about it. From the minute you were born—'

Harlow winced.

'To what you're doing now. The owl sanctuary.' He peered at her. His eyes were not unkind, but now the implication he'd researched her was not benevolent as it had been a moment ago. He could find out what he wanted, about anyone he wanted. He was probably even aware of her financial situation and was afraid that might be the reason behind this visit.

It wasn't.

'Yes,' she said in response. 'The owl sanctuary.' But he'd explained nothing to her yet. What was the 'nasty' story that would explode in the press if she pushed this?

She felt very small sitting in the chair in front of him in this vast room. Her hands in her lap were limp and useless. She needed to do something with them. She picked the tumbler of water back up, blinked a couple of times and cleared her throat. She had to do this. It was likely her only chance to face him. 'Tell me what happened.' It wasn't a question. There was no room to get out of it. A straightforward demand. How would this political lion respond to this one?

Nigel sighed. 'Your mother. She was my teacher.'

CHAPTER 36

Harlow

Friday 4 p.m. — 43 hours earlier

Whatever she'd been expecting, it hadn't been that. This man was one of the most powerful men in the country and he'd just told Harlow that his teacher groomed him when he was a child.

'I was sixteen and considered myself an adult.' He leaned back. Sighed. 'Worldly-wise, at that age. I knew even then that I would go into politics. My parents had sent me to the finest school they could afford. They struggled to keep me there, but it was important to them I get the best start in life.' Nigel's demeanour relaxed a little. The secret was out and now all he had to do was tell his story.

Sixteen! Harlow's stomach twisted into a huge knot. Nowadays, what her birth mother had done would have landed her in jail — even in the eighties, surely it must have seemed wrong. So this was where she had come from. What Nigel had said was more than true — the world would go crazy for this information. She didn't want that.

'She was my English Lit teacher,' Nigel went on, unaware of her revulsion. 'It wasn't anything dramatic and romantic. It was slow. We would talk after class about what we had been discussing in lessons. I loved school. Loved learning. I wanted all the knowledge. I was a proper nerd. But a reasonably good-looking one.' A slight blush crept up his face as he accepted his gene pool had bestowed on him clear skin, bright inquisitive eyes and a great head of hair.

Harlow imagined he was a bit of a looker in his youth. But still . . .

'One day her hand brushed my arm. I didn't think too much of it at the time, but later I fantasised about it. That quick touch. I made more effort to speak to her after class. Was more talkative and quicker to smile.'

He was taking some of the blame for the relationship on himself. That was all levels of wrong. He should recognise that at his age. Yet he seemed determined not to put the whole responsibility on her mother.

'It progressed from there until one day, I walked her to her car after the last lesson of the day. She had a bunch of books to mark, so I offered to carry them. But once at the car I climbed into the passenger seat. She didn't object. She started the car and we drove somewhere quiet while we talked. That was our first time.'

Silence dropped over the large bright room like a dark winter night suddenly closing in. Harlow had no words. She felt sick. In her wildest dreams she had never imagined this would be her beginning. She'd thought her mother might be young, single, a girl who couldn't cope, maybe, but not this. Never this.

Nigel's eyes were kind. 'It only happened a couple of times and then she stopped it. But by then it was too late.'

Harlow's stomach twisted again. She clutched her arms around her waist, begging her body to hold it in.

Nigel leaned forward, concern etched on his face. 'Do you want me to continue?'

Did she? She'd come this far; she might as well hear the rest. She closed her eyes, the pressure accumulating in her head, then opened them again. Nodded. There was no going back.

Nigel appeared resigned. She was here. In his home. He'd been found and the secret he'd held onto for all these years was finally out. 'She planned to give the child — you — up for adoption, but the thought of the scandal coming out terrified me. My parents were out of their minds. I'd had to tell them as one of my friends had seen me with her in her car. I'd managed to talk it away, but if he'd found out about the pregnancy, he'd have jumped to a difficult conclusion.' He looked down at the floor. 'They threatened your mother from the very start. Told her if she went ahead with the birth or adoption they would report her to the school. Not only would she lose her job, but her entire career, she would never work again. The police would even be involved. My parents were desperate, as they saw it back then, to protect me, and having a baby would ruin my future. Your mother was left with little choice but to leave you at the hospital. So there was no official record of your birth. Nothing that could come back on me. My parents' desperation for my future was like a real living, breathing thing.'

Unlike me. Harlow's jaw tightened. These people were her grandparents. The very people who should have fought for her safety. And yet they were the ones who had instigated the whole scenario. To save the prospects of their precious son. But what about her? Had anyone checked up on her? Followed her life? Did they care at all? The sickness she felt hardened in the pit of her stomach. A stone that was being polished with every word that came from Nigel's mouth.

It was as though he could see the change in her. His shoulders drooped. 'It mortified me, Harlow, believe me.' His tone had changed, from the confident, in-charge MP, to that of a less bold man, one who was unsure of his situation and the way it was playing out.

Harlow had little sympathy.

Nigel continued. 'But it was all out of my hands. I was a child.'

Though her adult logic agreed with his point that he was a child at the time and the adults had all the power, Harlow's emotional response butted up hard against the comment. This man was involved in creating her and his family had caused her to spend her life not knowing who her parents were. Wondering what she'd done to be dumped the way she had been. Thinking it was all her fault. So many emotions were swirling through her, there was no way to bring it under control and make sense of it. Harlow blinked hard.

Nigel persisted. 'The adults had taken control. They spoke in hushed whispers when they thought I was out of earshot. But I wanted to know the truth and eavesdropped at every opportunity. You were my child, and it shocked me to my core when I figured out what had happened.'

Harlow was speechless.

'She left the school before the summer holidays, hiding her expanding waistband until then. But I could see it. I knew. She told me she'd start life again in another school, I didn't have to worry. My education and life could continue. Then that was it. I couldn't communicate with her. My parents had all the control. I had to carry on and pretend it had never happened. The shock of it all brought my grades down for a while. It was all such a bloody mess.'

Harlow gaped at him.

'I'm sorry.' He reached out to her. The realisation of what he'd said, the insensitivity of it, connecting with him. 'I didn't mean it like that. I just wanted you to know . . .'

Harlow drew back.

'What happened affected me. There was no way to express it, though. My parents had me locked down hard. I was either at school or at home under curfew.'

'What about me?' she whispered.

'I was a child myself,' he said again. 'I couldn't do anything. I didn't know how to keep track of you. Though when I was older, an adult, and I had connections, I tracked you down. Found out a wonderful couple had adopted you and moved to Devon. You were by the sea. You had a good life. I checked in every so often. I am so proud of you, Harlow.' Tears pricked his eyes.

196

Confusion shook Harlow to her core. Unable to make sense of what she'd been told. He'd found her? How many laws had he broken to do that? And how long ago? He'd found her and yet he hadn't made contact with her. She'd been abandoned yet again. The hurt sliced through her chest like a razor and she inhaled rapidly. She pushed a hand onto her breastbone in an attempt to release the pain. 'And now?'

Nigel dropped his head into his hands. 'I can't give you what you want. Look at who I am. If this comes out, the scandal will destroy any chance I have of becoming prime minister. It's my dream, Harlow. You have to understand that. There is no higher office in the land. It would be a privilege and an honour to win the next election. Can you even imagine it?' His eyes were wide now at the thought of his bright future, and when they alighted on her she saw the shadow she had cast upon it.

'I don't want to take anything away from you,' she said.

'You don't understand,' he was pleading now. 'Your mere existence puts it all in jeopardy. All it needs is for one person to find out. My family are in the dark, Harlow.'

She squirmed in her seat. 'Justin knows.'

Nigel paled. 'What do you mean? He hasn't said anything. I saw him this morning.'

'I spoke to him yesterday. He was already aware. Maybe your parents said something.' She really didn't care.

Concern washed over Nigel's face. Perhaps he was wondering if he could still keep her a secret from his wife, or if she already knew about his past. That was his problem. It was clear he wanted nothing to do with her.

She rose from her chair.

Nigel followed suit. 'I'm so sorry. I hope that knowing the truth about your origins helps slightly.'

Did it? Probably. She was even more grateful for her mum and dad, that was for sure. They had given her everything. They'd made her the person she was today, not this man in front of her, who was more concerned about his career than his blood. And she was a pretty decent person, if she said so herself. She'd call her dad and tell him how great he was. But this man here . . . she would walk away and never look back.

CHAPTER 37

Claudia

'Do you want a brew?' Dom rubbed his face. 'I could do with getting out of here. It's suffocating.'

Claudia took in a deep breath. The phone call with Paul Cunningham had been emotional. 'I think a cuppa is a great idea and we can debrief while we're at it.'

They rose from their chairs and manoeuvred themselves out of the space that was pretending to be an office and walked together to the kitchen.

'I'm calling the hospital. I want an update on Russ.'

Dominic switched on the kettle. 'Didn't Sharpe say she would fill you in on how he was doing?'

'She said not to bother Maura. I'm not doing that.' Claudia snapped back at him. The fatigue and the unknown danger of the investigation gnawing away at her nerves. 'I'm sorry,' she said, sitting on a chair at the table in the corner. Phone already at her ear.

Krish walked in, a tray in his hands, complete with empty mugs ready to be filled again. He was on the tea run. His face lit up when he spotted Dominic and Claudia. Claudia pointed to the phone she was holding, but smiled up at him. He grinned at her and placed the tray at the side of the sink, setting the tap running to wash up the dirty dishes.

With the sound of the kettle coming to boil, Krish washing his pots and Dominic and Krish holding a hushed conversation, Claudia struggled to hear the nurse at the other end of the line. She asked after Russ, telling the nurse she was his manager and not a relative, even though this would reduce the amount of information coming her way.

'There's no change,' the nurse said. 'It would be helpful if you allocated one person to phone for updates. We really are rather busy here.'

Sharpe must have called.

Claudia apologised, explained how anxious she was and thanked the nurse for his time.

He mellowed a little. 'I understand Mr Kane's injuries might be connected to his role in the police and that you're all concerned—'

'It's DS Kane,' Claudia interrupted.

The nurse was silent. Russ was just another patient to him. Someone to care for. His rank, his job, had no bearing. Claudia had to calm down. But the stress was building up.

'I apologise,' she said.

Krish and Dominic stopped talking. She shook her head.

'As I was saying, he's getting the best care we can give him, but we need to use our time to focus on him and not answer calls all day.'

Claudia thanked him and said she would liaise with her supervisor about checking on Russ and ended the call.

'What was that about?' asked Dominic.

'Was that about Russ?' asked Krish. 'How's he doing? We've been told very little this morning. We're all in shock. It's all going to shit.' He rubbed at the mug in his hand with the tea towel distractedly.

He looked drained. Was that the same jumper he'd had on yesterday? He was probably feeling pretty rough and jumbled up. They all must. Claudia really should stick her head in their current incident room and speak to them. After all, she was still their DI, and responsible for them. This was only a temporary secondment. It should have been the first thing she did when she returned to the station, but she'd been so amped up after the night at the hospital and after the meeting with Sharpe and Dominic at Albie's that she'd wanted to get straight into the job. She'd let them down. It was the last thing she wanted to do. Especially after Russ. Guilt flooded her system.

She pushed her phone back into a pocket. 'I'll come into the office and, if it's okay with DI Carlyle, I'll update you all when I've got a brew in my hand, but yes, that was the hospital. Russ is in critical condition. They operated on him last night and he's currently in ICU being cared for. Please don't call. They've strongly suggested only one person check up on him.' She sighed as she remembered the nurse's rebuke.

'He's going to pull through, though?'

Claudia had no idea. 'He's receiving excellent care. Let's hope for the best.'

'What the hell happened last night? Sharpe wasn't particularly forthcoming in her email this morning.'

'Let me come through and I'll give you a briefing. But be warned, I don't have a lot of information.' She had to be careful she didn't bring them in on anything relating to the case. No one else should be placed in danger. Not because of her, anyway.

* * *

In the incident room, Claudia found DI Carlyle stooped over a desk, deep in conversation with another officer. She waited until he was finished. Carlyle, a short stocky guy with a smattering of freckles across his face looked up at her, then straightened himself. 'Claudia. I'm so sorry to hear about Russ.' He reached out and touched her arm. 'How is he? Any further news?'

'Actually Phil, that's why I'm here. I wonder if you wouldn't mind me taking a minute to update my team?'

'Oh, not at all. Have at it.' Carlyle waved a hand over the room.

Expectant faces peered up at her. They were strained, pale, visibly tired and drawn. The hit-and-run on a colleague had knocked them for six, and they didn't even know the half of it.

To them, it was a case of bad driving, where the motorist had driven off for fear of facing the consequences of their mistake. But Claudia and Dominic knew better — that the driver had been lying in wait for Russ, wanting to hurt him, to send a message to back off from Sophie Sinclair. How long had they been staking out his house? Hours? It had been a late shift for Russ last night. No one would have known at what time he'd arrive home. And if he'd not gone for a walk — if he'd gone straight inside from his car — what would they have done then? How would they have made the attempt on his life? The thought made her shudder.

So many questions and yet they had no answers.

And here she stood, in front of her team, who were expecting her to tell them everything. They wanted the truth, and she wasn't in a position to give it to them. Claudia shivered — someone had walked over her grave.

This was spiralling, and being out of control was not where she wanted to be.

'You want answers,' she said.

The wall of silence very much said yes.

'Information is thin on the ground at the moment. As you know, Russ was the victim of a hit-and-run last night. He's currently in ICU in a critical condition.'

Voices rose. Claudia held up a hand. 'I have no prognosis. At this stage, I'm told, it's a matter of waiting to see. I can't tell you if he's going to be okay. If any of you pray, I'd suggest now would be a good time to say your prayers. Otherwise, send all the positive thoughts you can. He's not in a great position from what I can gather, but Russ is a fighter. A strong, healthy man. And if anyone can pull through this, it's him.'

'What about the investigation into the driver?' Lisa asked.

'Being led by another team.'

'Why not us?' Rhys wasn't happy.

'You know we can't — it's a conflict of interest and we're already stretched across two investigations as it is. But we'll give the investigating team any help they require.'

'That goes without saying, boss.' She'd never seen Graham so tired. As an ex-soldier, he was usually the healthiest and fittest of the lot of them. But he was physically depleted today.

'DCI Sharpe has started a whip-round for Maura and Maisy, so please give generously to that. It'll help with any immediate concerns Maura has. Though of course Russ will stay on full pay.'

'What do we do now?' It was Rhys again. Never one to shy away from the difficult questions.

'We continue working our cases. And I'll keep updated with the team investigating the hit-and-run and inform you as and when I know anything of substance.'

She got nothing back from them. This told her they weren't happy. Better unhappy and safe than in the same position as Russ. She couldn't bear that.

Claudia thanked Carlyle with a nod of her head and walked out of the incident room, deflated. Her team silent behind her. Did they blame her in some way? Feel she was abandoning ship when they needed her most? If only she could explain her concerns to them. But it was out of her hands. Someone else was in control of the game now and she had to play carefully.

CHAPTER 38

Back in their broom cupboard Claudia turned to Dominic, getting straight back to business. 'What did you turn up while I spoke to Paul?'

Dominic took the pen from his desk and scratched the top of his head with it. 'I did some more research on Sophie Sinclair.'

'And?'

'To be honest, I didn't find much. She's not on social media. Or if she is, it's all very private. There was no link between Sophie and Harlow that I could find, either.'

'What does she do for a living?'

'She's a university lecturer, in Psychology.'

'Interesting subject.' Claudia pursed her lips. Sophie Sinclair might know about the human psyche, but it didn't mean she was a killer. But as Claudia's job had taught her, you very often couldn't spot a murderer — short of a confession, you had to rely on the evidence rather than gut instinct to tell you who was guilty. Murder itself could be dispassionate, but most of the killings she had worked on could be classed as emotional reactions to stressors. The Artist — she shuddered as she remembered him — had the outward appearance of being a cold-blooded killer, but even he, when they'd dug deeper, had stressors in his life — the loss of a relationship and a career that didn't work out the way he wanted it to. Admittedly, when people were stretched to breaking point, most didn't turn into killers.

She thought back to the interview with Sophie Sinclair. There wasn't much to consider. The blank face and the no comment responses on the recommendation of her solicitor. It was the best legal advice she could have had. Any lawyer in their right mind would have advised her the same way. Let the police prove their case.

But they couldn't.

Claudia tapped her fingers on the desk. 'Sharpe emailed me the name of the DI leading the investigation into Russ's attack. I'll look it up and call them.'

She was restless. They didn't seem to be making any headway, and she was running out of ideas.

When she logged onto the computer, the front page of the Intranet had changed. It now informed the force of the serious incident involving DS Russell Kane late yesterday evening, outside his home address. That the service was looking at the matter as suspicious and were investigating.

Claudia's throat tightened, and she tried to swallow the lump that had lodged there, but it was fixed in place. Emotion swelling to the surface, she continued reading. There was an official force-wide collection for Maura and Maisy and any amount, however small, would be warmly welcomed. The article ended with a link to an online book of well wishes. Once everyone had the chance to write in the book, it would be sent to Maura so she could read through it and hopefully gather some strength from all the positive thoughts coming from Russ's colleagues.

Claudia clicked through to her emails. There was a preliminary report from Nadira on the PM with several results attached. The rape kit had been completed. 'PM confirms that Harlow wasn't raped.'

'At least she didn't have to endure that.'

'Now we just need a motive.'

* * *

Tara Price, the investigating officer on the hit-and-run, was sympathetic but business-like when Claudia called.

'I know Russ is one of yours, and you're impatient for results, but without him being conscious to help us it's slow going. The witness has been reasonably helpful, but it was dark and she can't give us the make of vehicle or provide any description of the driver. She was too high up to see inside the car. There are no tyre tracks as the driver didn't even attempt to brake, which tells us one thing . . .'

'What's that?' Claudia already knew the answer.

'Whoever was driving definitely meant to hit Russ Kane. It wasn't an accident. So when we get our hands on them, we're throwing the book at them. It's attempted murder.'

Claudia let out a breath. So long as Russ hung on it was an attempt. Fear plagued her, but she wouldn't give it a voice. Russ was a strong man. He would fight to be well again. He had a family to get back to. The other possibility was not an option. It would have no room in her mind. Russ was her right hand. No matter that she had two detective sergeants, and that Dominic was her other. The truth was, she favoured Russ. She'd worked with him longer. Of course, she had a different relationship with Dominic. He was her father. But Russ and she had a working rapport that allowed Claudia to relax because Russ could pick up some of the strain.

Now it was her turn to carry his strain. All he had to do was recover. All. Like it was as simple as that. She didn't know just how serious his injuries were, but hospitals didn't throw words like critical around lightly. 'The accident investigators, did they find anything that could help?' she asked.

'We recovered Russ's clothing and we've submitted it to forensics for priority testing, so we're hoping for results pretty quickly. It may be some particles from the car can be found on him. The hospital allowed us to swab Russ himself once he'd been operated on. We've also submitted those samples. We are doing everything we can, Claudia. Please don't think otherwise.'

Guilt niggled at her. 'I'm sorry. I'm not trying to tell you how to do your job. It's just—'

'You're worried about your detective and you want whoever did this to be brought to book.' Matter of fact.

'Yes.'

'Trust me. We might not have worked with Russ, but he was one of us. We're all feeling it, Claudia.'

This was true. Whenever a colleague fell in the line of duty or otherwise, the whole force mourned. She thanked Price, who promised to update her the minute she had any results or positive information to impart.

The question was on Dominic's face. Claudia gave him the little she had.

Dominic tipped his head back and stared at the ceiling before speaking, gathering his thoughts. 'Whoever is behind this thought it through and knew what they were doing, waiting for him in the night when no one would be about.'

'We might strike lucky with trace evidence.' Claudia was hopeful. 'He was hit at force. There had to be an exchange of particles between Russ and the vehicle. We might even be able to identify the car or locate where it's been.'

'We might.' Did he believe what she'd said or was he simply agreeing with her to prevent any kind of argument? It wasn't like him to be so accommodating. He was usually one to be up for a fight. But he seemed to want to keep the temperature of their relationship down for the moment. And who could blame him? Everyone was hurting. It didn't help anyone if they were at loggerheads with each other.

They worked in silence for a few minutes. The tension of the case simmering in the room quietly but taut like a string on a violin. Then Dominic jerked his head up. 'I have something.'

'What is it?' Claudia's heart thundered in her chest.

'The phone records I sent off earlier, they've come back. We know who Harlow called on Saturday morning. Before she went out alone.'

He really did have something. 'What . . . who is it?'

'Dawn Sinclair.'

Claudia frowned. 'Any relation to Sophie?'

Dominic shuffled through some papers on his desk and waved the one he wanted in the air. 'The voters' register for Sophie's address. Three voters, all with the same surname. I'd guess she still lives at home with Mummy and Daddy because she's certainly not old enough to have a child on the register.'

Claudia jumped out of her chair and grabbed her coat from the back of it. 'Let's go, then. Dawn Sinclair has some questions to answer.'

CHAPTER 39

'How safe do you think this is?' asked Dominic as they waited for the door to open.

'What, attending the house of a person of interest in the murder of Harlow Cunningham, after we've been warned off?' Claudia shrugged, though she didn't feel as nonchalant as she appeared.

'That's exactly what I mean. Look what happened after you brought Sophie in.'

She didn't need reminding. But it was because of Russ that she'd follow this investigation to the ends of the earth now. No one would dictate what the police could and couldn't investigate. It wasn't how these things worked.

'Well, I imagine she'll know some details if Sophie has told her about her visit to the police station. We need to find out how much she knows and anything further.'

The door opened and a woman with greying hair and red-rimmed eyes stood in front of them. This was the mother. An idea prickled at the back of Claudia's mind.

'Dawn Sinclair?'

The woman nodded. As Claudia introduced herself and Dominic, a wave of anxiety washed over the woman's features. She'd seen it before in witnesses faced with the police, but Claudia wondered if there was more to her nervousness.

'Can we come in?' Claudia asked. 'We'd rather not have this discussion on the street.'

Dawn appeared startled, but allowed them in. 'What's this about?'

A dog approached, a golden Labrador, his nose pushing up to Claudia's leg. She leaned down and rubbed his head.

'I hope you don't mind dogs?'

'It's fine.' Claudia looked back up. 'Can we sit and talk somewhere?'

Dawn led them into a living room and the dog curled up next to her on the sofa.

'Do you know someone by the name of Harlow Cunningham?' asked Claudia when they were all seated.

Dawn flinched. Claudia had hit a nerve. The idea starting to take form.

'Mrs Sinclair?'

'Please call me Dawn.'

She was playing for time. 'Dawn?' Claudia pushed.

'It's delicate.' Dawn played with her hands in her lap. Fidgeting until she stopped and hugged the dog, stroking his head.

'Do you know Harlow Cunningham is dead?' Dominic's voice was hard and brutal.

Claudia stared at him, but she understood why he'd done this. Their position in this case was so precarious he believed they needed to push on and get to the bottom of it as quickly as possible. His compassion and sensitivity were long gone.

Dawn stopped moving. Then her eyes welled, before an avalanche of tears cascaded down her cheeks. Well, that answered that question. But in what capacity did Dawn know Harlow? The idea in Claudia's mind was now a question.

Claudia checked for tissues. Dawn was sobbing uncontrollably. The dog was whining. Rubbing his nose into his owner's leg. But Dawn was oblivious. Her hands pushed into her face.

There were no tissues in sight, so Claudia ran out of the room and found the kitchen. She returned to the living room with a couple of sheets of kitchen roll. Dawn took them gratefully, dabbing at her face with the scrunched-up paper.

Claudia gave Dawn some time to gather herself, mouthing the word *tea* at Dominic. He huffed but made his own way into the kitchen where he clattered about as he searched for the items he needed.

'Do you want to tell me about it?' asked Claudia as Dawn's sobbing subsided a little.

The woman swiped at her eyes and dried away the tears as Dominic walked in with a mug of something steaming hot. He handed the drink to Dawn, who took it from him, surprised.

'I've sugared it,' he said. 'It'll help.'

She thanked him.

'Harlow?' Claudia prompted as Dawn cradled the steaming mug.

Dawn shook her head. 'I can't. I'm sorry.'

'Why not?' Dominic stared at the woman, disbelief clear to see on his face. 'We know she called you on Saturday.'

Why couldn't she speak to them? What was stopping her? Was she under pressure as they were? Under threat of violence? Had she been told of Russ's circumstances?

'All I can tell you is her calling me had nothing to do with her death.'

'You need to let us be the judge of that,' said Claudia.

'I spoke to my daughter . . .'

Ah, Sophie.

'And like her, I won't be disclosing anything about our family. This is a personal matter, and I'd appreciate it if you could leave me to grieve alone, please?'

Dawn was trying her best to be hard and competent, but the sadness oozed from her. There was a personal link between Harlow and Dawn, and Claudia wanted to know what that was. And why was Dawn grieving, when Sophie had appeared fine? And didn't you only grieve for people you knew?

'Did you speak to Harlow in person the week she died?' she asked.

Dawn bowed her head. The move hid her expression but spoke volumes. She had seen Harlow. Dawn may have even been the person Harlow visited on Saturday after she made the call. But what was it about? Harlow's death had clearly upset Dawn. This was a reaction to the murder of someone you cared for.

Dawn placed the mug on a coaster on the small table and rose from her sitting position. 'I'd like to be alone, please.'

They were being kicked out. The most polite kicking-out they'd ever been on the end of. But being kicked out was certainly what was happening.

Claudia stood and Dominic followed suit. They had no choice but to leave. There were no grounds to force their presence on this woman, even in the middle of a murder inquiry. Police didn't have the power to demand entry to a citizen's home. There had to be specific circumstances and none of these applied here and now. They had to withdraw and do it with grace.

'Thank you for your time.'

Dawn showed them to the door. 'I'm sorry I couldn't help.'

Claudia wasn't sure how sorry she was.

'You chose not to help,' said Dominic. His patience with this case long expired.

Dawn looked affronted, but didn't correct him. She kept her silence. The golden Labrador stood behind her like a sentry, guarding his owner.

Before she stepped over the threshold, Claudia turned to Dawn. 'Can I ask, do you work? What do you do for a living?'

Dawn Sinclair bristled. 'I don't see what that has to do with anything. I'm retired. I used to be a teacher.'

Ah, like mother, like daughter. Sophie was a university lecturer.

Once the door was closed behind them, Dominic rounded on Claudia. 'What the hell?'

She held up her hands. 'We can't make her talk to us.'

'That reaction,' said Dominic. 'To Harlow's murder. She was most definitely close to Harlow.'

Claudia considered Dawn's tears, her reaction, the thoughts that had run through her own head. 'Harlow was the one who chose Sheffield as a location for the reunion. Paul tells us she was originally abandoned here. Her friends told us she went out alone while she was here. Dawn's daughter, Sophie was angry with her. To me, it's all adding up to one conclusion . . .'

Dominic was also still thinking it through. 'Sophie was not just angry, she was furious with Harlow when she caught up with her in the West Park Grand Hotel. A completely different set of circumstances and reactions to what Dawn displayed today. It was strange.'

'Agreed. But family might not react the same way to new information they're not expecting . . .'

'You think Harlow found her birth mother? Dawn?' Dominic sucked on his cheek. 'She's old enough. She's upset enough at Harlow's murder. But if she was her mother, why wouldn't she tell us? And, how the hell did Harlow find her in the first place?'

'Mmmm, that's the difficult question. There's no paper trail with an abandoned baby. But before we jump to conclusions, let's canvass the neighbours.'

Dominic zipped his coat up. 'Here?'

'Yes. Let's find out if anyone saw Harlow here on Saturday, after she called Dawn. After all, Chloe said she went somewhere before they went out as a group. Some neighbours can be extremely helpful. Much to the annoyance of those who would rather have their privacy.'

Dominic grinned. 'I like your thinking.'

'Do you have a photo of Harlow on your phone?'

'No. You?'

Claudia pulled her mobile out of her pocket. 'Yes. I'll send it to you. We'll split up to do this. That way we'll get it done faster.' She tapped at the screen and Dominic's phone pinged as the image arrived.

'Got it.'

'Okay, I'll do this side of the street, you do the other and we'll meet up when we're finished. I don't expect the homes further out to have seen anything, but let's be thorough.'

They parted ways and Claudia knocked at the house next door to the Sinclair's. As she waited for it to be answered, Dawn Sinclair appeared again from her own door.

'What the hell are you doing?' she hissed.

'Please go inside,' said Claudia coolly. 'This is a police investigation.'

A woman was dead and a detective was fighting for his life, but Dawn had stalled their investigation and refused to cooperate. She had expected them to slink off with their tails between their legs. Now she was spitting feathers. Inside, Claudia was grinning from ear to ear. She couldn't care less about this woman's frustration.

'You can't bother my neighbours. This is police harassment.' Dawn huffed out her chest and crossed her arms. The pure level of entitlement just oozed from her. It pleased Claudia when she could work around people like this.

'It's a murder inquiry, Mrs Sinclair,' Claudia replied. 'And asking questions isn't harassment.'

At that moment, the door opened, and an elderly gentleman leaning heavily on a walking stick greeted her, his white hair sticking up at all angles. Dawn vanished back into her own home as he appeared.

'I'm sorry to disturb you.' Claudia hoped he hadn't struggled to get to her.

He smiled. 'Not at all, dear. I don't receive many visitors. It's lovely to have someone to talk to. What can I do for you?' His stick wobbled and he shifted position, steadying himself. Claudia fought the urge to reach out to support him.

He hadn't asked for her help so it would be rude to lean into his home and touch him that way. He'd say if he was struggling. At least she hoped he would, anyway.

Claudia showed the man her identification and introduced herself.

'Oh, police.' He looked up and down the street. His grey eyes crinkling at the corners as he focused. 'What on earth has brought you to my door?'

Claudia pulled her phone out of her pocket again and angled the screen towards the man. 'Can I ask if you've seen this woman in the last week?' It was wrong to lead witnesses, so she couldn't provide him with the day or date. Not that she had one, she would only be guessing. So by broadening the timeframe for him he could give her his truth. Because witnesses all had a different version of the truth.

He leaned forward a little more, stick wobbling again. His eyes narrowed as he took in Harlow's features. 'She seems familiar. Like I said, I don't get a lot of visitors so, when there's any activity outside, I tend to people-watch. My living room is at the front of the house, you see.' He pointed to the side. Claudia saw the large window and hoped he would say he remembered Harlow.

The man shook his head. 'I'm sorry. My memory isn't what it once was. I'm getting on.'

Claudia smiled as though she hadn't noticed. 'You live alone?' Maybe there was someone else in the house who had seen Harlow.

'Oh yes. I lost my wife six years ago now.' His eyes crinkled again as he peered at Claudia. 'If you have someone special in your life, can I suggest you hold them close, make the most of them. Because one day, it'll all be over and you'll find yourself sitting alone, staring out the window, people-watching. It's no life. And not the life you once had.'

Suddenly Claudia felt so very sad for this man in front of her. So much so that she did what she'd held back from doing a minute earlier and reached out to him, placing her hand over his, the one clinging to the walking stick. It wobbled beneath her touch. His skin papery soft. It felt as though she could tear it if she wasn't gentle enough. She rested her hand lightly. His face softened even more. Claudia doubted he had been touched in such a gentle way in some time, and she wished she had a moment to go in, to sit and talk to him about his life. Spend some quality time with the man who took his comfort in the lives of others through his window. Better inside than out here on his doorstep where it was cold. He was thin, with little to protect him from the outside temperature, though an oversized knitted cardigan hung off his frail frame. It wouldn't do him any good to be out here for long.

The man sniffed.

But she had her job to do.

Claudia removed her hand and took her pocket notebook out, asked for his details for her records, and then gave him her contact card. 'If you think of anything . . . after I've gone,' she said. She grabbed his hand one last time. 'Or for anything at all.'

He was silent, but his face told her everything. Claudia's heart broke a little as she walked away.

CHAPTER 40

Claudia watched as Dominic moved along the houses on the opposite side of the road. There were several where residents weren't home. After all, this was a weekday, people worked. They might have to come back later if nothing came of this.

She knocked on another door. Dawn was still hiding inside. Better she was out of the way.

It was freezing and Claudia stamped her feet in an attempt to warm herself, pushing her hands into her pockets. There was barking coming from inside the house and then shouting as the owner tried to control the dog before responding to Claudia. Eventually, a young woman opened the door.

'Hello?'

'Sorry. DI Claudia Nunn.' She produced her identification. The woman checked it.

'Can I ask if you've seen this person around over the past week?' Claudia angled her phone so the woman could examine it.

There was a frown of concentration. More barking coming from inside the house. 'What's this to do with?'

'She was recently murdered and we're trying to trace her footsteps prior to her death.'

'The woman in the news?' Her eyebrows lifted in surprise.

'Can you help?' asked Claudia, not wanting to go into the specifics of the case.

'Yes. Yes, I've seen her.' She shivered. 'Won't you come in? It's freezing out here.'

'Thank you.' Claudia welcomed the invite into the warmth. It was a truly bitter day.

The home was warm and welcoming. The woman shut the dog in what Claudia presumed was the living room, and ushered her into the kitchen where tall stools surrounded an island.

'Can I take your details for our records?' asked Claudia, notebook and pen out again.

'Yes. I'm Fara Gambo.'

Claudia scribbled the woman's name down in her book. 'Can you tell me about it?' A frisson of excitement swept up her spine. The Sinclair women might not have been helpful, but their neighbour was about to reveal more than they wanted the police to know.

Fara pursed her lips. 'It was last Saturday. Early, I'd been walking Looby and was on the way home when I saw her knocking on Dawn's door. I had a bit of a nosy at her as I'd never seen her before. Because of her age, I presumed she was there to see one of the girls, but I noticed only Dawn's car was in the drive, and it was Dawn who answered and let her in. I can't tell you anything further.'

'What time was this?'

'I'm not sure. Nine-ish.'

Claudia made another note. 'Was there anyone else with her?'

'No, she was alone.'

'And you're certain it was her?' Claudia pulled her phone out again and scrolled to the image of Harlow, handing the handset to Fara, who stared down at the smiling face of the now deceased woman.

'Yes, it's her. I can't believe she's been murdered,' Fara whispered, with that faraway stare people got when thinking of something even remotely painful or socially difficult. 'You never expect anything like this to happen on your doorstep.'

It hadn't happened on her doorstep, but Claudia understood what she meant. 'Did you overhear what was said between Harlow and Dawn?'

Fara shook her head. 'It was all very quick. Was that her name — Harlow?'

Claudia confirmed the dead woman's name.

Fara continued. 'Harlow knocked. As I said, I paid attention to her because I'd not seen her around before. We were nearly home—'

'We?'

'Me and Looby.'

'Ah.' The dog. 'Sorry, carry on.'

'We were nearly home, so I got a good look at her. She seemed nervous, like she didn't want to be there. Then Dawn appeared at the door and let her in. I never saw her again.'

Claudia thanked Fara for her time, then gave her a card with her contact information on. Though now she thought about it, she wasn't entirely sure if this was a good idea. It might have been better to scribble down her mobile number on a piece of paper. Her card had her office details and if anyone got wind that she and Dominic were still investigating Harlow's murder, then the cat would well and truly be set amongst the pigeons. The same went for Dawn's other neighbour. She'd have to mention this to Dominic. It was possible he'd have already considered this.

The door had just closed behind Claudia when her mobile phone rang. She pulled it from her pocket. Caller ID gave nothing away.

She answered.

'Claudia, what are you doing?' It was Sharpe. She didn't sound happy. But she had a lot on her plate.

'We've been to speak to Sophie Sinclair's mother. Harlow Cunningham called her on Saturday.'

'Yes, I know where you are. It was a rhetorical question.' Sharpe sighed down the phone.

Claudia could see Dominic leaving an address over the road and waved him over. He crossed towards her.

This could only be bad news. Claudia waited the DCI out. 'We've had a call.'

Shit. 'About?' Like she needed to ask. What was it with this job? Was everyone connected? And how the hell were Dawn and Sophie Sinclair connected to anyone?

'About you harassing the Sinclairs and then their neighbours.'

'Their neighbours?' Wow, they really were scraping the bottom of the barrel. But there was something these people didn't want Claudia and the police to find out, that was for sure.

'Are you harassing the neighbours, Claudia?'

'We're canvassing the neighbours. Does that count?'

Sharpe sighed again. 'I'm doing my best to provide cover for you, but you're not making this easy. Whoever is behind this has more power than we're used to being up against. Connelly phoned me with his knickers in a right twist. Even though he gave the go-ahead after they targeted Russ last night. Someone high up is behind this, Claudia. You have to stop what you're doing there, I'm afraid.'

'You're serious?'

Dominic had reached her and frowned at the frustration on Claudia's face. She shook her head: it wasn't good, and he frowned again. A dash of anger lighting up his eyes.

'I don't know how to help,' Sharpe said. 'I promised you we'd fight this. We'd get whoever was behind this and who-ever targeted Russ. But we're being blocked at every turn. It's being made to look like official and proper actions, second-ments and acting on complaints of harassment, but we can see the reality of an investigation being blocked. Do you have enough from what you've done so far?'

Claudia thought about Fara. She had placed Harlow at Dawn's address and in Dawn's company. But she wasn't sure what it gave them exactly. 'Harlow was here on Saturday, visiting Dawn. We have a witness who confirms that.'

'Okay then. Do as requested and leave the area. We can go back and get a statement from the witness at a later date should the need arise. For now we keep looking for all the strands that will link the investigation together.'

The cold was seeping into Claudia's bones. It added to the exhaustion she felt. 'You really want us to leave?'

Dominic scowled. 'What the hell?'

Claudia waved him away, but he didn't move.

'You're kidding, right?' he said.

She waved him away again, but his scowl only deepened.

'I am serious, Claudia,' Sharpe went on. 'Yes, Connelly and I agreed you should continue with this. But we have to work within the parameters we've been given. Please don't make this more difficult for us. Connelly isn't happy and the shit rolls down the hill to me and you know what happens then . . .'

Claudia ran her free hand through her hair. The shit would continue to roll downhill towards her. There was no choice but to follow orders. 'We're being stopped at every turn,' she complained.

'I know. I'm sorry. Connelly was furious. Apparently, he'd had a real dressing-down because of this complaint. He was informed that if he couldn't get you under control, then you would be controlled by other means.'

'What the fucking hell does that mean!' Claudia roared.

Dominic stepped back, eyes wide.

'I mean it, Maddison, what the fucking hell?' She was still shouting. Heat flushed through her body and her muscles tensed, knuckles whitening as she gripped the phone. She'd never been so angry in her entire life. How fucking dare they threaten her? And through her superintendent? What the hell?

The other end of the line was quiet as Sharpe listened to her explosion. When Claudia had finished, Sharpe spoke. She was subdued. 'That was why Connelly was furious, Claudia. Not because of the dressing-down he'd received, but because of the threat they made to you. He wanted me to pass on his concerns and to say that you should show caution in your daily activity. When he challenged the intimidation, the person doing the talking denied it was a physical threat against you but was a threat against your career, but after Russ, we have to be cautious.'

'And did Connelly tell you who was behind this warning against my . . . career?'

A beat of silence. 'No. He was discreet. What he said is that this is top level, Claudia. There was no room for him to manoeuvre.'

Claudia looked around her at the quiet residential street in the middle of the week. There was no sign of any potential threat near her, but there hadn't been anything obviously threatening to Russ last night, or he wouldn't have stepped out on that road. 'Okay, we'll move on. But I'm not happy about any of this.'

'Me neither, but we have to proceed carefully.'

'Okay.'

'Claudia?'

'Yeah?'

'Watch your back.'

CHAPTER 41

Harlow

Thursday 2 p.m. — 69 hours earlier

The hotel lobby was quiet. It was that unusual time when people had already checked out if they were leaving that day and only just arriving if they were checking in.

Harlow had been here since yesterday and was glad she'd chosen this hotel. It was clean and comfortable, and she could easily relax in it. She glanced at her watch for what felt like the hundredth time but in reality was probably only the tenth. She was waiting for her friends to arrive. They could check in at two p.m. and they'd all promised to be here as soon as they could, to make the most of their long weekend. After all, they hadn't seen each other in over a decade. Would she even recognise them all?

Harlow smoothed down an invisible crease in her jeans. It had taken several outfit changes for her to decide on what she was wearing. Jeans ripped at the knee, tan boots and an oversized white shirt, tucked in at one side. It might be freezing outside, but here, in the hotel, it was cosy and snug.

Harlow was rigid in her chair. Her insides were vibrating. Her excitement and nerves were at top level.

She sipped at the glass of wine in front of her. Yes, it was early, but the drink was necessary to steady herself. What if they didn't recognise her? Had she changed? What if she'd changed so much they no longer liked her? Harlow wasn't sure she could bear that.

The entrance door opened and a guy, tall and confident, with a weekend bag in one hand, strode into the lobby. Harlow watched as he walked over to the reception desk to book himself in. She strained to hear as he gave his name, but she was too far away. It didn't matter, though. She'd recognise that face anywhere. This was Brodie Keep. The skinny kid out of the group. You couldn't call him that now. He'd filled out nicely. He'd grown into a man. No longer a spindly boy. Of course, it was bound to happen. She shouldn't be surprised. But the spindly kid walk was gone and in its place was the confident stride of an assured adult male. Harlow couldn't wait to meet him, to say hello to him, and to catch up with him.

She sipped her wine again and waited while he checked in and then, when he was done and walking towards the lifts, she rose from her chair and tentatively approached, her ankle still tender from this morning. But it was the fear of how he'd see her that was still uppermost in her mind. Of course she'd love him, but what about his reaction to her?

'Brodie?'

He stopped and peered at her. Then his face lit up. 'Harlow!' He dropped his weekend bag, which gave a deep but cushioned thud as it hit the carpeted floor, and wrapped her in a bearhug.

He smelt of cinnamon and of being outside. Harlow wrinkled her nose. It was good to be here, in his embrace. The scent of him invading her. They'd never been an item, but the group as a whole had been incredibly close and it was within this hug that Harlow remembered that bond and relaxed into it. Not realising how much she had missed it and missed them all.

Eventually, he released her. 'Harlow. Wow. It's been so long.'

It had and she didn't want to be released. The warmth of his arms was a good place to be.

'I know those two people canoodling by the chairs,' someone laughed from behind them.

Standing behind Brodie, in a dark chocolate knitted wrap, was Chloe Martin.

When Harlow locked eyes with her, Chloe left her suitcase where it was and ran towards her, wrapping her in another hug. She could get used to these. It had been a long time since she had been in the embrace of another human, and it felt so good.

This time it was sweet. Gentler, more effervescent. Curls tickled her face and she brushed them away. 'Chloe, it's so good to see you.'

Chloe grinned and ran to Brodie, leaping up to wrap him in an equally jubilant hug, which he returned.

'Oh my,' she gushed. 'I've been waiting all day to do that. Are you the first ones here? What time are the others due? I can't wait to put my arms around them.' She was talking at a hundred miles an hour.

Harlow linked arms with Chloe in an attempt to calm her. Soothed herself by the physical contact. It felt natural to be close to her friends already. Chloe smiled across at her.

'We're the first ones here,' Harlow said. She pointed to the table behind them. 'I have a small glass of wine which I needed to settle my nerves.'

'Oh darling, you required your nerves settling?' Chloe grinned again. 'Nerves or not, wine sounds like a fabulous idea. Putting my clothes away can wait a little longer, at least until everyone gets here. I don't want to miss anyone's arrival. Let's go and grab a drink, Brodie.' And with that Chloe grabbed Brodie with her free arm and marched the three of them over to the bar, not letting go of Harlow and leaving her suitcase in the middle of the lobby. Harlow winced every couple of steps as her ankle twinged. She'd take a couple of painkillers through the weekend and it should stop bothering her. It wasn't that bad.

'Your . . .' Harlow pointed at Chole's abandoned suitcase.

'Don't worry about that. Who's going to run off with it?' The energy coming from Chloe was contagious and soon Harlow's nerves settled and she was just excited about the weekend ahead.

Harlow, Chloe and Brodie sat down in the lobby chairs, bags and suitcases on the surrounding floor, and drinks on the table, celebrating arriving safely, waiting for the rest of the gang to join them.

'I can't believe we're finally here,' gushed Chloe. 'It's so good to see you both.' She eyed Brodie. 'And you've changed.' She laughed and Brodie laughed with her.

'I bloody hope so. For the better?'

'Oh definitely. Don't you think so, Harlow?'

Harlow was too embarrassed to get into that conversation. She smiled at the pair and turned towards the entrance where, just at that moment, an elegant, slim, tall woman was gliding through the foyer. 'Ashanti.'

Chloe put a hand to her mouth. 'Oh my God. She's stunning. I follow her on Instagram, but she's so much more beautiful in real life.'

As one they rose and rushed over to Ashanti, who was now booking in at reception. They crowded around her amidst much squealing. The receptionist did her best to continue her task at hand although it was difficult while surrounded by such excitable guests.

Harlow couldn't believe she'd pulled this off. That, one by one, they were all coming back together. A warm glow surged through her, nerves long forgotten.

Ashanti collected her key card, then hugged Harlow hard. 'You did this, sweetie. Thank you.'

Tears pricked at her eyes. She wouldn't get emotional. This was about the joy of seeing each other again. Nothing more than that.

'What did she do now?'

Chloe squealed. There was a lot of squealing happening. The receptionist winced a little.

Harlow turned. Jay was standing behind her with his bag draped over his shoulder. He'd matured into a man as Brodie had, though he was slimmer than she'd expected. Drawn. She was so pleased to see him, she threw herself at him and wrapped him in a hug. He reciprocated. 'It's so good to see you,' she whispered to him. She had a strong urge to make sure he knew how important he was to her.

Jay nodded quietly without saying a word, then broke away and said his hellos to everyone else. There was something under the surface Harlow didn't recognise. Whatever it was, she hoped Jay would talk to her this weekend. She'd missed him over the years. He'd been the first of them to marry and had slipped away from them, into married life. But prior to that, she'd had a strong relationship with him. She'd find time to talk to him alone. Repair the bond. Return it to what it once was. And in doing so, be there for whatever was bothering him. Because Harlow was sure Jay was not bringing his A game to the party. Though she could talk.

She wasn't just here for her friends. She had an ulterior motive. And maybe if she talked to Jay, and they confided in each other, she might just tell him what that was. Though her revelation was pretty big. Harlow wasn't sure anyone would get their heads around the whole truth of it. Maybe some of it. She could tell them a partial truth. But all of it? She would see how the weekend went. Though after this morning Harlow wasn't sure she had the nerve to continue with her plans.

'Hey, earth to Harlow?' Jay laughed at her. 'You seemed a world away. You okay?' He leaned into her. So close she could smell the warm citrus of his aftershave.

She smiled. 'I'm good. Just thinking how great it is to have us all together,' she lied.

Brodie wrapped an arm around Jay's neck. 'It's all because of you, Harlow. None of us reprobates could have organised this.'

Jay stuck an elbow in Brodie's stomach. 'Speak for yourself.' He laughed. 'Though no, Brodie's right. We might have been able to do it, but it wouldn't have crossed our minds. Life just ticks on and we forget to do the important things like this, so thank you, Harlow.'

They all had drinks now, so they raised a glass in the air. 'To friendship,' they all shouted. And Harlow was at once both grateful to have organised the weekend with her friends and afraid for what lay ahead.

CHAPTER 42

Claudia

It was almost closing time at Albie's when Claudia and Dominic walked through the door, but Sharpe had grabbed a table and already had drinks waiting for them.

As Claudia sat down, her phone buzzed. A message from Matt, her ex. He'd heard that Russ had been hurt. Was she okay? She shoved her mobile away.

'Any news on Russ, ma'am?'

'He's still classed as critical and in ICU,' Sharpe told them. 'Maura hasn't moved from the ward all day and the grandparents are caring for Maisy.'

'What about the investigation into the hit-and-run?' Claudia asked. 'Have they updated you?'

'I contacted DI Price before I left the office. It's slow going. Nothing will happen at pace, Claudia. They're waiting for forensic results and as you know, it takes time. Though the samples have been classified as a priority due to it being an attack on an officer. It should speed things up a little.'

Claudia tucked a strand of hair behind her ear. 'I can't bear all this hanging around and not knowing anything. I want to kick in doors and pull in offenders. Interview them, charge them and put them before a court. Make them pay for what they've done to both Harlow and Russ.'

Sharpe didn't disagree.

'Harlow was into something significant for all this to rain down on us, for investigating her murder. We haven't yet ascertained what that is. Her friends didn't seem to know. As for what we've learned today: Dawn Sinclair is Sophie's mother. Harlow called Dawn on Saturday morning and, although Dawn herself refused to answer our questions, a neighbour places Harlow at Dawn's door and entering the property at Dawn's invitation the same morning as the call. That was as far as we'd got before you made contact to stop us interviewing further neighbours. We think Harlow may have found her birth mother but there's absolutely nothing and no way to corroborate that.'

'Give it a rest,' Dominic growled. 'We have to move forward, not keep griping about what we don't have.'

Anger flared like a beacon in her skull. 'What the hell?'

'Stop it,' Sharpe snapped before they could even get started.

Claudia glared daggers at her father. How could he do this to her? He was here to support her, not turn on her at the earliest opportunity.

'I won't have this,' Sharpe continued. 'This is the most demanding job we've ever come across. I won't have us bickering among ourselves about how we deal with it. It only serves to strengthen their, whoever they are, strengthen their position. We can't allow that.'

Claudia's boiling rage simmered down slightly. Sharpe was correct. They had to work together. Could Dominic do that?

'I'm tired. I'm sorry,' he said.

Claudia gave a curt nod.

Sharpe watched them. 'So we have linked two new people to Harlow. Sophie and Dawn Sinclair. Try to pin down their whereabouts on the morning of Harlow's murder. Check the hotel lobby CCTV again, see if either of them pop up on there. They have vehicles, check ANPR, parking tickets, speeding tickets, anything that has them out of the house that early on a Sunday morning.'

Claudia sighed. 'Of course. Though I think it'll be a rule-her-out-exercise as far as Dawn goes. She was pretty cut up as far as I could see.'

Sharpe gave a quick nod. 'Go home, get some rest and come back and review this with fresh eyes tomorrow.' She sipped at her coffee.

'How am I going to sleep? With Russ battling for his life, Maura in turmoil and Paul Cunningham oblivious to the fact someone somewhere is fighting to keep his daughter's killer free,' Claudia remonstrated.

'And he doesn't know what she's into that might have got her killed?' asked Sharpe.

'He hasn't got a clue. To him, she was the same girl she always was before she left home last week. Nothing had changed.'

'Something had definitely changed,' said Dominic, draining what was left in his mug. 'You don't get murdered and cause this much havoc if nothing has changed.'

'Indeed.' Sharpe steepled her fingers. 'There's nothing to be done this evening that can't be done tomorrow. Sleep on it and come back to it tomorrow. Murder inquiries can drag on at the best of times.'

Claudia rose. 'I need a shower. I need to wash the day off me.'

Dominic followed suit. 'Do you want me to stay over?'

'I'm not a child. No, I don't want you to stay over. I'll be careful, but I don't think they'll try anything again. I think attempting to kill one officer is enough of a warning shot, don't you?'

Dominic grunted.

'I certainly hope so.' Sharpe was the last to rise. 'Take care of yourselves and I'll see you tomorrow.'

* * *

She recognised the car parked in front of her house as soon as she was close enough to see it. Pressure tightened like a buzz saw in her brain. This was the last thing she needed.

'Matt, what the hell are you doing here?' Claudia climbed out of her car as Matt met her from his. 'This is the bloody second time this week.'

His face was pinched. His lips pale. 'I heard about Russ. It's all over the force. No specifics, but there are some weird rumours doing the rounds simply because there's no information. And you know cops, if they don't have the facts then they'll fill in the holes themselves.'

He stepped closer to her as she headed to her front door. She wasn't about to stand outside discussing this. Secret was secret and she wouldn't put Matt in danger just to curb his curiosity, if that was all he was here to do. Nosy fucking cops.

'I'm so sorry about Russ,' he said as she unlocked the door. 'How's he doing? There isn't much news on the intranet other than they'll update us as soon as they know anything more.'

She stepped into the house. There was a low hum as the heating had recently kicked in on the timer. January was a cold month so she liked to take the edge off the chill for when she arrived home from work.

Matt followed her, and she allowed him in. The door shut with a small click. 'He's critical, as the intranet says.' Claudia pulled her coat off and threw it at the back of a chair. Exhaustion suddenly sweeping over her. He acquiesced and took another chair, slumping down in it, his legs wide open, hands swinging loose between them. 'Claudia, tell me, what the hell happened?'

Claudia closed her eyes. 'Matt, why are you here? I don't see you for an age, then it's like you live here again.'

The heating ticked quietly around them.

'The rumours. Something doesn't feel right. No one can give a solid reason for what happened to Russ. He's a sensible guy, he's not just going to get hit like that. So I worried about you. I still . . .'

Matt chewed the inside of his cheek.

Claudia opened her eyes. 'It's being investigated. That's all I can say.' She wished he would leave, though, so she could run a bath, pull on her pyjamas and climb under her duvet. She had never wanted her duvet as much as she wanted it right now. She seriously hoped that Sharpe was right, that a good night's sleep would give this whole situation a different slant in the morning. It didn't seem feasible, but Claudia would try anything. It was as though her body were made out of solid concrete. Moving was just too much effort.

'There's also a rumour about your case, that someone is trying to shut it down. Add that rumour to Russ being put in the hospital and it stinks to high heaven. So I thought I'd better check and see how you were doing.' He leaned forward. 'So,' he said. 'How are you?'

Oh, they'd moved on from Russ and were talking about her now. Was he going to leave at some point? Maybe if she gave him what he wanted he would get up and go home to his wife. 'I'm tired, Matt. It's been an unbelievable couple of days. All I want is a hot bath and to crawl into bed.'

Matt nodded his understanding. 'I get that. I've got a bag in the car. I'm staying here tonight. You run a bath, I'll make you something to eat while you do that and then you can go to bed.'

Jesus. 'What? No.'

'I'm not taking no for an answer. No one believes a vehicle accidentally hit Russ on his own street. Your case is being messed with. It stinks to high heaven. I won't get a minute's rest if I think you're in danger. So I'm staying over.'

Claudia was wide awake now and sitting bolt upright. 'And your wife?'

Matt had the sense to look sheepish. 'She's not best pleased, but I explained it's for your safety and nothing else. That the other person who would do this for you is actually in the hospital. She couldn't argue with that.'

Dominic could do it. But she'd sent Dom away. She hadn't believed anyone would make any other attempts after

232

warning them off with Russ. Matt was going overboard and she wasn't about to explain her job to him.

'No.'

'No?'

'Get out, Matt.' She stood. 'This is ridiculous. If we were still together, you could protect me as much as you wanted, though to be fair it sounds a little old-fashioned. But you're married to someone else. So please go home to that someone else and tell her you love her and are there for her before she divorces you, because I really couldn't bear it if you were on my doorstep any more than you already are.'

Matt was surprised. Where he was concerned, Claudia had always been a bit of a pushover. Their relationship had never been acrimonious. But her tone now was clear. She wanted him out.

'You're sure?'

'I want to go to bed, Matt. Please go.'

'You want me to cook for you first?'

Claudia pointed to the door, exasperated. 'Out.'

He stood and walked over to her, wrapping his arms around her for a moment. 'Call me the minute you need me. I'll be here.' And with that, he let go and walked out.

Claudia locked the door behind him and leaned back against it, grateful for the peace she was finally left with. His offer had been kind and generous, but this was the toughest case of her career and she needed to keep her wits about her. Having her ex-husband around playing the returning hero wouldn't help her. Instead, it muddied waters that had long ago been cleared. Better to keep the clean lines in place. Besides, she would never do that to another woman. No matter how innocent the situation was. She would have to actually be on her death bed to accept help from Matt, and she was far from being in that position.

CHAPTER 43

The bath was deep and soothing. Gone was the hard-arsed cop she portrayed through the day. Here there was a beautifully fragranced candle burning on the windowsill and a glass of wine balanced on the edge of the bath. She really could do with one of those wooden bath trays. That way she could also bring her book in while she soaked, without fear of dropping it into the water and destroying it. The glass would be safe and the whole thing would look fabulous. When the investigation was over she would get one.

Once out the bath, Claudia dressed in her softest pyjamas, made a mug of tea and took it to bed, opening her novel to the place she'd last read to and settled down. Her mind gradually slowing with the evening routine.

Claudia was enthralled in the story but eventually her eyelids became heavy, her hands drooped, and she was unable to go any further.

She placed the book on her bedside table and turned off the light, leaving the room in darkness other than the soft glow coming through the curtains from the street lamp outside. The road was a quiet one, and relaxing was easy. Claudia curled up on her side and closed her eyes. Sleep came and took away the stress of the day.

A dull thudding broke through the blackness, then stopped. What was it? Claudia lay still, head deep in the pillow, face scrunched in the soft fabric, fogged by sleep. But aware of something, a sound, a feeling. She struggled to grasp hold of what she'd heard. What had woken her up? Sleep was pulling at her, dragging her back into its grip. The banging came hard again. Insistent.

Claudia strained to open her eyes, but her body fought against her. The need to stay in deep sleep was strong. But that banging . . . it was unrelenting. Like someone trying to rouse her.

Claudia shook her head a little, without actually lifting it from the pillow. It was too heavy for that. But she definitely needed to clear her brain.

Then there was a smashing sound. Sharp and clean. Glass splintering.

Claudia shot upright in the bed. What the hell?

She should have allowed Matt to stay over. Someone was attempting to get into the house.

It was in that briefest of moments as she listened to her window shattering on the floor and thought of her ex-husband that her nose twitched.

What was that?

It was like rough bark in deepest dankest winter being cut up by a chainsaw. A coarse scent from the mix of hacked-at wood and the hot fuel of the chainsaw. A raw smell that snagged on the hairs in her nose.

In fact, it wasn't just her nose.

The room had a weird haze to it. Like there was a film over her eyes. Claudia blinked, but it didn't clear. She blinked again. Still, the haze remained. The smell stronger. Her mind struggling to catch up to what her senses were screaming out at her.

Why was her mind so slow? What the hell was happening? Was she stuck in a dream? A nightmare? She didn't think so. Claudia was certain she was awake. But it was as if she was wading through mud.

Then it hit her. Slammed into her like a truck.

Shit.

She jumped out of bed. Her legs like jelly, she stumbled and was on her hands and knees. Claudia could feel the carpet burn as her knee skimmed the floor. Her head woozy. She had to get a grip and get it quickly.

The house was on fire and she was still inside it.

There was shouting from downstairs. Someone screaming her name, but no one was coming. No sound of feet on the stairs. Though her mind was foggy, it was more alert than when she'd first come round. Whoever was down there had managed to wake her. They'd given her a fighting chance of getting out of this alive. But the fire must have taken hold. They couldn't get to her.

Shit.

She had to get out of this herself.

There was a glow underneath the closed bedroom door that terrified her to the pit of her stomach. Fear clenched at the soft spot at the base of her skull. Icy and sharp, providing her with the level of alertness she needed to get out of this.

She crawled on hands and knees to the door and placed a palm against the wooden barrier. Raging heat emanated through to her skin. The fire was too close. The sound of the roaring flames perforated the fog in her head now. By keeping low to the carpet, she was aware she had a better chance of surviving this. The fire department would be en route.

But what to do? Cower in here or attempt to help herself?

She couldn't stay in here, curled up on the floor, waiting to die.

How the hell would she get out of here?

Plumes of smoke drifted in through the gap under the door and quickly, as Claudia crouched on the carpet it swirled upwards around the room, clogging up her eyes and making it difficult for her to breathe. It was thick and cloying, like she could reach out and grab it, not just breathe it in. She thought of the harm it was doing to her lungs.

Someone was still shouting below, a distant sound through the fug of the smoke and the roar of the fire. There was no going out the front of the house. She had to find another path. Claudia looked at the window.

It was the only way.

But she was on the first floor, one storey up. She'd be injured if she jumped.

She'd die if she stayed put.

Sirens blared in the distance.

Claudia dropped her head to the carpet. They were coming for her. She could wait here for them. They'd pull her out.

Her throat hurt, as if small claws were gripping her throat as she breathed. Grabbing and pinching and clinging to her while she did the simple act of breathing. She wiped her eyes with the back of her hand in an attempt to clear her vision. The bedroom was getting darker with the smoke. Her throat getting thicker, the claws digging in more painfully. She coughed again. This time the pain was in her chest as well.

She had to get out of here.

She had to get off the floor.

Claudia peered up at the window.

It seemed far away. So very, very far away from down here on the carpet. The soft, soft carpet. It would be easy to close her eyes, wait for the fire fighters to enter her home and pull her out. But she shook her head. The bottom of the door was glowing. She was hot. She had no idea how much time she had left in this room.

Of course she should have pulled her quilt from the bed and shoved it at the gap in the door, but she'd been leaden and foggy since she'd woken. She must have been inhaling smoke as she slept.

The sirens had stopped, she realised. Blue lights spiralled through the window. All she had to do was get up off the carpet and make it over there. It didn't matter if she broke her leg jumping. She'd be alive.

With all the effort she had inside her, Claudia pulled herself bodily, arm over arm, knees digging into the floor, pulling, pushing, getting herself over to the outside wall of the bedroom. Away from the incoming smoke and the burning heat that was building up. It would all breach the thin barrier that was her bedroom door any moment. She had little time, and she had to move.

Terror was a wild animal. But it was one tamed by a choke hold around its neck. She was trapped in the most frightening way possible, but she could see a way out. Scary as it was, it would save her life.

Claudia leaned her forehead to the carpet, grateful for the path ahead. Grateful she would soon be out of this house. She'd never wanted to leave her own home so badly. The place she'd shared with Matt. If only he'd stayed. If he'd been here this might have turned out differently. But no, she couldn't do that to his wife. She was at home waiting for him. Claudia relaxed. She'd done the right thing. Of course she had. Matt was a married man, and Claudia was not that woman. If only . . .

She was warm and cosy. Comfortable. She was losing her train of thought . . . something about Matt . . . Married . . . Never mind . . .

Smashing glass, a thud as something landed hard at her side, woke Claudia from her dreams. Her eyes widened. She was in her bedroom. Burning. She was so hot. Shit. It was boiling in here. She coughed. Her chest on fire.

What was that?

Her name.

The rough bark of her name in someone's mouth.

Her dad.

He was down there.

There was a brick at the side of her.

'Claudia! Get up! Come here!' His voice was hoarse.

She was underneath the window. The rush of cold air soothing her skin. She reached up and grabbed hold of the windowsill. Still coughing. Her chest and throat hurt with every breath.

Then she was standing. The air frigid on her skin.

Below was her father, another brick in his hand — where had he got them from? — his hair wild, his face red and furious.

'Claudia!'

The blue lights of a police vehicle. Not the fire service. Claudia's heart plummeted. She opened the broken window and climbed onto the windowsill so she was sitting on the edge, the heat of the burning house at her back. In the distance, more blue lights were coming her way. The fire service.

They were too late. She had to jump. The heat and the smoke were a wall of terror that she needed to escape.

'I'm coming, Dad.' Tears poured down her face.

'Wait a minute,' he shouted. 'They're here.' He pointed behind him as the fire truck pulled into the street. The blue lights split the night into fragments. Cracking it into pieces combining with the orange reflections of the flames.

'No. I can't wait.' The fire was at the door. The heat too much to manage. Fear bearing down on her.

'Claudia, no.'

Firefighters were climbing out of the truck in all their protective gear. They shouted to the driver, pointed up at Claudia. The truck moved slowly towards her.

Slowly. Slowly.

'No,' she shouted. 'It's too hot.'

Dominic ran closer to the house. Ran in the way of the truck — just as Claudia flew from the window.

CHAPTER 44

Claudia didn't think she had seen Dominic so furious before. He was close to wearing a hole in the linoleum of the hospital floor the way he was pacing in front of her bed. Some of his anger was aimed at her and she wasn't happy about that.

'It was a choice between being eaten alive by the fire—' She coughed to prove a point. The oxygen mask fitted on her face hissed consistently, regardless of whether she relaxed and breathed 'normally' — would she ever breath normally again? — or if she coughed her lungs up.

Dominic stopped pacing for a moment, horror contorting his features. He waved his hands in the air in a way that suggested he wanted to do something to help but didn't know what, and she shook her head, still coughing. She pressed her chest with both hands, hoping the gesture would ease the pain in her lungs a little, but it didn't. The smoke had well and truly entered her body and was clawing away at the soft tissue inside her.

'Or breaking some bones,' Claudia finished when the coughing had stopped. 'I preferred the option which meant I'd still be alive at the end of it.'

Dominic resumed his pacing, then paused again. A deep frown furrowed between his eyes. All the stopping and starting was driving her mad.

'You have no idea of the fear involved when fire is bearing down on you like that,' she said.

'But you could have hit your head on the concrete ground when you jumped and then you'd be dead anyway.'

'I took that risk.'

'I'm glad you did,' a voice from the door said.

Father and daughter turned. Sharpe was standing there, more relaxed than when she'd attended for Russ's emergency, in tracksuit bottoms, trainers and a jersey top. She still looked good.

'Do you think you lot can stop getting me out of bed in the middle of the night, please?' She wrinkled her nose as she came into the room. 'It's doing no good for my beauty sleep.'

She perched on the end of Claudia's bed. 'So, you didn't hit your head, but you did—' she waved a hand over the cast on Claudia's foot — 'this.'

Claudia took a deep breath, which only made her cough again. The pain deep in her lungs hurt like a blunted knife carving out her insides.

Distress creased the lines on Sharpe's face as she heard the acrid coughing. 'My God, what the hell have they done to you?'

Eventually Claudia recovered enough to speak. 'I broke a couple of small bones in my foot when I jumped. Apparently it could have been worse, but Dad was there to catch me and he took most of my weight.' They weren't in a work setting, even though this was Sharpe, so Claudia was happy enough to call him dad. 'I inhaled some smoke. They want to keep me in overnight. Possibly longer.' She pulled a face at that.

'Two of you? First Russ and now my detective inspector. This is outrageous.' Sharpe was incensed.

Dominic turned on her. 'What are we going to do about it, is what I want to know?' His cheeks blazed red where his anger flared. He'd already been building up before Sharpe had arrived and now she'd mentioned there'd been two of them intentionally hurt and one of them was his daughter, Claudia could nearly see the steam coming out of his ears like a comedy rabbit or some such cartoon imitation of life. She clenched her jaw. If he saw her smiling at his fury, he would explode. One thing Dominic did not do well was control his anger. Especially when it was righteous anger, and this was well and truly in that box.

Claudia leaned her head back against the mound of pillows that hospitals tended to provide you with and listened to Dominic huff and puff. Sharpe however was silent. She was thinking things through.

The oxygen mask continued to hiss up between the gap on Claudia's cheek. Fresh air whistled past her eyes. It was heavenly and she, for the first time in a long while, relaxed. She'd lost everything she owned and yet she was feeling surprisingly calm. Probably due to the fact that everything was totally out of her control now.

'Well?' Dominic was still pacing.

'Please stop,' said Sharpe, who had only witnessed it for a couple of minutes. Claudia had put up with it for so much longer.

'What?'

'That pacing. You're doing no good with it. Stand still and have a real conversation, will you?'

He stopped in his tracks. Again, Claudia wanted to smile, but kept it to herself.

'Where will you stay when they let you out?' Sharpe asked of Claudia, ignoring Dominic's question about the investigation.

'With me,' said Dominic.

Claudia couldn't help but roll her eyes. 'I have friends, Dad. You might think I'm just my job, but I do know people. I'm sure someone will put me up.'

'That's not the point.' It was practically a snarl. 'Are these friends capable of protecting you? Willing to have their own home burn down? Be put in harm's way for giving you shelter?' He glared at her. His intention was good but his delivery was harsh and Claudia had the urge to curl up under the covers and hide from him. Like a small child once again.

Though she'd never been afraid of him as a child. Her child-hood had been a good one. But the fury emanating from Dominic at the danger she'd been in was off the chart.

On this issue however, about putting her friends in the path of danger, he had a point.

Claudia shrugged.

'That's it, you're staying with me.'

'Well, for now, I'm staying here,' Claudia reminded him.

That glare again. 'Then I'm staying as well. I'll sleep on that chair.'

'There's no need for dramatics,' Sharpe told him. 'I'm not going to take risks with Claudia's life. There will be a uniformed presence outside your room, Claudia, just as there is outside Russ's room. When you're discharged we'll assess the situation again.'

Dominic was appeased by that.

'I don't think they'll come back to finish the job,' Claudia said. 'I think they attacked me because we spoke to Dawn. Like the warning shot with Russ.' She was tired and wanted nothing more than to close her eyes and sleep but this needed her attention.

'A warning shot doesn't kill the person it's warning off.' Dominic was pacing again. 'This was attempted murder.'

Sharpe looked him up and down and then turned her attention to Claudia. She gave her a smile and Claudia returned it. Grateful to her boss for her calm presence in this situation. 'I realise it's a little odd to call these warning shots, Dominic. But Russ has been safe since his arrival at the hospital. I don't think the intention is to finish off what they started. Killing a police officer is not the desired out-come. I think all they want is for the police to step away from the Harlow Cunningham investigation and because we're not, they're making an attempt to incapacitate the officers involved. Though they've been playing with fire . . .' Another look at Claudia. 'Quite literally, in Claudia's case. Both of these attacks have been life-threatening. For that reason I think we're dealing with someone who doesn't particularly think things through. They're rash. Action before thought. Childish, almost.'

The room fell silent as the three of them considered what Sharpe had said. No one they'd come across in their investigation had fallen into this profile.

'So you aren't treating this as attempted murder?' Dominic was not letting up. 'Whoever attacked Claudia waited until she was in bed and then set fire to the house. Whoever attacked Russ waited outside his house and ran him down.'

Claudia really was tired.

It was Sharpe's turn to glare and boy did she do a proper job of it. Dominic winced. Her tone was glassy when she spoke. 'You do not attempt to kill two police officers and expect the police force to back off because you want them to. That is *not* how this works. In response to your question, yes, these are being investigated as attempted murders. Whether that offence gets knocked down to a lesser crime when it comes time to charge is another matter, but two officers nearly died and that is not acceptable. My comment was not how I see this, but how I believe our offender sees this. I believe, he, or she, hoped that after Russ was hit, we would back off. They have little faith in the police.' Sharpe stared hard at Dominic. 'Little faith in me. This is not over.'

Dominic's shoulders slumped. The spiral of anger and excitement he had built up in himself was released as he realised they were not letting this one go. Claudia closed her eyes a moment, unsure if she could continue. The hissing barely registering now, her exhaustion complete.

'This latest attempt has rattled the powers that be considerably. Whoever is behind this doesn't wield enough power that the bosses will allow them to kill their officers. It's coming down the line that all hands will investigate the fire at Claudia's, the hit-and-run on Russ, and the murder of Harlow Cunningham. Let's just say there is blind fury and a little panic that they allowed it to get this far.'

'Bloody hell.'

'The team's back on it?' Claudia asked, eyes still shut.

'The team have been removed from Carlyle's investigation and placed back in your incident room and they've been read in on what you've been doing. They're conflicted in their feelings. Not happy that you went behind their backs, that you didn't tell them your thoughts on what was happening, but understanding of why you did it and then furious at what it led to. They're itching to come in and start work but I told each and every one of them to get a couple more hours' sleep then head in. They'll make a start on running down Dawn and Sophie to see how they link to Harlow and if they were anywhere near the murder scene on Sunday. There's enough staff with the night teams working the immediate scene.'

Claudia opened her eyes. The team was back. She didn't have to run around and be secretive any more.

Sharpe jumped off the bed. 'Now you're up to date and I can see you're alive, I'm going back to bed for a couple of hours' sleep myself. I just need to organise the uniforms, then it's beauty sleep for me. I'll see you in the office bright and early, Dom?'

He looked at Claudia.

She waved a hand at him. 'Go. Better to get to the bottom of this than sit and babysit me. Besides, I'll already have a babysitter.'

He nodded at Sharpe. 'I'll be there.'

'Good. Let's get this bastard.'

CHAPTER 45

It was finally quiet. Sharpe and her father had gone. There was a lone officer standing outside Claudia's door as promised. Exhaustion took her, and Claudia slept.

It was the sleep of the troubled. Smoke and fire came for her. A figure with no face approached her. Walking closer and closer and yet she could never make out any features. Cold, hard hands wrapped themselves around her neck while the flames danced.

Claudia screamed and bolted upright in her bed. Her back was cold with sweat. Her hip jolted in spasm as she jumped into a sitting position, but her foot stayed where it lay neatly in its cast. Heavy and leaden.

The scream caught in her throat and she coughed hard. Pain tore at her chest. Tears pricked at her eyes. What a state she was in. Claudia tried to steady her breathing. Slow it down and calm the coughing.

The officer on the door ran in, fear on his face, his hand gripping his airwave radio, ready to request support. Of course, he was aware of everything surrounding Claudia. The threat on her life. The attempt on Russ. The murder inquiry. It would have the whole force talking now. And here he was guarding one of the most prominent people on the case and she was screaming in the night. Terrified didn't quite cut it.

'I'm sorry,' she said through the whistling oxygen mask that the nursing staff had insisted she sleep in, regardless of the discomfort it caused.

She coughed repeatedly, more tears leaking down her cheeks. 'A dream,' she clarified to the wide-eyed officer.

He gave an embarrassed smile, though Claudia didn't know who the embarrassment was for, himself or for her, dressed in a hospital gown, a state no subordinate should ever have to see her in, and he slunk out, pulling the door quietly to. Damn her body and damn her mind.

She rubbed with the heel of her hand at her chest until eventually the coughing subsided. The fatigue of the last couple of days pulled at her brain and she slid back down into the bedcovers, ready to give herself to sleep again. The turmoil of the case and the problems it brought with it would all wait for the morning. Right now, she needed to rest.

Claudia closed her eyes. The scent of disinfectant filtered through the mask. That hospital smell that was familiar to anyone who had ever stepped foot into a medical building. The hushed voices of the nurses along with the groaning of a patient in a ward somewhere outside her private room, and a machine on creaking wheels, was the soundtrack of the night as Claudia drifted back to sleep.

It was the very same soundtrack that was still playing when she woke again. This time in a more relaxed manner. No screaming. No fire. No smoke, and most certainly no hands around her neck, put there by a faceless being. It was not quite light, but the hustle and bustle of the wards outside Claudia's room was loud. Lights were on and people were talking loudly.

Claudia might be out of action, but she had a plan for today. She pulled off the oxygen mask and hooked it onto the wall, turning it off at the source. She grabbed the hospital dressing gown the staff had provided, knowing all her worldly belongings had gone up in flames, and wrapped it around herself. Her chest hurt as she moved, but she wanted to get this done as soon as she could. Before anyone could tell her otherwise. While the hospital staff were busy with their morning tasks.

Gingerly Claudia slipped off the bed onto her good foot, waving the broken one in the air above the floor.

She searched the room. In the corner was a wheelchair.

Shit, she hadn't thought this through.

Claudia hopped across to the wheelchair and dropped into it heavily, her chest feeling like it was hosting an entire house of bricks in there. It was so heavy and uncomfortable when she moved.

But what now?

'Hey,' she whispered through the door.

No response.

'Hey.' She tried again. Her chest heaving with every breath. Her throat raw.

Nothing.

'Officer.' She imagined the inside of her throat, red and blackened with a layer of skin removed. The pain was immense.

A face peered around the doorframe. A different one from the cop who had run into her room last night. This was a female officer. Tall, her cheeks flushed. 'Oh,' she said on seeing Claudia in the chair. 'Is everything okay?'

'I need you to take me to see DS Kane if you don't mind? I don't seem to be able to make this thing wheel around by myself. I think they're meant to be pushed. Would you mind?' She spoke as quietly as she could. It helped with the pain in both her chest and her throat.

The officer walked into the room.

'It's not in your job description—' Claudia started, voice low.

'Not at all.' The cop moved behind Claudia, grabbed the handles and took the brake off.

Oh, there was a brake. That made sense.

'I know what you did,' said the cop. 'Going after whoever hurt DS Kane and continuing the murder investigation into that woman when someone wanted you to stop.' She paused as though she'd spoken out of turn.

Claudia let her hands fall into her lap. Of course she'd known it would get out but she'd never expected it to go round this fast. What was this cop saying? She knew what she'd done, but what?

The cop pushed her towards the open door. 'Are you allowed to leave?'

Claudia admitted she wasn't sure.

'It's okay, ma'am. I have your back.'

There was a moment of silence and Claudia wondered what the cops and civilian staff were saying about her and Russ, as well as Dominic, Sharpe and Connelly.

'What you did was incredible.'

Well, she hadn't expected that.

Nobody seemed to notice them as they rolled down the corridor. 'What you did, when you were up against everything that could be thrown at you, you didn't back down. Not everyone could claim they would do the same thing. Some would step away and say this was just a job and not worth their life. Especially after the attack on DS Kane.'

Claudia wanted to cry. It was something she now realised she hadn't yet done. And yet here, locked into a wheelchair, unable to do anything for herself, being pushed by a younger officer, listening to her admiration, the emotion caught in Claudia's throat, which didn't help the problems already lodged in there. Should she have tried to bring the oxygen mask with her? It was too late to go back now. They had made a run for freedom. She endeavoured to take small and shallow breaths.

'I think more people than you might believe would have risen to the challenge.' She turned and looked at her saviour. The one helping her escape her room. 'What's your name?'

The officer blushed, her already flushed cheeks darkening. 'Meg Edwards, ma'am.' Her footsteps echoed down the hallway as they approached the exit. The wheels of the chair squeaking as she pushed Claudia in front of her. All the while, her shoulders were back, pride in her stance.

'Meg, thank you. It's the support of people like you that allows me, Russ, Dominic, DCI Sharpe and Detective Superintendent Connelly to stand up to the pressure we're fighting against.' Suddenly awkward, she asked, 'How is Russ this morning?'

'I've heard he's awake.'

Claudia let out an audible sigh, which came out more like a croak.

'You've not spoken to him?'

'No. No, I've not.'

Meg raised her speed. 'Let's get you there then, ma'am.'

Within a few minutes, the pair of them were standing outside another ward, staring at the closed double doors and the uniformed officer with his arms crossed.

'He's not in the ICU?' Claudia whispered to Meg, trying not to attract the attention of the new officer, even though he was staring directly at her.

'No, ma'am. They moved him to this ward last night. Just before they brought you in.'

Shit, Sharpe hadn't mentioned that. Though Claudia supposed she'd had plenty of other things on her mind at the time.

'Tony . . .' Meg inched Claudia closer.

Tony lifted his thickset frame a little higher.

'You know who this is.' Again, a couple of inches closer. The tone in her voice brooked no argument, but neither did the look on Tony's face. He was here to protect Russ, and Claudia was pleased he was doing his job. She just wished it wasn't at the expense of her seeing her closest colleague and friend.

'Of course I know who this is,' Tony said, staring down at Claudia in her wheelchair. She hated being so defenceless and desperately wanted to stand. In fact if he didn't move in the next ten seconds she would rise out of the chair and give him a bollocking. Detective inspector to police constable. For what, she hadn't yet decided, but it would come to her. One thing was for sure, she would not sit here and allow herself to be intimidated this way.

'This is DI Nunn, the woman who stared down the barrel of a metaphorical gun and wasn't afraid of those who wanted her to back down.' The cop's smile lit up his face. 'What can I do for you both?'

Meg stepped forward and punched him on his arm. 'What the hell?'

His grin widened. 'I'm in awe. Cut me some slack.'

'We're here to see DS Kane,' Claudia whispered. 'I believe he's awake now.'

'I haven't seen him myself, but that's what they're saying.' He stepped aside. 'I'm sure he'll be dead pleased to see you.' His smile dropped. 'I'm sorry. I didn't mean to say that.'

'Don't worry. Neither of us died and we're mighty glad about that. Thank you,' she said as Meg wheeled her past and into the new ward.

They found Russ in another side room. They put cops in single rooms, to protect their privacy from any press who might be lurking about or any other potential dangers.

His door was ajar and Claudia could see Russ propped up on a pile of pillows. Machines attached to him were beeping happily, or they sounded happy enough to Claudia's ear, and bags of fluids snaked their way into his body. There was a cast on one of his legs and an arm. He was pretty badly beaten up. His face was bruised, one eye swollen and blackened. The cheek underneath as swollen as the eye. He'd been hit hard and had gone down hard.

He appeared to be sleeping but as the door creaked when Meg pushed it wider to fit the wheelchair through, Russ's one good eye shot open. At first it appeared he couldn't get his bearings and had no idea who was in the room with him. Then gradually he focused and saw Meg. Confusion reigned. He didn't know this cop. Then his one-eyed wonky gaze slid down to the wheelchair, and he spotted Claudia.

'What the hell?'

Claudia thought exactly the same thing. Russ looked to have lost at least half a stone. Dark shadows circled his red-rimmed good eye and his good cheek hollowed out his face. What the hell, indeed.

'It's good to see you, too,' she said instead, giving away none of her shock at his appearance.

A weak smile played across his lips. 'I'm sorry. I can't sit up. You okay if I stay where I am?'

Claudia lifted a hand. 'I'd be annoyed if you tried to move. Stay there.'

'What the hell, again, Claudia? What are you doing in here?'

He sounded tired. Weak.

There was no sign of Maura. She had probably gone home for some rest last night, when they'd moved Russ to a main ward.

'Like you, someone took umbrage to the fact we were looking into the Cunningham murder.'

'You're kidding.' His eyes widened. 'What happened, Claudia?'

'Fire. While I was sleeping.'

'Shit. Your house. Your stuff.'

She hadn't dwelled on that. Had tried not to think about it. About how much she'd actually lost. She shrugged. 'It's just stuff. You and me, we're more important.'

'What the fuck. What's happening?' He was trying to move. Pain etched across his face.

'Stop it,' she snapped.

Meg came from behind the chair, ready to do something, but what?

'Cool it,' Russ said to her. 'I don't know you. You're not putting your hands on me while I'm half-naked.'

'Well, get your act together and lie still.' Claudia wasn't happy with him. 'Or I give her permission to call for a nurse to come and whip your arse.'

Russ looked suitably chastised and held up a palm. 'I'm staying put.'

Meg shuffled back behind Claudia.

The machines continued to beep around Russ.

'Practically the whole force is on the case now,' Claudia said, her chest hurting, wishing again she'd brought the oxygen with her. 'What, with the investigations into your hit-and-run, my fire and the Cunningham murder inquiry back on track, whoever is behind all this has a lot of workforce coming his way.'

'It's all back on?' Russ sounded surprised. 'No more sneaking around?'

'It's more than back on. They're furious and out to get whoever did this. You don't try to kill cops and get away with it, no matter who you are.'

Russ closed his eyes. 'I'm not sure I'll be a cop again.' His voice was quiet.

The words hit her like a brick wall.

'Don't say that, Russ. You might have a long road ahead, but you will be back. Trust in the medical profession.'

'They took my spleen, Claudia.'

She stared at him. He was obviously feeling the pain of the hit-and-run, he was in a bad way. 'It's not the end of the world . . .'

The pair surveyed each other from their respective positions. Russ laid out on the bed and Claudia in her wheelchair. Both struck down by an unknown person who didn't want the Harlow Cunningham murder investigated.

'I don't know,' Russ said eventually. He sounded half asleep. One of these machines was probably filling him with pain meds.

Claudia motioned for Meg to wheel her closer and took his hand.

'Russ, whoever did this to you will be in a cell awaiting trial one day, I promise you.' She kissed his hand and placed it back on the bed.

And with that, she left him to sleep again. His body needed a chance to rest and to heal. The journey ahead for him was long and arduous.

CHAPTER 46

Claudia left Russ's room bereft. She'd talked of fighting to the end of this case, but his mood was low. He was in pain and no one would tell him how his injuries would play out and what his recovery plan would be. It was difficult for him to look ahead.

By the time Meg returned Claudia to her side room, her chest was heaving and painful and she was coughing more often.

As Meg pushed her back through the door, a nurse followed them inside with a loud tut.

'And what do you think you're doing, unhooking yourself from the oxygen, young lady?' The nurse crossed her arms and jutted out her chin, clearly not amused.

'I had to see my colleague,' Claudia said, with as much authority as she could muster.

The nurse laughed, a bitter sound. 'You're not a police officer in here, Claudia. You're a patient. So don't try that on with me.'

Claudia shrank in on herself and the nurse surged forward, practically pushing Meg out of the way. She grabbed Claudia by her arms. 'Let's get you back into bed, shall we?'

Claudia was secretly grateful to her. Her body ached. Her chest heaved, and she was coughing like a lifetime smoker — which was what had probably drawn the nurse's attention in the first place.

Once she was under the covers, the nurse attached the oxygen and Claudia sucked in the cool air greedily.

'Why do police officers make such terrible patients?' The nurse complained. 'You're nearly as bad as doctors.' She tutted again, but there was a twinkle in her eyes. 'Look, I know you have a tough job, one that landed you here. God knows I could never do what you do for a living, but you won't get back out there until you take some care of yourself and allow the oxygen to do its work and give your lungs a little time to rest and recuperate. Then you can do whatever it is you need to do so badly.'

Claudia looked up at the woman, who was only doing her job, as Claudia desperately wanted to do her own. 'I'm sorry. I wanted to see my colleague . . .'

'Russ Kane.' She patted Claudia gently. 'A friend is on his ward.' The nurse pulled over the blood pressure pump on wheels that was standing in the corner and wrapped the cuff around Claudia's arm, then pressed the button on the machine. The cuff hummed into life and inflated, tightening and squeezing. 'He's in bad shape,' she continued, 'but with a little time, he'll mend. He's in the best place.' She recorded the blood pressure reading, removed the cuff, wrapped it all up and returned the apparatus to its place.

'He'll be okay?' Claudia clarified.

'I can't go into his medical details,' said the nurse, 'but have some faith in the team here and in your colleague.' Next, she pushed a thermometer into Claudia's ear. It beeped, and she noted the temperature. 'He's a strong young man. That will benefit him.' She pulled the blanket up to Claudia's waist and patted it down. 'If you're lucky, you might be out later today or tomorrow morning. But you have to do as you're told and rest up.' The stern look returned.

'I promise,' said Claudia meekly.

The nurse smiled and turned away, but stopped suddenly. 'I hope you find whoever did this to you and Mr Kane.' And with that, she was gone, off to minister to the rest of the patients on the ward.

Claudia leaned back on her pillows, the oxygen blowing gently into her nostrils.

It was only now she allowed herself the time to think about what had happened. Not only had someone tried to kill her, but they'd destroyed all she owned. She had no home. She was in the dark as to how much damage the fire had caused as an ambulance had whisked her away as soon as she'd escaped, but she doubted the building was habitable. All her clothes were in there. She had nothing to wear. Everything, all her possessions were gone. She didn't even have the pyjamas she'd been wearing because they were smoke damaged and had been binned when the nurses had stripped her. A sickness curled in her stomach.

What would she do?

Of course, her friends would be there for her and she was insured. But it was her best friend, her father's wife, Ruth, who would have been the person who would have had her back. She'd have provided her clothes to walk out the hospital. She'd have been there to support Claudia in her hour of need and she'd have shut Dominic up when he said anything stupid. But Ruth was gone, and this was a fresh wave of hell that washed over Claudia now.

How had they got to this place?

Everything had spiralled to this point. First Ruth had been murdered, then an unusual case resulted in Claudia killing a man, and now she lay here, alone, with a uniform officer guarding her because of the risk to her life. Well, they said these things came in threes. She'd had her fill. She wanted it all to stop, and she wanted to get off the ride.

What would Robert, her therapist, say about all this?

A rattle of wheels interrupted her thoughts as a trolley banged into the side of the door and a cheery voice shouted it was time for breakfast. Claudia attempted to drag herself out of her reverie and put on a smile for her visitor.

* * *

The day dragged, as days in hospital often did. Claudia texted Sharpe several times for an update. She was an impatient patient and an even worse side-lined detective inspector. When Sharpe didn't respond immediately, Claudia took to texting friends just to make sure her phone was actually working. It was a welcome distraction when a fed rep turned up. Several female officers in the force had responded to the news of Claudia's home attack by donating various items of clothing. The women had been generous, which was always the case when an officer was down. The fed rep had four huge bags full. Claudia asked for her thanks to be conveyed. There would come a time when she could buy her own clothes, but right now, these were gratefully received.

When Sharpe's updates eventually came through, they gave little away. There were three separate teams working in tandem, as she'd been told: one on the hit-and-run, one on the fire and her own team back on the Cunningham murder. It was slow going. *And rest up*, said Sharpe. She would tell her when she had something positive to say.

Claudia slammed her phone onto the bed in anger.

'It's not going well?' a small voice said from the door, which wasn't Meg's.

Claudia looked up.

'Ma'am,' said Meg, her hands twitching by her side. 'Dawn Sinclair would like to talk to you, if you're up to it?'

'I'm sorry, I pushed past your officer.' Dawn's face was pale. She was pulling a coat around her slim frame and holding it tight around herself.

'It's fine.' Claudia was speaking to Meg. She liked the girl. But Dawn Sinclair took it as accepted that she could enter the room.

What the hell did she want? To own up to her relation-ship with Harlow. They'd already made that leap. Whatever it was, Dawn Sinclair looked like a frightened woman.

Claudia's phone buzzed with another incoming message from Sharpe. She held up a finger. 'Give me a second.'

Dawn Sinclair hovered by the chair at the side of Claudia's bed. Claudia flicked through to Sharpe's message.

Had a visit from Dawn Sinclair. Interesting conversation and have information we can move on. Will phone you shortly.

So Sinclair had been into the police station and yet had come here as well to talk to Claudia herself. And whatever she'd said had actually been useful. Claudia was interested now. She placed her phone on the bed.

'Why have you come to the hospital, Mrs Sinclair? In fact, I have to ask how you were aware I was in the hospital in the first place?'

Dawn Sinclair grasped the back of the chair. Her fingers white with tension. She cleared her throat. 'I . . . erm . . . I . . . I . . .'

Claudia waited her out.

Sinclair started again. 'I had a visit, early this morning, from a very angry DS Harrison . . .'

Her father had been to see her?

'He . . . erm . . .'

Sinclair was obviously shaken by what Dominic had said and maybe by what she was about to say next. A shiver ran down Claudia's spine.

'DS Harrison said there had been a fire at your address, your home, last night and that it nearly killed you. He told me you were his daughter. He was very angry — and rightly so.' She paused, collecting herself. 'I'm so sorry, DI Nunn.'

'Why should you be sorry, Mrs Sinclair?' Claudia's voice was cold. If Sinclair was apologising she didn't think she liked where this was headed.

'I have information that I should have given you when you visited me. I was afraid, and it was that fear that silenced me. But it also put you in harm's way and I won't allow anyone else to be put at risk. Not for my mistake.'

Claudia took another deep breath.

'Your mistake?'

'Yes.' Sinclair searched Claudia's face. For what, Claudia was unsure. 'Do you mind if I have a seat? I'm not sure my legs will support me through all of this.'

Claudia wanted to make the woman stand, but if she was to get to the truth then she had to ease this along as best she could. She agreed.

Dawn Sinclair smoothed the back of her skirt as she seated herself in the plastic bowl of a hospital chair. The legs scraped a little on the hard floor as it moved under her. She was twitchy. Afraid of the slightest sound. Claudia wondered what on earth she was here to spill.

'It's a story from long ago,' the woman said, 'but it ripples through the generations to today and to Harlow coming to Sheffield.'

'You knew her?' Claudia asked.

'Not in the way you're asking,' said Sinclair.

Claudia waited.

'I am her birth mother.'

The room was still. Claudia's breath paused in her chest. Dawn Sinclair was Harlow Cunningham's birth mother. It had been a supposition, created by several different pieces coming together. To have it confirmed by Dawn pulled the picture together. Harlow was in Sheffield to find and talk to Dawn. But how had that got her killed?

'It was a long time ago. I was a newly qualified teacher, and I fell for a student. He was of age, but he was still a student.'

Claudia started to cough. Meg stepped in and Claudia waved her away, grabbing at the glass of water on the bedside table, taking a sip and steadying herself. 'Sorry. Continue.'

'I intended to give the baby up for adoption, but the boy's family found out. They were furious. They had plans for their son. It was a private school, you see. He could go places.' She paused. 'He went places,' she whispered, so quietly Claudia wondered if she'd heard her properly. 'They didn't want a baby attached to him. They applied so much pressure. Threatened to inform my employers, go to the press, everything that would destroy me. They didn't want me to have the baby or gave it up for adoption, leaving a paper trial right back to their son.

'I was young, myself. I hadn't long finished teacher training and I didn't know what to do. I was overwhelmed by the pressure they bore down on me. Little did I realise if the boy's parents did any of those things, like going to the press, that they'd have also hurt their own child in the process, not just me. But I was an emotional wreck. In the end, it became too much and I succumbed. I left my baby somewhere safe but unrecorded. Neither I nor her father were linked to her. I got a job elsewhere and I tried to get on with the rest of my life. I married and I had two daughters with my husband. It was the fear of destroying this family, the family I created afterwards, that prevented me giving you the truth earlier. But I've come to realise that it's time to acknowledge Harlow. She was my daughter and I let her down. Not just in the beginning, but at the end. Your father's anger made me realise that.' She gave Claudia a weak smile and Claudia thought she should remember to thank her dad.

'I have to face my family's anger head on. My daughters have already found out and, as you're aware, are furious with me for my actions. Though Sophie attempted to protect me, I think it was more about protecting me and her father as a couple, in turn protecting her own version of what her family is. Sophie is the youngest, you see, she's rather spoiled, I think.'

A tear spilled onto Dawn's cheek. 'It's Serena I'm worried about. She came home early from a week away with her partner after seeing the news. She was distraught. I didn't understand why at first. So wrapped up in my own grief. Until she told me of her meeting with Harlow.'

This surprised Claudia. 'When was this?'

'Oh, a couple of months ago apparently. Yes, it came as a surprise to me too. Serena said she did one of those DNA test things you can buy and upload to a website, to find obscure relatives around the globe. Instead she found a sister. Harlow had done a DNA test and uploaded the results to the website in case any blood relatives did a test. She hadn't been able to think of any other way to trace her biological parents as there just wasn't a paper trail.' More tears flowed. 'Serena and Harlow matched. They talked. Harlow told Serena of her beginnings. They'd had lunch in Cambridge, a middle ground. Serena said Harlow was wonderful and she promised to keep Harlow's presence to herself and allow Harlow to approach me herself, telling Harlow she'd make herself scarce that weekend and go away with her boyfriend. Not that she lived at home with us but she'd rather not be around. And Harlow for her part kept it from her dad. She told Serena he was still grieving hard for her mum. She didn't want to pile this on him. Not yet anyway.'

Dawn sucked in a deep breath. The emotion of her family story tearing through her. 'Serena contacted Harlow at the last minute, hours before she arrived in Sheffield, to say she'd been unable to keep her a secret from her sister, Sophie, and she was so sorry. Sophie wasn't as open to a relationship with her as Serena was. Sophie's fear was what this would do to me and her dad. Harlow had to tread carefully.' Her voice broke and Dawn sobbed.

Meg stepped into the room and handed her a wad of tissues she'd found somewhere. Dawn took them gratefully and quickly mopped up her face. 'They're entitled to their feelings. And I have to hope we can work our way through it.'

'You pretended she never existed,' said Claudia, thinking of the new family Dawn had around her.

'Not at all,' shot back Sinclair. 'I thought about her all the time. Wondered if she looked like my girls. Was afraid that she might look like my girls. It's a bitter circle.'

'Why is she dead, Mrs Sinclair?' Claudia asked.

A tear slipped down Dawn Sinclair's cheek. 'Because of who her father is, I imagine. I have no proof of who killed her, but there is real power behind her father.'

'And who is that?'

'The man destined to be our next prime minister.'

CHAPTER 47

Harlow

Thursday 10 a.m. — 73 hours earlier

Her father, or rather the man who had fathered her, because her dad was waiting for her back in Devon, wasn't home until tomorrow. Today, though, she was meeting Justin Winters, his son. Justin was an MP in his own right. Spoiled little brat if the press were to be believed. Though perhaps that wasn't surprising. He was one of the youngest people to be elected to Parliament at the tender age of twenty-three. But she'd make up her own mind on his brattishness.

What she wanted from this encounter, Harlow wasn't sure. But she'd arrived in Sheffield yesterday and had itchy feet. Waiting until tomorrow, when Nigel was home, didn't feel like an option. If there was an opportunity to meet her birth family now, then she would take it.

Justin Winters was her brother by blood, after all. Maybe he'd be pleased to see her. Maybe he'd ease the pathway to his father. Their father.

When he opened the front door to his high-rise apartment, she found herself face to face with a male version of herself. Justin Winters had the very same eyes. The shape of them, the colouring. His hair, though short, was swept to the side, dark like hers. His chin jutted out ever so slightly in a tiny point. It was like looking in a mirror. If he saw the resemblance, he didn't react to it.

She'd told him she was coming, but Justin Winters stared at her as if he hadn't been expecting her. There was no warmth or welcome in his eyes. He didn't step back to allow her access. He crossed his arms in frosty distrust.

'Harlow Cunningham,' she said, for want of anything else to say.

'I know,' he replied.

Her stomach twisted. She hadn't expected a cheerful family reunion, but this was something else.

'Can we talk?' she asked nervously. Would he send her away without allowing her access after agreeing she could visit?

He finally stepped aside and Harlow walked into the property. It was all glass and polished chrome, in a wide-open space, with a huge glass wall overlooking the city below.

Justin closed the door and then stood beside it, arms crossed over his chest again.

Harlow swallowed back her anxiety. She would not allow this man to intimidate her. He was no better than her. Just because he'd been brought up in wealth. Not given away. It didn't make him any more of a person than her. She had a family who loved her. 'You know who I am?'

'Of course I know who you are.' He almost spat the words at her.

Harlow wanted to run out the door, into the corridor and into the lift that had swept her up here so silently. Regret coursed through her. Was this the reception she would receive from his father?

Her father.

She wished to escape this hostile man, but he was blocking her route out, standing in front of the door she'd just walked through. What to say next? 'Do you have any questions?'

She had plenty herself, but maybe he had some of his own. After all, he wasn't part of her story. This must be as much of a shock to him as it had been to her when she'd found out, not the truth, because her mum and dad had always been honest with her about her beginnings, but the details, the who, from Dawn's daughter, Serena. There were two daughters, Harlow learned. Serena and Sophie. This made them her sisters. She had family. And here in front of her, she had a brother. It was nearly too much to take in.

Serena, the one who had contacted her, believed in truth and not secrets. She'd hated that the story of Harlow's birth had been covered up all these years.

Harlow wondered how Serena's relationship with her mother was now but dropped the thought quickly. At least Serena had a relationship with her mother. It was more than Harlow had at this moment in time. Though that could change. But Harlow couldn't help but be bitter at the way things had worked out. Not for the parents who had adopted her, though. They'd been the one good thing in all this and for them she'd be always grateful.

She looked at Justin. It was all such a minefield.

Justin's top lip lifted in a sneer. 'I have one question . . .'

The breath paused in her chest. This could break the ice.

'What do you want?' he asked.

What did she want? What did he mean, what did she want? Surely he didn't think she wanted anything from the family other than to know them? Her mind whirled as she attempted to put together a coherent response. How could she tell this young man that she wanted nothing from his family but to spend a little time with them? Maybe get some answers about what had happened back then? Why she'd been left the way she had, why no one had wanted her. Wouldn't any person who'd been abandoned that way want the same?

'I want to see Nigel Winters. I want to get to know you all and I want some answers,' she said eventually.

He laughed then, but it was more like a coughing sound. A bark. A dismissal.

Harlow felt her cheeks flush. How she wanted to escape.

This wasn't what she'd expected at all. She'd imagined her brother would be as inquisitive about her as she was about him. But this man in front of her was hard and brittle. If this is what his lifestyle had done for him, she was glad she hadn't been brought up with him. Harlow squirmed, eager to leave, but he was still in the way. Arms across his chest. A barrier. Chest puffed out like a peacock.

'You expect me to believe that?'

'It's true.' She took a step forward but still he didn't move and the closeness to him made her uncomfortable, so she stepped back again, wrapping her arms around her body.

'You're here for what you can get out of my father. You know who he is and what he could do for you. You've come from nothing and you want more.' The sneer was back. 'But don't think you can arrive cap in hand. My father's not in Sheffield. You missed him. He won't be here until tomorrow. Poor you. Do you have any idea what you will do to my father's career if this gets out?' The truth of the matter came next. 'Or my career, come to think of it.' Justin's face was nearly puce. Suddenly it was clear to Harlow. It wasn't his father he was protecting. It wasn't the family fortune. It was his own name and his own future in the political world. He saw himself following in his father's footsteps and one day leading the country. Harlow watched the idea as it shaped in his eyes. Clear and bright. He wouldn't allow her to get in his way. 'You're to leave now and if I see sight or sound of you again, then you'll regret it.' This time he stepped forward. His breath on her face. Hot and sweet. 'Do you hear me? You. Will. Regret. It.'

An icy chill slid down Harlow's spine. 'Let me out.'

This time he moved to the side. She grabbed for the door handle, her movements jerky and uncoordinated. Her hand slipped as she went for it and she stumbled, her ankle twisting slightly. She held the cry in and swung for the handle again, this time making purchase and pulling it open. She was half-way through when Justin's low voice behind her, crackled.

'If you come near my family again, or if I find out you're nosing around, I will break you.'

CHAPTER 48

Claudia

Claudia couldn't wait for Sharpe to call her when she was ready. As soon as Dawn Sinclair had gone she grabbed her phone and dialled. Sharpe picked up immediately.

'I said I'd call you later. What don't you understand about that?' She was blunt, but there was no real anger in her voice.

'Dawn Sinclair paid me a visit.' Claudia didn't need to say anything else.

'Did she, now? So you're up to speed then. It's thanks to Dominic's little tirade at her that we're where we are at this moment. The fire at your house gave her the push we needed.'

'Nigel Winters?' Claudia had been blown away by the revelation.

'We've put in a request for his personal phone records, the authorisation has been signed, and we should have something back in the next hour or so. Then it's just a matter of trawling through his messages and calls to see if there's anything incriminating.'

'There's also his work email account and phone, but I'm not sure he'd involve his MP accounts.'

'Hold on to your hat, Claudia. We're all over it. Let's see what his personal accounts give us before we go there, shall we? Everyone has their head down and is doing what they can to sift through Nigel Winters' life. They're tearing it apart. His movements over the weekend. Matching it up with the CCTV we have around the hotel. Everything is happening. I'll keep you updated.'

'What about that DNA trace we found under Harlow's fingernails?'

'That's something we're trying to figure out.'

And with that, she was gone. They had so much to do. All Claudia was doing was slowing them down.

'Meg!' she shouted through the door.

Meg popped her head around the frame.

'Could you wheel me to the nurses' station please? I need to get out of this place.'

Following a debate with a nurse and a junior doctor, Meg finally wheeled Claudia out of the hospital to where Dominic was waiting with the car running and ready to go. From the bags of clothes that had been delivered she'd selected a pair of jeans and a sweater. There were even a couple of pairs of trainers to choose from. At times like this, Claudia was reminded, the force turned into a family.

Dominic took her crutches, slung them on the back seat, and supported her into the vehicle. 'They've said you're good to leave?'

Claudia looked to Meg, who stared at the floor in response. 'I'm as good as I need to be.'

Meg pulled the chair out of the way of Dominic's vehicle. 'Thank you, Meg, for everything.'

'Take care of yourself, ma'am. If I can be of any more help, just shout.' Meg flushed again and Dominic slammed the door closed on Claudia, walking around to the driver's side and climbing in.

'Back to mine?' he asked.

'The station?' she said hopefully.

'You're kidding, right?'

'You can't lock me out now.'

'Sharpe and Connelly would have my hide if I took you into work today. Rest, Claudia. Someone just tried to kill you. Don't worry, we'll keep you updated. It's all systems go. Everyone is working so hard — we nearly have the answers we need.'

With that, Dominic drove Claudia to his house. His words about putting her friends at risk had sunk in and she agreed that while Harlow's killer was still at large, she would stay with him, but once this was over she would sort out other arrangements. Dominic grumbled, but dropped her off before returning to the station.

Claudia grabbed some cheese on toast and a mug of tea from the kitchen and made for the living room so she could lounge in front of the television and watch the news.

She was uncomfortable in her father's house. How could he live here after Ruth's murder? Her skin crawled just thinking about it. But he'd told her it had been their home and was filled with warm memories as well as the bad. So Claudia left him to it.

The cast on her foot hindered her movements. With a crutch under one arm and a plate balanced on top of the mug in her other hand, it was a slow and frustrating journey. And it was a journey. Something that shouldn't even register in her mind, moving from the kitchen to the living room, was an entire expedition to her now. Claudia ground her teeth at the ridiculousness of the situation and only let go of the tension when she finally collapsed onto the sofa, placing the plate and mug on the coffee table in front of her. A trail of tea drops lay in her wake where her balance had been off.

Claudia switched the television on and leaned back, flicking through channels until she found the news. If her team, or one of the teams working any part of this case, broke this, it would quickly hit the national press, and she wanted to witness it as soon as it did. Especially if she couldn't be the one to force his door in.

It made her sick that he'd done this to her and to Russ. He'd put her out of action and now she was unable to do her job. But she trusted in her colleagues. They would bring him down.

She chewed on her toast, ignoring the crumbs that tumbled down her jumper, and thought of Russ. How he'd said he might not return to policing. Claudia couldn't imagine a world where she didn't work with him. It didn't seem possible. She'd worked alongside the man for years. He'd been her right arm. Whoever was behind all this would pay for what they'd done.

Claudia finished her food, leaned back, and closed her eyes. The sound of the television now a background noise. Nothing was happening. Yet so much had happened in her world. She was exhausted. Forty winks wouldn't hurt.

* * *

The ringing of her phone brought her round. Her mind was fuzzy from where it had been drifting into sleep. Claudia slammed her hand around her, searching for her mobile. The sound rang out, but she couldn't find the source. Eventually she found it down the back of the sofa.

The caller was Sharpe.

'I thought you'd want to know,' she said without preamble. 'There's a text conversation between Nigel Winters and his son Justin where Justin says he's sorted the problem. His dad doesn't need to worry about her any more. This is Sunday morning.'

Claudia rubbed her face. Her mind struggling to catch up. She was sure she'd only just that second closed her eyes, but the room was hazy. She blinked. It was still fuzzy. Claudia realised it was getting dark. She hadn't only just closed her eyes. She hadn't only had forty winks. Claudia had been asleep for hours.

No wonder she was finding it difficult to latch on to what Sharpe was saying to her. Something about a conversation between Nigel and his son and it had to do with Harlow. 'I'm sorry,' Claudia said. 'I didn't quite catch that.' She hoped Sharpe didn't realise she'd woken her up. 'Something between Nigel and his son? We think the son is involved?'

There was a sigh down the line, but Sharpe's tone was patient. 'Justin told his dad he'd sorted the problem, and he doesn't need to worry about her any more. This is on Sunday morning so we're taking it that he's referring to Harlow.'

'So they don't name her?' Claudia had caught up. 'It's not enough, we need evidence.'

'Claudia, I've found out from the chief constable that the leaders of all political parties have their DNA taken in case of assassination attempts, if someone plants a bomb for example, where they only have DNA to work with.'

Oh. They had a sample recovered from Harlow's crime scene.

Sharpe continued talking. 'They keep the DNA profile on a database that only certain people can access—'

Shit. 'How do we go about—'

'If you let me finish.' Though Sharpe had attempted to keep her tone even through her conversation with Claudia, it now snapped. Claudia understood. Sharpe was in a pressurised situation. They were dealing with the leader of the opposition party. This was not run-of-the-mill stuff. 'Some of the people allowed access to the DNA database include chief constables.'

Claudia realised she was sitting with her mouth open. She shut it. 'Is the chief constable going to cross-reference it with the sample we recovered from the crime scene?'

'She said that now we have the text message, we have enough grounds for her to do this. We should have the results in a matter of hours.'

Claudia couldn't breathe, and it wasn't just because of the smoke damage to her lungs. No wonder things had panned out the way they had if the leader of the opposition had been driving it. Power like that could open and close many doors. It answered a lot of questions.

It was as though Sharpe had read her mind. 'The chief also said she was contacted in the night by a very distressed acting assistant chief constable. He told her he would be handing in his resignation the following morning, but that she needed to know he had moved staff from your investigation onto another at the behest of Justin Winters. When she asked why he would do this, he started to cry and told her Justin had set him up. He's a married man, but he was about to leave a bar one night after a drink with a friend, when a young woman stopped to talk to him. One thing led to another . . . she was very young and attractive and made him feel . . . I don't know, what is it older men crave?'

Claudia shook her head. 'To feel young again?'

'Maybe that's what she said. Anyway, apparently there are photographs and Davidson loves his wife.' Sharpe's tone was disbelieving but she continued. 'They have grown children and young grandkids. It would tear the family apart, etc. He was an easy target. He didn't think it was much of an ask, moving a few staff around.'

'And Justin was the one who told his father he'd sorted the "problem"?' The fog of waking was gradually clearing, but a deep-seated headache was making itself at home. If what Dawn had told her was true, Justin Winters was Harlow's brother. This was an ugly case.

'That's the way the text reads.'

'But we're going after Nigel?'

'To get the DNA compared we're going with the suspicion that as Harlow's father and leader of the opposition and most likely the next prime minister of the country, Nigel Winters would not want Harlow screwing up his life, so was behind whatever happened to her and directed everything. We'll do the test and go from there.'

Claudia hung up, having extracted a promise that someone would update her as soon as they had answers. Sharpe was calling Russ next. As police officers and victims of this man, both of them deserved to know what was happening, regardless of the fact that neither of them could be in the station working the case. Something that was driving Claudia to distraction.

Three hours and forty-seven minutes later Claudia's phone rang again. She wasn't asleep this time, though she was still slouched on her father's sofa and getting pretty fed up with being there if she was honest. The headache was burrowing a hole in her temple. She picked up immediately.

'It wasn't Nigel Winters.'

Claudia's stomach dropped like a brick through water. 'You're sure?'

'Of course I'm sure. I can read, Claudia.'

It was a stupid question and one she regretted asking as soon as the words were out of her mouth. But she'd been so sure Nigel Winters had been behind Harlow Cunningham's murder and the attempts on the lives of both herself and Russ. To have it come back as a negative result like this was disheartening, to say the least. 'I'm sorry.'

'Don't be. That's not all I have to say.' Sharpe was taunting her. Claudia held her breath and waited for what was to come.

'It might not be Nigel Winters, but his DNA on the database was a familial match with that seized at the crime scene.'

'You mean . . .'

'That's exactly what I mean.'

'That it was his son? Justin?'

'We have our man, Claudia. Want to come in to watch the arrest?'

CHAPTER 49

Claudia wasn't allowed to be a part of the team that was taking down Justin Winters. Not with difficulties breathing and a broken foot. But she could enter the property when he was secured. It wasn't exactly protocol, but as long as she didn't ask him any questions in relation to the investigation, then both Sharpe and Connelly had signed off on it.

It was late by the time they were organised. Their first stop at Justin's apartment drew a blank. Justin wasn't at home. But a very helpful concierge informed them that Justin had gone to his parents for dinner.

The procession of police vehicles changed direction towards Nigel Winters's address. Claudia just hoped no one inside the apartments had peered outside their windows, into the night, and photographed the marked vehicles below, sending the image to their neighbour, or worse, posting it online.

Darkness cloaked them as they drove to Nigel's. An air of anxiety at the way this job had exploded and excitement at closing such an extraordinary case filled the vehicle. In the lead van was the arrest team, consisting of staff taken from her unit, uniformed cops, plus a couple of officers from the protection team to make sure that nothing went awry during the operation. The level of tension was off the scale. There were no political jokes. No bad puns. Everyone was taut. This operation had the possibility of going wrong in the most spectacular of fashions. And Claudia was here to witness it all.

The line of vehicles pulled up outside the property. A couple of external security lights flickered on, as the protection officers had advised.

They weren't here to do this in secret. There were to be no doors put through. They'd walk in, speak to Nigel, find Justin, then make the arrest and walk out with him.

Like they'd said earlier, so much scope for things to go wrong.

But everyone knew their roles.

Sharpe was pleased the house was at the top of a long driveway, as there'd be no one with a camera that would put the arrest straight up on the internet tonight. She wanted to control the narrative. As would Winters as much as he could in his position, she imagined.

The door opened immediately. The protection officers had informed them that, as well as security lights, there were CCTV cameras in operation. Winters had seen their arrival.

Nigel Winters, head of the house, stood in the doorway with his hands in his pockets, looking for all he was worth like a relaxed host greeting visitors at a dinner party. Not like a man who had just witnessed via his home security system a fleet of police vehicles, both marked and plain, trail into his property.

'Officers?' He didn't know who to address.

Because of the size of the operation and because of who they were here for, Sharpe was making the arrest herself. It would have been Claudia had she been in better health. But it wasn't to be.

Claudia clenched her teeth yet again in the back of the car, with the window down so she could hear what was being said, while she waited on the sidelines.

Sharpe introduced herself and produced her identification.

'How can I help the fine officers of South Yorkshire Police today?' Nigel's cool was still in place, though a little frayed at the edges.

Sharpe had her back to Claudia so she couldn't hear every word, but she heard her ask if his son was home.

The frayed edges pulled apart a fraction more. 'What's this about?'

Sharpe stepped forward and Claudia didn't hear the response. Winters crossed his arms.

'Sir?' Sharpe took another step closer. She had a warrant for Justin's arrest in her hand. It wasn't necessary. You didn't need a warrant to arrest someone, but because of the sensitivities of this case, Sharpe had gone down this route. Better to have a strong paper trail, she'd told Claudia.

In the bright light of the security bulbs, Nigel Winters paled and Sharpe stepped past him and into his home. Winters pulled a phone out of his pocket and made a call. Most likely to his solicitor. Justin would definitely need one.

Claudia waited. More members of the team, including her father, entered the house and still she waited. She didn't think she had ever been as frustrated in her whole career. This man had destroyed her life, and she was left outside. Told to stay away for her own safety because she wasn't fit for duty. His fault.

The driveway stayed lit up by the security lights as officers came and went from the house. And still Claudia waited. Her foot throbbed and still she waited.

Eventually her phone rang as she sat there festering about the situation, nearly consumed by the anger.

'Yes,' she shouted into the handset.

'You can come in now. He's been arrested and is sitting in the living room on the right. He's not very happy,' said Sharpe.

'On my way.' Claudia grabbed a crutch and rammed open the car door. As fast as she could, she was over the gravel and at the front door. She took a deep breath. This was it. The man who had killed Harlow Cunningham and tried to kill her and Russ. They had him.

CHAPTER 50

Claudia watched Robert, who was sitting opposite her with his long legs crossed and his glasses perched on top of his head. Again, he was waiting for her to respond to a question. Always waiting. He was a patient man, as he needed to be with her as a client. She didn't give him anything easily. Cops were not renowned for being talkative, emotional souls; they witnessed too much of the dark side of life and had to box it away for their own protection. Claudia was no exception.

'Claudia?' he prompted.

'Sorry.' She'd drifted off. Lost in her own self-reflection about how bad she was at self-reflecting. How ironic was that?

'The end of the investigation?'

She scratched her head, tucked her hair behind her ear. Anything to keep her hands busy, if only for a second. 'Yes. Justin Winters admitted after a couple of days' worth of interviews that he killed Harlow to protect both his father and himself, and that his father knew nothing of his actions. He had tried to close the police investigation down by setting up a situation he hoped the acting ACC, Davidson, would take advantage of: a young available woman in a bar, and when he did, photographs were produced and pressure was applied. Davidson has been suspended pending a gross misconduct hearing, where the likely outcome will be dismissal. It's been, as you well know, plastered all over the press. You can't get away from any of it.'

Robert silently listened. There was no reaction from him.

Claudia continued. 'Justin, for his part, was disappointed to be informed that it was impossible to completely close a newly opened homicide investigation, but he did the best he could to curtail it, again of his own volition. The attempts on the lives of me and Russ were him and him alone. Nigel was horrified when he learned of what his son had done.'

'I saw he'd stepped down from his position as leader of the opposition.'

'It was untenable for him. So while Justin was attempting to protect him, all he's done is destroy his father. He'd have been better off letting Harlow run with things and seeing how it panned out. The public is more forgiving of a variety of misdeeds nowadays and besides, it wasn't Nigel's fault. It was Dawn Sinclair's for having sex with a student and his parents, who are long dead, for the pressure they applied to her. They don't get to witness the fallout of their actions. They went to their graves believing they did the best by their son.' The end of her nose itched and Claudia rubbed it, irritated at the intrusion to the peace that usually came with being in here.

'How did Harlow's father take all this? Not only was his daughter murdered, but she was killed by her biological half-brother, and done in the name of her father. That must be hard on a parent.'

Claudia sighed.

'It was tough?'

There was a pause before Claudia spoke again. 'I could have left it to Devon and Cornwall police to update Paul, but I felt it was our responsibility—'

'Whose responsibility?' Robert didn't take his eyes from her.

Claudia scowled at him. 'My responsibility. Okay? I thought it was my responsibility to give him the truth of the situation. To relay what had occurred and why.'

'You couldn't drive . . .'

'Sharpe drove.'

Robert raised an eyebrow and Claudia nodded. 'I know. It surprised me as well. But she really came through for us during all this.'

Robert allowed silence to expand in the room until Claudia filled it again.

'It was horrific.' Tears sprang to her eyes. Tears she had not shown Robert in their many hours together. But what she had witnessed, shared with Paul, it was brutal and demanded tears. She swiped at them angrily with the back of her hand. 'That's it. That's all you're getting on Paul.'

Robert nodded. 'Okay. Thank you, Claudia.'

Claudia let out a breath. Her shoulders sagged from the tension that had accumulated there.

'And Russ?'

Claudia sighed. This never stopped. Was she really here for this pain? 'He's out of hospital.'

'How do you feel, Claudia?' Robert's voice was quiet.

'Like my world is tumbling in around me. How do I deal with it all?'

'By doing what you're doing. Talking about it. Bringing it out into the open, examining it, seeing that it holds no power over you in the here and now and can't hurt you.'

He made it sound so easy. She scratched at her arm. 'I've moved out of my dad's and in with a friend. My house was insured and is being repaired. It'll take a little time, but I have good friends.'

'How's your relationship with your father at the moment?'

For all Claudia's twitching, Robert hadn't moved an inch. He remained still and serene.

'I returned to the office, restricted with my foot. No going out and about for another couple of weeks, so there's the usual work stuff with him. Though he's happier because Russ isn't there, which rubs me up the wrong way. And I don't know. Samuel Tyler's trial starts in a month. There's real tension between us because of it. I don't understand why, but whenever it gets brought up . . .'

Rain slashed at the window. The view was a wash of grey. It was almost unbearably bleak. Precisely how she felt. Would it be better to get therapy in the summer? Did it work better then? Sheffield wasn't a pretty city in the winter. The buildings were grey, the pavements and roads were grey, the skies grey, the whole thing had a washed-out look about it. Claudia fished in her bag and pulled out a knitting needle, then proceeded to shove it down her cast and scratch. Robert watched.

'You wouldn't believe how much it itches, simply because I can't get to it,' she said. 'Someone advised a knitting needle and boy, does it work.' She shoved it up and down a couple more times, then put it away.

'You're extremely fidgety this morning, Claudia.'

She scratched her head again. 'Am I?'

'You're processing a lot.' He held up a hand and tapped a finger with the finger of his other hand. 'The murder of Ruth is still an issue.' Another finger. 'The incident that resulted in you killing a man . . .'

She itched to bring the knitting needle out again but restrained herself for the moment.

'Now, on top of those two issues, you have Russ considering leaving the police, a man you admire and rely on.' He tapped a third finger. 'You're temporarily homeless.' A fourth. 'And the man who killed Ruth is about to go to trial.' Finally a fifth.

It was a good job she had no other problems, as Robert would need a third hand. She had to laugh, or she'd sit there and properly cry.

'My temporary living arrangements are not something that concern me,' she said. 'We can cross that off your list.'

He nodded. 'Okay then.'

'The first, Ruth, and the last, the trial, are combined into one, and once the trial is over, I am sure I'll be in a much better place. I can deal with this one.'

Robert assessed her. 'You honestly feel that way?'

'I do.'

'Okay then.'

'I can't do anything about Russ, but I'm a grown woman and a professional. Let's not go overboard with this. If Russ doesn't return to work, I'll cope. That leaves the initial problem I came to you for.'

'Killing a man.'

'Killing a man,' Claudia confirmed.

'Okay,' said Robert. 'Let's get you through this trial and we'll focus on that.'

'Once the man who murdered Ruth is behind bars,' said Claudia, 'I will sleep so much better.' She wondered how true this was. Would it be as simple as that? She'd been with so many victims and their families throughout investigations and trials, but never afterwards. Never found out how the aftermath affected them. If it brought closure. Was it the magic bullet that would heal her pain? Or would she be left wanting? She'd already survived so much. There was more than a little anxiety hiding in the run-up to the trial. She'd lied to Robert. But she had the strength to do this. Once this was over, it was done. She had faith.

Little did she know the true extent of the turmoil it would bring.

THE END

ACKNOWLEDGEMENTS

It takes a village to create a finished book and I want to take this opportunity to thank those people who make up my Claudia Nunn village. Those who made it all possible for you to read *She Knew Her Killer*.

Thanks has to go to my editor, Emma Grundy Haigh, who has believed in Claudia and Dominic from the start, and who is constantly calm. Something I definitely needed at various points in the process. Thanks also to Kate Lyall Grant for her sharp eye for detail. It wasn't always easy, but it was necessary. Thanks to Anna Harrisson for her copy-edit and timeline review and Emma Jobling for proofreading. To the whole Joffe team, who keep everything ticking over in the background, including, but not limited to, the social media accounts, the newsletter for readers, cover design, formatting, and contact with authors.

As always, my thanks go to my agent, Hannah Weatherill, who accepts that I email at odd hours and quickly gets back to me — in office hours! Who has shown nothing but belief and support in me. I'm so glad to have her by my side.

Thanks to Graham Bartlett for discussing historical police retention of material with me in relation to the search for Harlow's birth mother. It does make things so much easier when everything isn't electronically recorded!

Thanks goes to Kat Diamond for helping me resolve a plot problem as I was first outlining the story. The crime writing community is a wonderful supportive place.

To my family who watch me disappear to my desk on a daily basis: you mean the world to me.

And finally, thank you to you, the reader, who took a chance on the book.